DEATH'S DOOR

MERROWKIN BOOK 2

JENNIFER ALLIS PROVOST

Contents

Meeting The King

"Stop. Fidgeting."

I glared at Kevin even as I stilled myself. My brother, our parents, and I were standing at the end of a tunnel waiting for the golden gates of Kilstiffen to open up for us. We'd been out there for so long, I was beginning to wonder if anyone was home.

"Can't you just sing the gates open?" I asked my mother. She was a merrow, which meant she'd been born with a magical voice that could compel people and objects to do whatever she wished. Kevin and I had inherited that ability, although we'd just begun learning how to use our voices for anything other than regular singing. We hadn't yet got to the gate opening lesson.

"I can," she replied. "However, we've an appointment in the palace. The custom is to wait at the gates, and be escorted inside by the king's guard."

"Wouldn't want to mess around with these customs," I muttered.

"Be patient," Da said. "We'll be along shortly."

I blew out a breath, and resolved to continue waiting. Not that I had any choice in the matter, since those doors weren't opening by themselves. Stupid customs.

The whole reason we'd come below was because Mama was taking Kevin and me to meet her father the king, just as she'd promised. She was also due to return the golden key that controlled when the city rose and fell, which meant this was a momentous occasion for one and all. It had taken weeks of sending messages back and forth to arrange this meeting, and now the day had finally arrived. Here we were, waiting to experience all that Kilstiffen had to offer.

If the gates ever opened, that is.

And what magnificent gates they were. They were three times my height and almost as wide as they were tall, and the whole of them was covered in finely wrought designs featuring undersea scenes and elegant sea creatures. I wondered if the doors were made of solid gold. If so they must weigh a literal tonne, maybe more.

"You're fidgeting again," Kevin said.

"It's not my fault I'm nervous," I said to Kevin. "I've never been here before."

"You have," Mama said. "When you were three weeks old, I presented you to your grandfather, as I did Kevin before you."

"Events I cannot remember don't count," I grumbled.

"Don't fret, Meri girl," Da said. "Your grandfather was quite taken with you then, as he was with Kevin. He'll be glad to see both of you."

I looked up at Da, but before I could remind him that I was no longer an infant I heard gears turning. Finally, the gates opened up and four warriors bearing spears and shields stepped forward, and arranged themselves around us in a square. Mama took one look at them, tucked her hand into Da's elbow, and strode through the gates, past the warriors, and into Kilstiffen proper. Not knowing what else to do, Kevin and I followed.

"Shouldn't the men with the spears be going first?" I asked. Our escort was dressed almost identically as Seamus MacCreehy's enthralled warriors had once been, and their look was not inspiring confidence in me.

"You forget, Ma outranks them all," Kevin replied. "She can probably outfight them, as well." I opened my mouth to complain a bit more, but Kevin held up a hand. "Save your questions. Look around, Meri!"

I did, and noted that we were walking along a wide, flat causeway, not unlike the cobblestone paths of County Clare I'd been walking on my entire life. Then we crested a small rise, and I saw the city of Kilstiffen for the first time.

"Oh," I breathed.

"Quite a sight, eh," Kevin said, as he nudged me with his elbow.

Stretched below us were dozens or maybe even hundreds of white-walled houses roofed in shining gold. I could see verdant gardens packed with flowers woven between the crisp white buildings like a string of emeralds and rubies. An impossibly bright blue river meandered through the city, and encircled a many-spired palace with a roof clad in golden shingles. The palace's towers were covered with shimmering white tiles reminiscent of mother of pearl. Having grown up in a poor fishing village, I was awed by the casual displays of wealth everywhere I looked. I was also glad I'd listened to Mama when she insisted we wear our best clothes to meet the king. Even though my dress and shoes were brand new, I still felt a bit raggedy compared to my surroundings.

I was also amazed by the amount of light in the city. I'd expected Kilstiffen to be dark as a cave, what with its current location under the sea, but it was as bright as noon was above ground. The sky—or whatever was above us—was even a pale blue. Perhaps it rained down here, too.

Missing from the scene were Kilstiffen's residents. Save for ourselves and our escort, the city streets were empty, as were the windows and doorways of the many homes we passed. I found that odd; wouldn't the opening of the gates and the return of the king's daughter be a good reason to turn out? Apparently, these people had better things to do.

We crossed a silver and ivory bridge, then we ascended a gleaming white staircase and entered the palace. The interior was all polished white and grey stone, with colourful tapestries adorning the walls and thick red carpets on the floors. We walked through several outer rooms, each larger than the one that came before, then up a small flight of stairs and into a chamber so large it seemed the whole city could fit inside. The floor was highly polished white marble, and the ceiling was painted deep blue like the night sky, with lines and bobs of silver making up the zodiac and other constellations. In the very centre of the room was a throne, and upon the throne sat the king.

Mama had said many, many times that her father, King Steinar the Immoveable, was one of the kindest men she'd ever met. The man on the throne did not appear kind. He wore a crown of golden shards, his grey hair and beard were streaked with white like stripes of sea foam, and thanks to his scowl his brows were so low I had no idea what colour his eyes were. He was swathed in deep green silks and velvets edged in dark fur, and a pair of golden shoes peeked out from under his robes.

"He's like an angry Neptune," Kevin whispered. I bit the inside of my cheek, and tried to keep a straight face.

"Approach," the king ordered. We did, and I saw people assembled in the rear of the room behind the throne's dais. So there were others down here, at least in the palace. And here I was, worried that the king lived all alone.

We halted a few meters in front of the throne. Mama and Da stood in front of the king and bowed. Behind them, Kevin and I exchanged a quick glance and did the same.

"Aoife," the king boomed. "My youngest, fiercest child."

"My lord," Mama said. "Thank you for receiving us."

"When did I become a lord to you, instead of your father?" he asked.

"About the same time I was accused of treason," Mama replied.

The king's head drooped. "You know well that I never accused you. What's more, all now understand that you were the one in the right." He glanced up, and Mama smiled at him. "I'm told you have something for me?"

"Yes, my lord. Father." Mama stepped forward and withdrew the object she'd stolen from him over twenty years ago, which was the golden key to Kilstiffen. All of the green paint she'd covered it with had been carefully removed, and the key had been polished until it gleamed. The king gazed at her for a moment, then he descended the dais and claimed the key.

"My people, we are saved," he declared, holding the key aloft. "My daughter has delivered us from darkness. We will see the sun again!"

After the king had admired the key for a suitable amount of time, a few of the servants stepped out of the shadows and ushered us into an intimate dining room that, while much smaller, was every bit as opulent as the throne room. The dinnerware was made of cut crystal and heavy gold, and pearls the size of my palm and silvered coral were heaped in the middle of the table in lieu of a floral arrangement. The ceiling was painted like a noonday sky, and the surrounding walls were decorated with rolling green meadows. This room was lit by candlelight, and a clever person had placed the sconces near the windows to mimic the sun. If I squinted just so, I could pretend I was standing on Ireland's soil, rather than far below it.

Grandfather took his place at the head of the table, with Da and Kevin seated on his left across from Mama and me. At first I was relieved I didn't have to sit next to my grandfather, then I noticed Mama's straight spine and squared-off shoulders, and how Da's mouth was a slash across his face. I wondered if the king had purposefully separated them.

The king set the key next to his goblet and smiled. "I knew you'd do it, Aoife," he said. "Others were skeptical, but not me. I was certain you would stop MacCreehy and return the key to its rightful home."

"I had a great deal of help," Mama said. "I couldn't have completed my mission without Meri and Kevin, and Brian protecting our home."

I gulped down my panic. Why couldn't Mama have just taken all the credit? If there was anything I didn't need, royal scrutiny was it. Luckily, the king wasn't quite done complimenting Mama. "We are all lucky your children inherited your strength, and your wisdom. My dear Aoife, you remain our champion, and our guardian."

"As I always will be," Mama said. "My only regret is the length of time it took me to complete my mission."

"That is my regret, as well." The king's gaze slid toward Da. "I assume it was a great shock and surprise when my daughter returned to you."

"It was one of the happiest moments of my life, my lord," Da said.

"I'm certain it was," the king said. "Kevin, how is your singing coming along?"

"Good," Kevin replied, which was a complete untruth. Kevin couldn't carry a tune in a bucket. Realising he had just lied to the king, he added, "I'm still working on a few aspects."

The king grunted, and signalled a servant. Moments later, bowls of clam-scented broth were set before us. We watched as the king sampled a spoonful; when he nodded in approval, the rest of us picked up our spoons and began eating.

"Meri," the king said. I fumbled my spoon. "I'm told you've come into your voice."

I gaped at him. "Have I?" I asked, with a desperate glance at Mama.

"She surely has," Mama said, thus rescuing me from certain doom. "She commanded an army of enchanted stones to victory, and single handedly broke the merrows free from Seamus's thrall."

"That is quite impressive," the king acknowledged, but I wasn't interested in praise.

"How are the merrows?" I asked. "Did they all manage to return home?"

"They did," he replied. "Most came here, but a few went on to Evonium"

"Daveth is well, then? Can I see him?" I asked, before remembering one didn't make demands of a king. If my rudeness bothered him, he hid it well.

"He is doing very well," the king replied. "You learned some of their names?"

"I learned all of their names," I said. "And most of the soldiers' names, as well. Many were from my village."

The king nodded. "That is good, Meri. That is very good. Perhaps later, you will sing for me."

A servant whispered in the king's ear, thus saving me from an acappella performance over our soup bowls. The king stood, and my family and I followed suit.

"Come, all of you," he said. "The room is ready."

We rose and followed the king out of the dining room and into a smaller room. In this latest chamber, the ceiling and walls were painted in layers of rose and gold, with a floor of deep blue tiles.

"This room is like a sunset, the last was noonday, and the throne room was night," I said. "Why is everything in the palace painted like the sky?"

"To remind those who cannot go above on their own what the sky looks like," the king replied, his voice heavy with sadness. "To ensure that no one forgets the beauty of the sun and the sky." I pursed my lips, and resolved to keep my wonderings to myself.

The king approached a golden wall—honestly, Kilstiffen was packed with so much gold this latest installation may as well have been wallpaper—and opened a small hinged door in the centre. Beyond the door was a mechanism made of several copper gears, and into that device the king placed the key. We stood with bated breath for a heartbeat, two... Then the king frowned and removed the key, and shut the door.

"The window has passed," he said. "It will be another seven years before Kilstiffen may rise again."

Mama lowered her head. "Then I did fail."

The king placed his hand on her shoulder. "You did everything you could, with the little you had available," he said. "We've held out under the waves this long. A few more years will not matter overmuch. Now, let us return to our lunch."

MOTHERING

Our grand lunch in Kilstiffen featured course after course of every seafood imaginable. As a fisherman's daughter, I'd been eating seafood all my life, yet even I'd never seen so many sea creatures cooked up and served in the same meal. By the time dessert was served—which turned out to be a mound of shaved ice topped with candied kelp and surrounded by boiled prawns—I could hardly manage to look at it. Thankfully, it seemed that the king had also had enough.

"It pleases me that you and your family visited me today, Aoife," he announced. He gestured, and the attendants whisked our desserts away. "Do not let another fourteen years pass before you return again."

"Thank you for your hospitality, Father," Mama said. "It means the world to me to see you smile."

"Your smile pleases me, as well." The king stood, and we followed him out of the dining chamber and down a long, cold corridor draped in red fabric. Unlike the other tapestries we'd walked past, these were devoid of decoration.

"Why are all these tapestries plain?" I wondered aloud.

"This is a gallery, and those are curtains," the king replied. "When the city rises, we draw back the curtains so all may see the sun."

"Oh. I'm sorry you haven't seen it in so long, my lord."

The king faced me. "Apologise for nothing. If not for your efforts, we might have been trapped under the sea for all eternity. For your part in retrieving the key, I and every citizen of Kilstiffen thank you."

"Oh. Um, you're welcome."

The king smiled. "I notice that you're wearing Manannán's Pearl."

"Am I?" I asked, then my hand fluttered to my pearl pendant. I'd found it in the cottage at the bottom of our garden, and Da had told me that while it was Mama's necklace, she'd always meant for me to have it. "Isn't he supposed to be a sea god?"

"Yes," he replied. "Manannán mac Lir is the ruler of the Irish seas."

"Oh. I didn't know this was named after him. I thought the necklace was my mother's."

"It was, but as Aoife received it from her mother, so she passed it on to you," he replied. "As you will someday pass it on to your daughter. Wearing the pearl is somewhat of a tradition in our family."

"It's very nice," I said, then added, "my lord."

"I am not your lord," the king said. "I am your grandfather, and you will refer to me as such."

I saw the twinkle in his eye, and realised they were a pale, iridescent green. "I would be happy to, Grandfather."

The king—Grandfather—smiled. "That goes for you as well, Kevin."

"Yes, Grandfather," Kevin said.

Maybe having a king for a grandfather wouldn't be so bad, after all.

My happy mood faltered when we passed by the open doors to a large, oak-panelled room. Inside the room was a central podium, which faced rows and rows of chairs. Occupying the room were several people wearing black robes with tall cowls. The set-up, coupled with the sombre men in their dark robes, made me wonder if we'd wandered past a courtroom.

"What's in there?" I asked.

"That's the council of lords," Mama replied. "They enforce Kilstiffen's laws, and handle our relationships with the other sea kingdoms."

"Shouldn't they have come out to greet you?" I asked.

Mama pursed her lips. "It seems they didn't feel the need to."

After walking with us to the palace entrance, Grandfather bid us farewell, and the same four soldiers that had brought us to the palace escorted us out of the city. We took the same route away as we had upon our arrival, only this time, people lined the streets. At first I was glad, and eager to get a look at those who lived and worked below the waves. Then I realised that not a single one of them was smiling.

"What is happening?" I whispered to Kevin. One person after the next scowled at us, while several shook their heads in disapproval. Some even turned their backs as Mama walked past them. As for my mother, she kept her shoulders back and her gaze on the horizon, looking as regal as any princess ever had.

"Do as Ma's doing," Kevin said. "Just ignore them."

I did as Kevin said, and the walk out of Kilstiffen felt much longer than the walk to the palace had been. The four of us were silent as we passed through the golden gates, and as we climbed upward through the cave to the surface. The day had gone grey and misty, much like our moods.

After we returned home, Kevin ditched his suit and declared he needed to go into town. Da did much the same, and left to perform some sort of maintenance on his boat. That left Mama and I alone in the house. I did what I always did when I was nervous, and put on the kettle and started cooking.

"What are you making?" Mama asked, when she joined me in the kitchen. She'd changed out of the formal white and blue gown she'd worn below, and was now wearing a pink floral dress. Mama always wore dresses, even when she was working out in the garden. Unlike my mother, I was still wearing my dress from earlier, though I had nothing against trousers. Since I tended to spill food on myself whilst cooking, I only cared if my clothes were washable, and that there was an apron handy.

"I don't know yet." I surveyed what I'd set out on the counter: leeks, carrots, potatoes, cod, and the leftover bread from that morning. "Not fish," I said, and put the cod back in the fridge.

"Had enough fish earlier, eh?" Mama asked, and I nodded. "I'm sure you have many questions about Kilstiffen. Please, ask me whatever you'd like."

"Okay." I noted how Mama had pursed her lips, and stared at her hands where they lay folded on the table. Being that she'd been gone for so much of my life, mothering was new to her. I understood how she felt, since I'd hardly ever been mothered. But we were working on it, and each conversation we had was a bit less awkward. Sometimes, I talked with her as easily as I talked to Da.

The kettle whistled, and while I made our tea I thought about what I'd most like to know about Kilstiffen. When our mugs were ready, I delivered them to the table, and asked, "Where does all the light come from?"

"Of all the amazing things you saw this morning, that's what you want to start with?" Mama countered.

"The light might be the most amazing thing of all," I said. "We were far underground, yet it was as bright as midday."

"There are tunnels that run from the city up to the surface," Mama replied. "There is a system of glass and mirrors in place, and sunlight is reflected below."

"Huh." I leaned back in my chair. "I suppose that makes more sense than a giant lamp hovering overhead."

Mama burst out laughing. "Yes, I suppose it does."

"I also thought there would be more people about, especially when we arrived," I continued. "They're not very friendly to surface dwellers down below, are they?"

She clutched her mug and stared into her tea. "About those that were watching us leave. Not everyone in Kilstiffen was happy to see me." She scoffed, and ran a hand over her plait. "The council of lords would prefer to never see or hear of me again."

"But you're their guardian, and the princess," I said. "And you returned the key!"

"Aye, and I'm the one who stole the key in the first place."

"Do you still believe you did the right thing?"

"Yes, and I'd do it again, if I needed to."

"Then who cares what they say? If not for you, who knows what would have happened to Kilstiffen, what with MacCreehy's mad plans. They ought to be thanking you, the ungrateful lot."

She smiled. "Trust my wise daughter to see things as they truly are." Mama delicately sipped her tea. "School starts up again tomorrow, doesn't it?"

"It does," I replied. "Odd, for it to begin on a Tuesday."

"Aye, but that's hardly the oddest thing that's happened around here of late. Would you like me to walk to The Saints with you?"

"Thank you, but no need. Aodhan said he would pick me up at half past seven."

She tapped the side of her mug. "I wonder what the new headmaster will be like."

I shuddered. "Anyone would be better than MacCreehy."

BACK TO THE SAINTS

The next morning, school started up again. As soon as I was dressed and ready, I ran down the long driveway from my house toward the road. I wasn't rushing because I was eager to get to The Saints, but because Aodhan was waiting for me.

Ever since we'd simultaneously stopped MacCreehy's plan to permanently raise Kilstiffen, and rescued Aodhan's father from his existence as an enthralled warrior, Aodhan had taken to spending his nights at the surf shop instead of in the room he'd been allotted in my house. He'd ended up with that room after his mother, Mrs Dumhach, kicked him out of his family home, and Da offered him a place to stay.

But all of that was in the past, and now Aodhan's mother was genuinely trying to make an effort to get along with her first husband and rebuild her family, though things were understandably awkward. When Mr Sullivan had gone missing and been presumed dead all those years ago, his wife had mourned him, and eventually remarried. The fact that she'd married his best friend and business partner was the most awkward fact of the situation.

The Dumhach-Sullivan drama meant that Aodhan and his father ate at my house so often Mama had aired out the formal dining room, and Da had dragged the enormous old table out of the shed and polished it until it shone. The end result was a dining room fit for a king. That will come in handy if Grandfather ever stops by for tea.

The drama also meant that Aodhan and I didn't spend nearly as much time alone together as we once did. He was busy helping his father re-accustom himself to regular life after spending so many years as a warrior enthralled to MacCreehy, not to mention playing peace-maker between his bickering parents. I understood why we weren't together as much as we used to be, but I did miss him.

But this morning, during the ride to school, it would be just him and me.

I found Aodhan waiting for me at the end of my driveway in his new car. His last car had been left behind near the Shannon Pot on one of our earlier adventures, and by the time we'd recovered it, the poor thing was a bit worse for wear. Aodhan had sold it off, and got himself a larger sport utility vehicle, which suited him much better than the old compact car had. I thought it was a great deal more comfortable, too.

"Hello," I said, as I hopped into the passenger seat. "Have you been waiting here long?"

"Good morning. And no, I haven't been here long at all." Aodhan started the engine and pulled onto the road. "Are you excited to get back to school?"

"Wary is a better description." School had been closed ever since we'd rescued the jumpers from MacCreehy, who was not only a rogue merrow that put all of Ireland and Kilstiffen in danger, he was our school's headmaster, as well. He was also my mother's greatest enemy, though we didn't know that for a long time because Mama had sung a forgetting spell to my father. It had been done with Da's full permission, and his memories had since been restored, but it had made things confusing for a few years.

Anyway, what with the scores of jumpers we'd liberated and returned home, and a missing headmaster, the school had thought it prudent to shutter itself for six weeks while all of that was sorted out. In that time, they'd managed to locate and hire a new headmaster, who was a fellow by the name of Marcus Flynn.

"I hope this Flynn character is a regular bloke," Aodhan said. "I don't know if I can take having any more merrows in my life."

"You've got the same amount in your life now that you've always had," I said. "Originally there was me, Kevin, and MacCreehy. Now MacCreehy's gone, and my mother is back. Still only three."

"And what a good trade it was, swapping out that tyrant for your mother." Aodhan glanced at me. "How is she getting on?"

"Well enough." I decided against mentioning how she'd tried to make breakfast for me earlier that morning, and accidentally set the curtains on fire. Again. "She's so happy to be home I hear her singing in her room every morning and night."

"That's wonderful, Mer. I bet your dad's happy, too."

"He is," I replied. Da had hardly stopped smiling since Mama's return. "How's your dad? Will he be all right by himself today?"

"He thinks he'll have his entire life sorted out by sunset. Said he's going to go out on the waves and sit on his board, and wait for the sun and sea to tell him his next move."

"Will that work?"

"No idea. But since my mother seems terrified to be in the same room with him, and my stepfather is angry that he's back at all, it can't hurt."

I placed my hand on his. "I'm sorry."

"I know you are, but don't fret. He's here, and he's alive. Those are the most important things. Everything else will work out."

"You're a surfing philosopher, just like your dad."

Aodhan grinned. "I suppose I am."

We pulled into the student car park. While Aodhan found a spot, I gathered up my things. By the time the car stopped, I'd already grabbed the door handle.

"Meri, wait."

I turned toward him. "What for?"

Instead of replying, Aodhan slid his hand behind my neck and drew me close. His brown eyes searched my face, then he lowered his head and kissed me. His lips were warm, and gentle, and even though he hadn't asked first, I wasn't angry. Permission had been granted long ago.

When we parted he laid his forehead against mine, as his thumb stroked the nape of my neck. "I'm sorry, for just grabbing you like that," he said. "But I've been wanting to kiss you again for so long, and after everything that happened here we are at school ready to restart our classes, and I don't want things to go back to how they were before."

"Before?"

"Me mooning over you and you never noticing."

"I noticed." I grasped his right hand with my left. "I noticed all of it."

"But you always said you never wanted a boyfriend."

"What I didn't want was to be one of those mindless girls that only talked about boys," I said. "You, I like."

He grinned. My heart did a somersault in my breast. "I like you, too."

That time, I kissed him.

Aodhan and I entered Saint Senan and Conainne's Academy together. Right away, we learned that there was a mandatory assembly happening in the auditorium instead of our usual first class. That was fine with me, since my first class was chemistry and I loathed it.

"I'll show you some chemistry," Aodhan said, as he waggled his eyebrows at me.

I swatted at his shoulder. He caught my hand before I made contact and gently squeezed my fingers. "Let's just find some seats. And you behave!" I added.

We entered the auditorium and claimed two seats in the back row. The stage was empty, save for a man I'd never seen before who was seated on the far right side. He appeared to be middle-aged, with pasty white skin and equally pale hair; at our distance, I couldn't tell if it was blond or white. His folded-up legs told me he was also quite tall, and was as thin as a rail.

The bell chimed for our first class. The man on the stage glanced at the clock, then he stood and took his spot at the lectern. "Thank you all for coming," he began, then he gave the audience a rueful face. "Although, I suppose you had no choice in the matter."

A murmur of assent coursed through the auditorium. When it was quiet again, he continued, "Good morning. My name is Marcus Flynn, and as you're all no doubt aware, starting today I will be taking over as headmaster of this fine institution. I understand that there has been quite a lot of upheaval in your lives as of late, what with the disappearance of your prior headmaster, Mr MacCreehy, and the disbanding of a local cult. I hope to make your time here at Saint Senan and Conainne's Academy one of academic achievement and comfortable routine. Thank you."

With that, Headmaster Flynn ended his speech and walked off-stage. The student body sat for a moment in collective bewilderment, but he didn't return, and no other teacher stepped out to continue the assembly.

"That's it?" Aodhan asked. "All he could spare was a bare two minutes to introduce himself?"

"Did you hear him mention a cult?" I demanded. "They're saying the jumpers were off in a cult this whole time."

"I suppose that's easier to accept than 'your loved ones were held hostage these past few years by a lunatic who wanted to open a portal between here and the land of the gods'." Aodhan stood and shouldered his book bag, and then mine.

"Carrying my things now?" I teased.

His cheeks darkened, which made him even more adorable. "Make a fuss and it might not happen again."

"I'll remember that."

We made our way through the corridors, navigating between various clusters of students as everyone caught up with each other after our unscheduled weeks off. Some of them shot furtive glances at Aodhan and me, then resumed their whispering. Ignoring such occurrences was old hat for me, but I saw Aodhan tense beside me.

"Pay them no mind," I said. "Otherwise we'll have to talk to them, and I'd rather not be the one responsible for explaining the odd things that have happened recently."

Aodhan grunted, which I considered his agreement on the matter. We reached my history class, and lingered for a few minutes next to the entrance; after the new headmaster's short speech, we had plenty of time before the next class was set to begin.

With a sly glance, Aodhan surveyed the corridor. When he didn't find any authority figures lurking about, he withdrew his phone and began typing.

"What are you doing?" I asked. "Recording the headmaster's speech for posterity?"

"Definitely not. I'm updating the shop's social media accounts. I've started posting the surf conditions every day."

"Surf conditions? Like what?"

"You know, the air and water temperatures, wind direction, what time the tide comes in. Stuff like that. It makes the shop a bit more personal." He hit send and stashed his phone in his jacket pocket, then he moved closer to me and took my hand.

"Want to talk about what happened earlier?" he asked. "What happened in the car park, I mean."

"You want to talk here? In the corridor?"

He laughed softly. "Later, then?"

"Later would be grand. I want to tell you all about Kilstiffen, too."

"And I want to hear about it." He squeezed my fingers. "I'm going to go to the gym, see what's what with the team. See you at lunch, Meri."

"Lunch, then."

I watched Aodhan as he walked toward the gym. His movements were more graceful than a teen boy's ought to have been, perhaps on account of all the athletics he participated in. Or perhaps he had been born lithe and muscular, and this was his natural state. Either way, the view of Aodhan leaving was quite fine, indeed.

I realised I was gaping at Aodhan in the midst of a school day. I tore my gaze away from him, and saw Kelsey McGrath, one of the girls who'd bullied me for my entire school career, standing opposite from me. She was without her usual gang of mean girls, and instead of her standard perfect image, her auburn hair was unkempt, and there were dark smudges underneath her eyes. She was also gazing at the floor as if she was despondent. Hm, perhaps the rest of the bullies had turned on her. If you asked me, it would serve her right.

I opened my mouth to make a crack about Kelsey having lost her hairbrush or run out of concealer, remembered I was the better person, and entered the classroom instead. I'd just unpacked my copy book and pens when a student I'd never met claimed the desk next to mine.

"Hello," he said, as he thrust his hand toward me. "I'm Paul."

"Hello. I'm Meri," I replied. I kept arranging my things to avoid shaking his hand. In my experience, people who started out by being extra friendly with me always had ulterior motives.

"I'm new here," he continued, seeming unoffended. "I feel like everyone here knows everyone else, except for me, of course."

"That is an astute deduction."

"Well, now I know you, so I have one friend."

I turned and looked at Paul. He was tall, with brown hair and eyes, and was overflowing with so much enthusiasm he made Aodhan seem dour by comparison. And he was overstepping himself a bit.

"Class should begin soon," I said, and I flipped through my textbook to where we'd left off a few weeks ago, and made a show of looking over the chapter. Hopefully, this newcomer would take the hint and start bothering someone else.

Paul did not take the hint.

He also ended up being not only in my history class, he was in all of my classes and oh so excited that we would be spending so much time together. I wondered if I could appeal to the new headmaster for a complete change of schedule.

When lunch time rolled around, Paul followed me into the canteen. Not that I'd thought he would do anything different, but I'd hoped he would. Despite me pointedly ignoring him, he queued up right behind me, filled his tray with exactly the same items I had selected, and happily paid the cashier for both of our lunches.

"Thank you, but you didn't have to do that," I said. "I am perfectly capable of purchasing my own food."

"I'm certain you are," Paul said cheerfully. If he got any more cheerful, I might pop him in the nose. "I just wanted to thank you for being so kind as to show me around on my first day."

"Saying thank you would have been more than plenty," I muttered. I sat at an empty table, and Paul claimed the seat opposite me. Wonderful. Even more wonderful was when Aodhan strode up to the table, holding a tray laden with three times as much food as mine and Paul's were. He set his tray next to mine and stared at Paul as if he was an alien.

"Who's this?" Aodhan asked.

"Hi. I'm Paul." Paul stood and thrust his hand at Aodhan, much as he'd done to me. Aodhan leaned across the table and shook Paul's hand, albeit reluctantly. "It's my first day here at The Saints."

"He's in all my classes." I smiled at Aodhan. "All of them."

"Good to meet you, Paul. I'm Aodhan." Aodhan grabbed a chair and set it right next to mine. If he got any closer he'd be on my lap. Before I could comment on our unusual and unnecessary seating arrangements, Aodhan leaned close to me, and whispered, "Have you seen Kelsey?"

I drew back, wondering why he was concerned for the girl who'd gone out of her way to make my life a living hell for as long as I could remember. "I did, earlier. Why?"

Aodhan gestured to a table in the far corner of the room. Kelsey was sitting alone, and her tray was as empty as the seats beside her.

"Word is that Kelsey hoped her mother would be coming back with the rest," Aodhan said; I understood that by "the rest" he meant those we'd rescued from MacCreehy. "She even started going to the rescue centres set up by the garda, checking name rosters and all. Her ma never showed, and she took it hard."

"Then her mother must really be gone." I felt a pang of sympathy for Kelsey. My mother returning home after being gone for fourteen years was the best thing that could have happened to me. When Kelsey realized her mother wasn't coming back she must have been devastated.

"So she's down because she thought her mother was in a cult, and it turned out that she wasn't?" Paul asked. "You'd think she'd be happy she was wrong about that." He leaned closer to us, and added, "I hear that lot was into all sorts of nasty stuff. Heathen rites, and all."

I opened my mouth in order to dispute Paul's claims. Aodhan nudged my foot under the table, and I thought the better of it. "Yes,

Paul, it sounded quite awful," I said. "What else have you heard about the cult?"

"Oh, nothing really," he replied. "So, what does one do for fun around here?"

She Sold The Mustang

Paul followed me around like a lapdog for the rest of the school day. I tried very hard to not be annoyed with him; after all, it wasn't his fault he was a new student, and didn't know anyone besides me. I just wished he'd made an effort to make friends with a few other students.

After the dismissal bell had rung, I found Aodhan waiting for me near the main entrance. He was leaning on the wall, with his tie already loosened and his shirt untucked. His appearance was perfectly rumpled like a male model in a fashion magazine, not that I was going to tell him that.

I imagined how shocked Aodhan would be if I told him he reminded me of a model, and how his handsome face would be taken over by his big round eyes and eyebrows halfway up his forehead. Maybe I will tell him.

"Do you have practice now?" I asked Aodhan.

"Are you on a team?" Paul asked. Right, he was still following me. Unlike Aodhan, Paul's uniform was as crisp as if he'd just got dressed. His trousers even had that crease down the centre of each leg. It was as if Paul was Aodhan's perfectly bland opposite in every way, both physically and personality-wise.

"I run track," Aodhan replied, then he turned his attention to me. "It doesn't start up again until next week. Want to head over to the shop with me?"

"I'd love to," I said.

"You're going shopping?" Paul interjected. Again. "Whereabouts? In town?"

"We're not going shopping. I have a shop," Aodhan said, as he pushed off from the wall and slipped his hand against mine. "See you tomorrow, Paul."

Aodhan and I left Paul standing there, and walked toward the student car park hand in hand. We shouldn't have been holding hands like that on school grounds, but other than a few interested glances, no one seemed to mind. Soon enough we were in Aodhan's car, and we made the short drive to his family business, Sullivan's Surf Shop.

"How goes it?" Aodhan asked his store manager, Lorcan, once we entered the shop.

"Sales are a bit slow, but otherwise all is well," Lorcan replied. "Hello, Meri."

"Hello." I looked around the sales floor, and saw several customers milling about, but not the shop's founder. "Is Mr Sullivan here, too?"

Lorcan's face darkened. "He's still out on the water. At this rate he'll go hypothermic."

"Dad can handle it," Aodhan said. "Meri and I will be upstairs. Yell if you need us."

Lorcan smirked at Aodhan and me, then he resumed his paperwork behind the counter. Wondering what that was all about, I followed Aodhan up to the apartment.

"What's Lorcan's problem?" I asked once we were upstairs.

"He thinks we come up here to do things."

I almost asked him what sort of things he meant, but Aodhan's face made his meaning clear. "Does the whole staff think that way?" I squeaked.

"No, the rest are decent folk. Lorcan's an off one." Aodhan opened the fridge and rummaged for food. "Hungry?"

"Not after that." Instead of joining Aodhan in the kitchenette, I sat on the couch.

"Don't worry about Lorcan." Aodhan sat next to me and handed me a bottle of water. Since I wasn't thirsty, I set it aside. "He means well, just has no social skills. He also can't understand why anyone like you would be caught dead with someone like me." Aodhan smiled. "I wonder that, myself."

I stared at Aodhan, unsure if he really was that insecure and if Lorcan really was that much of an arse, when he laughed. "Anyway, you haven't told me about Kilstiffen yet, and I'm dying to hear about it."

"For starters, it's amazing," I began. "Everything is covered in gold, and they even have light down there!" I explained the system of tunnels and mirrors, and Aodhan shook his head.

"Wow," Aodhan said. "I figured the whole place would be lit by something archaic, like whale oil lamps or peat fires. Was there a parade or something to celebrate your mother's return?"

"The thing is, a lot of people don't seem to like my mother," I said. "The king was pleased with her, but there's a council of lords who think she was wrong to oppose MacCreehy. They blame her for the city not rising for over twenty years, and they're not really wrong. She is the one who stole the key in the first place."

"I'd probably be cranky too, if I hadn't seen the sun in that long. Can't it rise now that the key's been returned?"

I shook my head. "No. The window of time has closed. They'll have to wait for the next, which won't be for another seven years."

"Twenty-eight years, then." Aodhan flopped back against the couch. "That is a long time. Still, I wouldn't let those people bother you. They're just looking for someone to blame, and they can't blame MacCreehy since he's already been punished. People are always on the lookout for a scapegoat, and your ma being there fit the bill."

"True." I scooted closer to Aodhan and leaned against him. He put his arm around me. "And before you ask, no, my grandfather did not give me a tiara."

He smiled, and traced my cheek with his fingertips. "No matter. You don't need any diamonds or pearls about you. You're beautiful as you are."

I blinked, shocked and embarrassed and so incredibly happy he'd called me beautiful, but before I could give voice to any of that, he kissed me. I guess we just kissed all the time, now. I was all right with that.

"Sorry," he said when we parted. "I keep forgetting to ask first."

I wound my arms around his neck. "You could ask me now."

He affected a very serious face, and asked, "Meri, may I please kiss you?"

"Let me think about it," I began, then Aodhan scooped me onto his lap and squeezed me tight. I shrieked peals of laughter, and the tiny voice in the back of my head concluded that such noises were all the confirmation Lorcan needed of his theories.

In the midst of my squealing, a voice called out, "Someone getting murdered up here?"

We turned toward the voice and saw Aodhan's father enter the apartment. He was still wearing his wetsuit, and was navigating his surf board through the narrow doorway.

"Hey, Dad," Aodhan said.

"Hello, Mr Sullivan." Blushing, I slid off Aodhan's lap and moved toward the far side of the couch.

"Hey, guys. Meri, you don't have to move on my account," he added. I blushed harder.

"Dad, did the universe end up speaking to you?" Aodhan asked.

"She was quiet today, but I'm confident that she'll speak up when she's ready." Mr Sullivan propped his board against the wall. "Are your parents going to the open house tomorrow, Meri?"

"There's an open house?" I glanced at Aodhan, but he only shrugged. "Where? Somewhere in the village?"

"The new headmaster sent out a mass email. He wants to have a meet and greet at school with all the students and their families." Mr Sullivan regarded our blank stares. "I take it this wasn't mentioned at school?"

"The new headmaster gave a two-minute speech, if that, then he hid in his office for the rest of the day," Aodhan said. "Are you going to ask Ma to be your date for the meet and greet?"

Mr Sullivan frowned. "Did you know she sold my Mustang?"

"You once kept horses?" I asked.

"No, Mer," Aodhan said. "Dad's Mustang was an American car."

"Oh. Can't you buy a new car?"

"My Mustang was a classic," Mr Sullivan began, then he went toward the kitchenette, muttering about cars and loyalty as he slammed drawers and doors.

"It was more than just a car, wasn't it?" I asked.

"Way more," Aodhan said. "He sees it as more of his life Ma gave away."

"My heart breaks for him," I whispered. "He must be so lonely."

"He is, but he won't admit it," Aodhan whispered back. "Just keeps surfing and running by himself, waiting for my mother to magically be in love with him again."

For not the first time, I wondered if love was worth it. Then I remembered how I'd heard my mother sing every morning and night since she'd returned home to us, and how happy me and Kevin and Da were to have her back, and decided that maybe love was worth a little bit of effort.

"Mr Sullivan, would you and Aodhan like to have dinner at my house tonight?" I offered.

"Depends. Is your father cooking? Why that man doesn't own a restaurant yet is beyond me," he added.

"Of course Da's cooking," I said. "The only ones who cook in our house are he and I."

He grinned, and I instantly knew what Aodhan would look like in a few years. "All right, Meri and Aodhan, it's a date."

Da hadn't minded the addition of Aodhan and his father for dinner. Since he'd hauled out his largest pot that morning and made lamb stew, I wondered if he, or Mama, had been expecting them. However it had happened, soon enough the six of us were sitting around the table, with Da ladling out bowls of stew while Mama sliced the bread.

She wielded the bread knife much the same way she wielded her sword, which was both efficient and terrifying.

"Thanks for having Aodhan and me over again," Mr Sullivan said, as Da passed him a bowl.

"You're both always welcome here, Lucas," Mama said. "Brian always makes enough food to feed an army, which seems to be just enough for the five of us and one Aodhan," she added with a smile.

Aodhan accepted his bowl of stew, and said, "And an army marches on its stomach."

"Speaking of armies, are we all going to the open house tomorrow?" Da asked.

"I'm not," Kevin said. "I already did my time at The Saints."

"You've also got to make sure that stool at the pub doesn't float away," I said.

"What if it did?" Kevin countered. "A right tragedy that would be."

"Meri, Aodhan, did you have a chance to meet the new headmaster?" Da pressed on. "I imagine he's a fair sight better than MacCreehy was."

"I wouldn't say we met him," I said. "We all went into the auditorium, he told us his name, and sent us on to class. I might not even recognise him if I saw him again."

"Sure you would," Aodhan said, between mouthfuls of stew. "He's built like a lamppost and pale as death. Can't be too many around looking like that."

"Lots of people are thin, and perhaps he avoids the sun," Mama said.

"It's more than that," I said. "His hair's white. And so is his skin!"

"Perhaps he's an older man," she said.

"My two cents, it doesn't matter what his deal is as long as he's a regular guy," Mr Sullivan said. "No offense, Aoife, but I've had enough of merrows. The only ones I want in my life right now are you and your kids."

Mama smiled at Kevin and me. "I agree. And, while we're all together, Brian and I have something we'd like to tell you."

"Are you pregnant?" Kevin asked.

I smacked Kevin's shoulder. "Why is that always the first question out of your mouth?"

"No, Kevin, we are not pregnant, and Meri, don't hit your brother," Mama said, dividing her glare between Kevin and me. "Brian and I have decided to renew our vows."

"You're getting married again?" I asked. "Was the first time not legal?"

"Aye, the first time was legal, but a lot has happened since then," Da replied. "This can be a new beginning for us all."

I flopped back in my chair. "A wedding. How wonderful."

"Congratulations," Mr Sullivan said. "When will this be happening?"

"Oh, on about a month from now," Da replied. "We could have the affair right before Meri's birthday."

"As long as we don't tell anyone my birthday is coming up." What with my mother missing for so much of my life, birthdays had never felt like something to celebrate. "You know I can't stand people knowing about it."

"You never celebrate your birthday at all?" Mr Sullivan asked.

"Meri's version of a party is a new book and a cup of tea," Kevin said. "When she turned sixteen, Da took her to the bookstore and told her she could get whatever she wanted. It was like she'd died and gone to heaven."

"That was my best birthday ever." I'd got twelve books, a tin of tea, and a very cute tote bag.

"Wait, was there only books?" Aodhan asked. "No cake? Does that mean this birthday coming up won't have cake either?"

We laughed, and Da said, "Don't you worry now, Aodhan. I'll make sure Meri has a cake."

"Perhaps there will be a party this time," Mama said. When I looked at her in horror, she added, "A small one, with just us."

"A small party would be lovely," I said. "That would be a perfect day."

Later, after we'd finished the washing up, Aodhan and I went out to the back porch for some alone time. It was a bit chilly, so I'd thrown on a woollen jumper. Aodhan was wearing one of the dozens of hooded sweatshirts he owned with the surf shop's logo printed on it.

"Have you actually sold any of these?" I asked, as I tugged on his sweatshirt. This one was a bright blue, and had the shop's name printed on the sleeves. "Every day you're wearing a different one."

"Got to try out the stock," he said. "Besides, if I snag one off the sales floor, I can put the washing off for another day."

I wrinkled my nose, and imagined piles of worn hoodies mouldering away in the shop's laundry room. Before I could call Aodhan out on his deplorable washing schedule, he asked, "What do you really want to do for your birthday this year?"

"Oh." I leaned against the railing, and gazed at the decidedly unkempt back garden. If my parents were planning on holding their second wedding here, we would need to start working on this mess straight away. "I never really do anything for it."

"But this is a big one," Aodhan said. "Turning eighteen is a big deal. We should celebrate."

"Da said he would make a cake, and Mama mentioned a party."

"That's a good start." Aodhan slid his arm around my waist. "I just want to do something special for you."

I laid my head against his chest. "You do special things for me all the time."

"That's because you're special to me." We were quiet for a few minutes, then he said, "I've got it."

"Got what?"

"We can have a celebration with just you and me," he said. "We already know there will be cake, and after we've eaten it, we can go on a drive. I heard a new bookstore's just opened up in Cork. We could check it out."

I smiled; no one had ever understood me the way Aodhan did. "That sounds perfect."

Good Things

Wednesday morning started out much like Tuesday, which was wonderful. Aodhan picked me up at the same time, then we drove to The Saints and kissed for a bit in the school's car park. I had to admit, I was thoroughly enjoying this new phase of our relationship. Aodhan had always been kind and attentive to me, but now that he was holding my hand and stealing kisses whenever he thought no one was looking, I could hardly get enough of him.

But we couldn't hide out in his car all day, now could we? Reluctantly, we left the car, and Aodhan carried my book bag up the school's steps, then he handed it off to me and we went to our respective classes. That was when my day turned sour.

I turned down the west wing's corridor, and stopped by my locker to collect my chemistry book. I'd enjoyed not having that class yesterday, almost as much as I enjoyed missing it these past weeks while the school was closed. My other long standing bully, Sarah Haynes, was standing at her locker, which was unfortunately next to mine. Clustered around her was her usual group of sycophants, though her partner in all things evil, Kelsey, was missing.

"Heard you finally got a boyfriend," Sarah said, as the rest of her group snickered.

"Where's your better half?" I countered. If she thought I was going to discuss my and Aodhan's relationship with her, she was mad.

"Kelsey? That cow's gone as batty as you." Sarah slammed her locker shut and walked down the corridor, with her entourage following close behind. Glad to be rid of her, I closed my own locker—gently, like a normal person—and went on to chemistry.

Fortune laughed at me yet again. Our newest student, Paul, was in my chemistry class, just like he was in all of my other classes. However, the only open seat was clear on the other side of the room, which meant he was too far away to talk to me. I even managed to avoid him when we changed from our first class to our second. My happiness was short-lived, since he claimed the desk next to me in history class exactly as he'd done the day before.

"Good morning, Meri," Paul said brightly. "Is Meri a nickname of sorts?"

"Of sorts." I flipped to the relevant chapters in my history book and started reading.

"Did you do the reading?" Paul asked.

"I always do the reading."

"Then why are you reading now? I want to talk to you."

"And I don't want to talk to you. Thank you."

"But, Meri." Paul placed his hand on my desk. I slammed my textbook shut and glared at him.

"Stop. Please, stop." Paul opened his mouth, but I kept going. "Stop talking to me, following me around, buying me lunch, and everything else. Just stop."

Before Paul could react, Sister Nuala entered the room and called for class to begin. Paul shut his mouth, opened his book, and stayed blissfully quiet throughout the class.

Once class was over, I grabbed my things and darted into the corridor. Since my third period was free, I went straight to the library. I found an empty table in the stacks, pulled out my phone, and texted Aodhan.

Meri: In library. You?

Aodhan: Track.

Meri: Practice?

Aodhan. Just hanging around. Want company?

Meri: Sure.

I set my phone down and stared at the table's surface. I didn't have any homework to work on, since I hadn't been assigned any yesterday save for the reading those three chapters in history. I also didn't have any assignments lingering from before the break, since I'd already completed all of the work and handed it in. For the first time in my academic career, I had no reason to be in the library, except to hide from Paul and his annoying, too-friendly nature.

"But I am not hiding," I muttered.

"What was that?"

I froze, mortified, and debated fleeing the library altogether when Sister Mary Katherine stepped into the aisle. We hadn't seen each other since shortly after I'd broken her and the rest of those captured by MacCreehy free from his enthrallment, and I couldn't wait to talk to her. I stood and approached Sister, but stopped short.

"Meri, what's wrong?" she asked.

"I was about to hug you," I replied. "Is that okay? What with you being a nun and all."

"Of course it is," she said, then she embraced me. She was wearing her usual fuzzy pink cardigan over her habit, and she smelled like lavender. "Is everything all right?"

"Yes. No. I don't know." Sister released me and we sat at the table. "How are you doing, after everything?"

Sister wrinkled her nose. "Is that what they're calling it now? Everything?"

I shrugged. "I suppose it's better than saying you were all brainwashed by a cult."

"Yes, I'll agree with you on that. Did you know that the school didn't want to give me my position back? They claimed I might be a danger to the students."

"Is that why you weren't teaching yesterday?" I'd assumed Sister had wanted to take some time off before returning to work. Never in my wildest dreams would I have thought Sister would be denied getting her literature classes back. "I'm so sorry."

"About what, now?"

I took a deep breath. "How much do you remember about the time when you were enthralled?"

"I remember everything. I'm not so sure if that's a blessing or a curse," she added.

"Then you remember my mother. She was the woman in the gold chain mail, with the sword." Sister nodded, and I continued, "My family had a lot to do with MacCreehy going off the deep end and kidnapping folks for his army. I'm so sorry you and the rest got caught up in it."

Sister grasped my hand. "Meri, I'm sure you and yours were on the side of goodness. My situation will work itself out, eventually. Don't trouble yourself over me."

I bit the inside of my cheek, because I wanted to argue with Sister. Of course I wanted to trouble myself! She was suffering, and all over something she'd been swept into through no fault of her own. There had to be a way I could help her.

Aodhan came around the stacks, and halted when he saw Sister and me sitting together. "Am I interrupting anything?" he asked.

"Not at all, Aodhan," Sister said. "Meri and I were just catching up. Please, sit with us." Aodhan claimed the chair next to mine. "Now, I want both of you tell me everything I missed out on over the past few weeks."

"My dad's back," Aodhan said, his face split by the biggest grin.

"I thought he had passed," Sister said.

"We thought that too, but he'd actually been down below with you, having also been caught by that villain, MacCreehy," Aodhan replied. "When Meri freed all of you, she freed him, too."

"You see, Meri, you've already helped me, and Aodhan's father," Sister said. "In fact, you helped scores of people. Isn't that something to be proud of?"

"I suppose," I said. "I just can't help wishing none of it had happened in the first place."

"We can't adjust what's already happened, but we can choose how we react to it," Sister said, then she asked Aodhan, "How is your father readjusting to life above?"

"He's doing well," Aodhan replied. "I mean, it's a pretty awkward situation all around, what with my mother getting remarried and all, but we'll figure things out. I'm just so happy he's here. It's an actual miracle!"

Sister smiled, and patted Aodhan's hand. "Good things happen to good people. I want both of you to remember that."

"We will, Sister," Aodhan said, as he turned his smile toward me. "Promise."

After we'd spent some time talking with Sister, the lunch bell rang. She excused herself to return to her work, and Aodhan and I made our way to the canteen. We queued up for lunch as usual, but after we'd paid for our food, I spotted Paul standing with a full tray on the opposite side of the room, scanning the tables. The last thing I wanted was for Aodhan and I to sit down, and have Paul assume he was invited to join us.

I put my hand on Aodhan's arm, and asked, "Do you think we could eat out on the bleachers today?"

Aodhan's brow pinched, but he didn't question me. "Sure, Mer. Follow me."

We left through the canteen's side door, and Aodhan led me through the corridors and up the bleacher's steps until we were perched near the top. Once we were there, he put down his tray and took mine. When the trays were both on the seats, he faced me.

"Why do you want to eat out here?" he asked.

"It's a nice day." Panicked, I looked at his food, forgotten on the tray. Aodhan never forgot about food. "Isn't it?"

"Mer." Aodhan took my hands. "Tell me what's wrong. Please."

"Nothing's wrong so much as I'm annoyed," I said in a rush. "Paul's in all of my classes, and he won't stop talking to me and following me everywhere I go, and I just want him to leave me alone. Is that too much to ask for?"

"No. It's not." He tucked a strand of hair behind my ear. "Want me to talk to him, and tell him to quit it?"

"No," I said. "I would much rather avoid him, and hope he goes away."

"All right," Aodhan said, though I got the impression he would have preferred to haul off and give Paul a piece of his mind. "I won't confront him, but you have to tell me if he keeps bothering you. Deal?"

"Deal," I said, both grateful and relieved. "Will you eat now? It's not natural for you to ignore food for so long."

Aodhan squeezed my hands before releasing them, then we sat and put our trays on our laps. "What do you expect? You're so much more important to me than lunch."

I paused with my sandwich halfway to my mouth. "Really?"

Aodhan leaned over and kissed my cheek. "Really."

Unexpected Parents

That evening, Da, Mama, and I arrived at Saint Senan and Conainne's Academy at ten till seven. A large banner over the entrance declared it to be an open house, and bunting in the school's colours of blue and grey decorated the corridors that led to the gymnasium. A second banner in red and gold lettering hung across the gymnasium's double doors, welcoming us all.

"Headmaster Flynn certainly went all out," Da said. "I've never seen the school look so festive."

"Neither have I," I said. I pushed open the doors, and saw the room decked out as if the school was hosting a formal event instead of a simple meet and greet. Colourful streamers hung from the rafters, and one of the theatre teachers played music from a booth on the stage. People were standing in clusters around the room, though no one had started dancing yet. Thank all the gods for that bit of fortune. On the far side of the room was a long table covered with platters of snacks and neatly arranged stacks of napkins and cutlery. Of course, that was where we found Aodhan and his father. Both of them were filling up their plates as if they hadn't eaten in a week.

"Meri!" Aodhan called as he waved us over. Once we joined them, he said, "I had no idea there'd be food!"

"Think there will be enough for you?" I teased. Aodhan moved closer as if he would kiss me, then he caught sight of Da watching him and settled for giving me his goofy grin instead.

"Rose is handing out punch," Aodhan said, nodding toward a line of people.

"Oh, Rose is here?" I craned my neck to get a better view of that part of the room. Rose Fennimore was one of the school's few secular instructors, and I adored her. "Mama, want to meet my favourite teacher?"

"Lead the way," Mama said.

We queued up, and soon enough we were at the front of the punch line. "Rose, this is my mother, Aoife Murphy," I said, as I accepted a cup of punch. "Mama, Rose is my music instructor."

"A pleasure to meet you, Mrs Murphy," Rose said as she passed Mama a cup. "Word is that Meri comes by her voice from you."

"Is that what they say?" Mama asked. "I've been told you have a fine voice, yourself."

"I'm not bad, for an old teacher," Rose demurred. "Meri far out-shines me."

"I doubt that," I said, then I took a sip of punch and frowned. "Oh, that's rank."

Rose wrinkled her nose. "Aye, it's not the best. Something the headmaster no doubt picked up at a bargain. There's water at the other table," she added, nodding toward a cooler.

Mama and I moved on so Rose could hand out cups of that horrid swamp juice to those in line behind us, then we tossed our cups in the bin and grabbed a few bottles of water. I brought one to Aodhan, while Mama went in search of Da.

"Thanks," Aodhan said, as he accepted the bottle. "Think anyone's surprised to see your ma again?"

"There's probably a few blown minds." I spotted Mama and Da across the room, and watched as my parents made the rounds with my teachers and the other parents. It was fun watching the shocked faces of those meeting my mother for the first time, and of those who remembered the stories of my father rescuing her from a beach below the Cliffs of Moher all those years ago. Apparently, they'd all thought she was one of Da's drunken delusions. Well the joke was on them, since here was my mother in the flesh. Not to mention, Da hadn't had a drop of whiskey since Mama had returned.

"Look at your father chatting up Rose," I said, jerking my chin toward the two in question. Either Mr Sullivan thought the punch was palatable, or he fancied Rose. "Maybe he'll ask her out."

"Nah," Aodhan said. "Dad's still in love with Ma, for all the good that'll do him."

I spied movement at the door; speak of the devil, Aodhan's other parent had just arrived. "Aodhan, your mother's here."

"She is?" Aodhan spun around and waved at his mother. "Oh, no. She's brought him."

"Him who?" I craned my neck toward the entrance, and saw a very tall and imposing man enter behind Mrs Dumhach. He was wearing an expertly tailored black suit that looked as if it was worth more than my house. His shoes were so highly polished they gleamed like obsidian, large gold baubles at his wrists served as his cuff links, and a curved gold bar decorated his tie. All in all, he looked like a villain from a gangster movie.

"Is that your stepfather?" I asked.

"That's him, one Donn Dumhach."

"I don't know if he looks more like a zombie or a mortician." I clapped my hand over my mouth. "I can't believe I just said that."

"You speak the truth, Meri." Aodhan looked at his mother and stepfather and frowned. "I wonder where my sisters are."

Before we could speculate further, our new best friend, Paul, ran up to me and grabbed my elbow. Thankfully, my woollen jumper prevented us from making actual contact.

"Here, Father, this is Meri Murphy," Paul said. "This is the girl I told you about."

Aodhan's back straightened and his fist clenched; I hoped he wouldn't decide to punch Paul in the middle of a school event. I feared the only thing stopping him was the sudden appearance of the new headmaster, Marcus Flynn.

And that Paul had referred to him as Father.

"Wait." Aodhan looked from Paul to Headmaster Flynn. "You're the headmaster's son?"

"I am," Paul said, then he turned his back on Aodhan. "Meri, this is my father."

"Pleased to meet you," I said to the headmaster. I had no idea what to do other than be polite.

"And I am very pleased to meet you, Miss Murphy." Headmaster Flynn shook my hand. Up close, he was just as colourless as he'd seemed whilst onstage in the auditorium, and I could now confirm that his skin was as cold as a corpse. "You've made quite an impression on Paul."

"I-I have?" Before I could be forced into further small talk with the headmaster, Aodhan's mother and stepfather appeared.

"Hello, Aodhan, Meri," Mrs Dumhach said brightly. "Is this your new headmaster?"

"Uh, yeah. Ma, this is Headmaster Flynn," Aodhan said. "And his son. Paul."

Mrs Dumhach started chattering away at the headmaster, but he hardly noticed her. Instead, his gaze was locked with that of Aodhan's stepfather. The two stared at each other for a few heart stopping moments, then the headmaster turned away.

"Well, I'll leave you to it, Mrs Dumhach," Headmaster Flynn said; he clearly hadn't heard a word she said. "Come along, Paul." With that, Mr Flynn turned on his heel and walked away, with Paul trailing close behind him.

"That was rude," Mrs Dumhach said. "Donn, didn't you think that was rude?"

"Insolent is more like it," Mr Dumhach said. "He oversteps."

I glanced at Aodhan but he shook his head. I had no idea what was going on between Headmaster Flynn and Mr Dumhach, but I was certain I didn't want any part of it. Luckily, Da and Mama approached us, so I turned my attention toward them.

"Hello, everyone," Da greeted. "The Saints Academy certainly has come a long way since we were students, hasn't it, Bridgette?"

"It surely has." Mrs Dumhach smiled tightly; she was still sore about Aodhan and me getting in trouble—multiple times—while we were investigating MacCreehy, and her current plan seemed to be killing all of us with her extreme politeness. "Calliope, how wonderful to see you again. Will you be staying in town for a time?"

"I've no plans to leave," Mama said. "And please, call me Aoife. Calliope's naught but Brian's pet name for me."

"Is it?" Mr Dumhach asked. "What an interesting choice."

Mama looked up at Aodhan's stepfather. Her jaw tensed and her gaze went hard. It seemed that Mr Dumhach made everyone uneasy. "Brian came up with the name himself," she said. "I've no idea why."

"Your voice, perhaps?" Mr Dumhach pressed.

"Perhaps." Mama placed her hand on my shoulder and drew me toward her. "I'd like to visit with a few more of Meri's teachers. Good evening." As Mama, Da, and I walked away, I peeked over my shoulder toward Aodhan.

"We're leaving Aodhan all alone with those two?" I asked.

"He's hardly alone," Mama said. "He's with his parents."

"His stepfather is so strange."

"I agree, Meri. He certainly is." She paused, and asked, "What do you think of your new headmaster?"

"I think he's very odd," I replied. "What do you think?"

"I'd say there's more to him than meets the eye."

FOOLS FOR LOVE

Thursday morning passed much as Tuesday and Wednesday's had, with more of Aodhan and me kissing in the car park before class, and me doing my best to avoid Paul once I was inside the school. Being that we had all the same classes, I wasn't very successful. At least he didn't sit near me during chemistry.

I was on my way to the canteen—alone, having ditched Paul with a trip to the girls' washroom—when Aodhan appeared behind me and caught my arm.

"Ah, hello," I said. "Are you on your way to lunch?"

Aodhan scowled, and said, "He's telling everyone you're his girlfriend."

"Who—oh." Obviously, he was referring to Paul. My emotions warred between my increased irritation at Paul, and a new irritation with myself for wanting to apologise for something that wasn't in any way my fault. "Why would he say that? I've done nothing to encourage him."

"His sort doesn't need encouragement," Aodhan said. "Thinks he's entitled to any girl he fancies. I've been around guys like that my entire life."

I looked up at Aodhan and fluttered my eyelashes. "But you're not like that?"

"Stop distracting me with those eyes," he said. "Will Rose be all right with us eating in the music room?"

"Why would we want to eat in there?"

"It's raining, so the bleachers are off."

"I don't see why we couldn't use the room." There were plenty of desks and tables, and since it was lunchtime, no one else would be present.

"Good," Aodhan said. "Go on to the room, then, and I'll get lunch for both of us."

"Have you banned me from the canteen?" I demanded, irritated that Aodhan was telling me where to go and what to do. "First of all, you know I've done nothing wrong."

"No, you haven't done anything wrong, and I am the one who's banned." Aodhan ran a hand over his hair. "This isn't like yesterday when you wanted to eat on the bleachers just to get a few moments of peace. Right now, I'm so mad about what Paul's been saying, I don't know how I'll react to seeing that smug grin of his. My plan is to avoid Paul until I've calmed down, and can think rationally again."

He had a point; I'd all but ordered Aodhan out to the bleachers yesterday for much the same reason, and Aodhan hadn't complained a bit. Heart softened, I touched the back of his hand. "Why are you so upset?" I asked. "He's one person talking out of his arse. Leave it be."

Aodhan grasped my hand, then he rested his forehead against mine. "I know. You're right. I will leave it be, but for now, I just need to put some distance between us."

"All right," I said. I still wasn't pleased with his possessive behaviour, but at least he acknowledged it. "I'll see you in the music room, then."

"Thank you," Aodhan said, then he released my hand and went toward the canteen. I went the opposite way to the music room, and found the lights off and the door locked.

Rose must be out running errands, or getting her own lunch. I sang a low note, hardly louder than a breath, and smiled when the lock clicked open. I stepped inside the music room and let my eyes adjust to the darkness. I'd no sooner brought some chairs over to a table than Aodhan burst into the room carrying two trays of food, one stacked on top of the other.

"Where's Rose?" he asked.

"I've no idea. Eating on her own, perhaps?" Aodhan set down the trays. Our lunch amounted to chicken pot pies and two rather boring green salads. "You'd think with the amount of money our parents pay for our education, we'd have better lunches," I grumbled. Aodhan laughed through his nose. "What?" I asked.

"That's Dad and Ma's latest fight. He found out that my stepfather's paying for my and my older sisters' schooling, and he wants to take on the bills."

"Isn't it a good thing that your stepfather pays for school?" I asked. "Who else was supposed to do it?"

"Dad claims he left plenty of money for my sisters and me," he replied. "There's also revenue from the shop to consider." Aodhan took a bite of his pie and chewed thoughtfully for a moment. "I agree with you. Donal paying for our school was a good move on his part. Dad is just hurt, and sad, and..." Aodhan put down his fork and held his head in his hands. I reached across the table and squeezed his forearm.

"It's driving you batty, isn't it?" I asked.

"I should be happy," he said. "My father turned out to be not dead, and he's here. He's actually here with me. I've never wanted anything more than to talk to him again, go surfing with him one last time, tell him about track and all..."

"And, all what?"

"And now he's here, and him and Ma can't stop fighting, and my stepfather is pissed he's alive, and I don't know what to do." He cleared his throat, then dragged the back of his hand across his face. "I just don't know what to do."

I stood and went around the table, and put my arm across his shoulders. Aodhan turned toward me and hid his face against my midsection. I hesitated, but only for a moment, then I bent down and rested my face against his hair. Usually, Aodhan was the one comforting me. It was an unusual but not altogether bad feeling to soothe him for a change.

"None of us know what we're doing, not after everything we went through with MacCreehy," I said, as I stroked his hair; I liked taking care of him. "But it's all right. We'll figure it out."

"How?"

"Like we always do. Together."

After lunch, I made it to my next class and all the way to my desk without encountering Paul. Whilst en route to my second afternoon class—which was literature, the one Sister Mary Katherine should have been teaching—Paul caught up with me in the corridor.

"Meri," Paul said, and I cursed myself for letting my thoughts be distracted over Sister's current predicament. She would have admonished me herself, had she known I let my guard down.

I stopped and faced Paul. "Yes?"

"I didn't see you at lunch. Are you all right?"

"I'm fine."

He moved closer. "I was worried about you."

"No need to worry. I don't always eat in the canteen, so if you don't see me there tomorrow, it's fine." I forced a smile. "Really."

He placed his hand on my forearm, and I became intensely grateful for my blue uniform jumper serving as a layer between us. Not that Paul appeared to be filthy or otherwise unkempt, but I did want to keep some space between us. "Good," he said. "I'd hate for anything to happen to you."

I nodded, then Paul went on into the classroom. I looked up, and saw Aodhan standing at the far end of the corridor. His brows were pinched and his mouth was pressed into a thin line. I took a step toward him, but the bell rung. He shouldered his bag, then he turned and walked away. Since he was obviously sore about my interaction with Paul, I entered my class, fully intending to explain everything when I next saw him.

As it turned out, I didn't cross paths with Aodhan again until school let out for the day. I was walking down the main steps, intending to look for Aodhan in the car park, when he all but appeared in front of me. Before I could say or do anything, he pulled me close and kissed me.

Right there, on the school steps, he kissed me hard.

I'd never been kissed like that before. Okay, I hadn't been kissed very much at all, but Aodhan's lips were soft on mine, asking without demanding, patient and loving and everything I could have ever wanted. I'd never felt so adored in all my life.

We parted, and while I was still dizzy with endorphins Aodhan looked past me and smirked. I couldn't imagine who he'd be looking at—a team mate, perhaps—so I peeked over my shoulder to see who was back there. When I saw Paul Flynn gaping at us, my heart fell.

Aodhan hadn't been kissing me. He'd been marking his territory.

"What is wrong with you?" I hissed. "You care more about what he thinks than how I feel!"

Aodhan's gaze focused on me, and his eyes went wide. "No, Meri, that's not it!"

"Isn't it?" I shook myself free of him and stalked down the steps.

"Meri," Aodhan called.

"Stay away from me, Aodhan Sullivan," I yelled back.

By the time I'd walked home, Aodhan had called me at least three times. After the third call, I'd shut my phone off. He also drove past me twice, but was wise enough to keep going both times. I was absolutely not getting into a car with him, or going anywhere he was going. Walking would do me just fine.

When I got home, I stormed into the house, tossed my bag into my room, and stomped into the kitchen. Imagine my surprise when I found my mother putting the kettle on.

"Here for a bit of rage cooking?" she asked.

"I do not rage cook." I sat at the table, pouting.

"Oh, Meri girl, you most certainly do," Mama said as she took the seat opposite me. "Your father does, as well. Kevin rage eats."

"What do you do?"

"I stab things."

"Perhaps I should stab something, as well." I got up and went through the kitchen, searching for ingredients. I grabbed the sugar and vanilla extract, and set them on the counter. "Do we have any lemons?"

"Aye, your father just brought home a sack full of them for some reason." She watched as I tore the sack open and yanked out two lemons. "What are you making?"

"A lemon drizzle cake."

"Sour cake to match your sour heart?" When I didn't answer, Mama added, "Tell me what Aodhan did."

"He acted like he loved me, but it was all a show," I wailed, then I fell into Mama's arms and sobbed. "He kissed me, but not for me."

"For who, then?" Mama asked, as she stroked my hair. Between sobs, I told her about Paul claiming I was his girlfriend, and how Aodhan had kissed me in front of the entire school only to prove I was his.

"But I'm not his," I muttered. The kettle whistled. Mama sat me at the table, and started making our tea. "I don't belong to anyone."

"No, you don't, but you're more Aodhan's than Paul's." Mama delivered our mugs and sat opposite from me. "I'm surprised Aodhan didn't haul off and punch that Paul in the nose."

"He wanted to talk to him, and tell him to leave me alone." I recalled the several times Aodhan had said he would speak to Paul, and how I'd always told him to leave it be. "I told him not to."

"You forbade Aodhan from telling off Paul, so he proved that you're not available to that new boy in another way." Mama reached across the table and took my hand. "I'm not saying you don't have a right to be mad. You do, one hundred per cent. However, I also believe that Aodhan meant well."

"Then I should forgive him?" I asked. "Just smile and pretend none of this ever happened?"

"Absolutely not," she replied. "He upset you, and it's your right to tell him how you feel and demand an apology. However, I've seen how Aodhan looks at you. He loves you, and men in love tend to do the most foolish things."

"Did Da ever do foolish things for you?" I asked. "Or was he too afraid of you?"

"Brian has never been afraid of me," Mama said. "No matter how mad I ever got, or how I screamed and railed at everything under the sun, he never felt a drop of fear. Of course, I never screamed and railed at him, regardless of what annoyances we were dealing with. Brian was always the one keeping me sane. And there was the time he punched a man in the face over me."

"He did?" My father was the calmest, kindest man on the planet. Until that moment, I hadn't thought he knew how to make a fist. "Why on earth did he do such a thing?"

"Oh, Brian thought the man was trying to garner an invitation into my bedchamber," Mama replied.

"Was he?"

"Well, yes," Mama admitted. "The man in question was a prince from another sea kingdom, and there was talk of us being a good match for one another. Neither I nor your father agreed with that assessment." Mama paused to sip her tea. "This happened in the palace in Kilstiffen. It was all quite awkward."

"I'm sure." I gazed at the ingredients I'd assembled on the counter. "What should I do about Aodhan? Have him lay out Paul and be done with it?"

"If you think Paul deserves a whack, do it yourself," Mama replied. "As for Aodhan, give it some time. Let your anger settle, then see where you are. Aodhan is a good one, and I see how happy he makes you." Mama frowned a bit, and added, "Whatever you decide to do, make sure you're not acting out of anger. You don't want a few words said in haste ruining something so important to you."

I nodded, since I thought much the same. "I will."

The Party

On Friday morning, I attempted to walk to school instead of being driven there by Aodhan. He had other ideas.

I left my house extra early so he wouldn't be waiting at the top of the driveway for me when I began my walk. That part of my plan went off without a hitch, until Aodhan passed me on the road as he was on the way to my house. I'd hoped him seeing me walking by myself would have given him the hint to leave me alone. When I heard him screech to a halt, then turn the car around to creep along the road behind me, I knew it hadn't.

We continued on that way, with me pretending there wasn't a large black vehicle rolling along the road behind me, until Aodhan had enough. He swung the car around and stopped it directly in my path.

"Meri," he said, as he leapt out of the car. "Please, talk to me!"

"I'd rather not." I walked around the car and had every intention to keep on walking. Aodhan grabbed the strap of my book bag and dragged me to a halt.

"So, what, I make one mistake and you're never going to speak to me again?" he demanded.

"I don't want to talk to you while I'm still angry." He let go of my bag, and I turned to face him. His hair was wild, and he looked like he hadn't slept a wink. I couldn't deal with any of that, so I wrapped my arms around my stomach and looked at his feet. "I don't want to say something I might regret."

"Yell at me if you want." He stepped closer, his hand hovering near my elbow, but he refrained from touching me. "Scream, yell, hit me if that's what you need to do. Just don't shut me out."

"I don't want to scream or yell or hit." My voice caught at the end. "I don't want to be mean to you. I just want to calm down, and I haven't yet. You don't have to wait for me," I added.

"I'll wait," he said. "I'll wait forever, if you need me to." I nodded, then I turned to continue on to school. "Mer!"

I paused, and glanced over my shoulder. "Yes?"

"Let me drive you to school. Please." When I remained rooted in place, he added, "I won't talk."

"All right." Aodhan held open the door for me. "Thank you."

Aodhan got behind the wheel, and we drove in silence to The Saints. Despite what I told him, I wasn't mad any longer. I was sad, and confused, and wondering if we'd rushed into a relationship. I felt very strongly for Aodhan, and I wanted to be with him, but not if it meant him acting like a possessive creep and having a small meltdown every time a boy talked to me. Then again, I didn't want to be without Aodhan, either.

"I just don't know what to do," I mumbled.

"What was that?" he asked. Right, Aodhan and his magic ears picked up everything I said, whether I wanted him to or not.

"Nothing." He frowned, then he pulled into the student car park. "Thank you for the ride."

"I'll drive you home, too. If you want." We got out of the car, and Aodhan stood there with his hands in his pockets. "Mer, I'm sorry. I hope you can believe me."

"I do believe you. I'm sorry, too."

With that, I walked into school alone.

I kept to myself all day, and spent the lunch period in the depths of the library. No one took any notice of my behaviour, since I'd always been a loner. I daresay the only person who would have thought I was acting out of the ordinary was Aodhan.

He kept his word and left me alone during the day, and either couldn't find me during lunch or didn't bother looking. I don't know why the thought of Aodhan not looking for me tied my stomach up in knots, since I was the one who told him to leave me alone in the first place. I'd wanted Aodhan to leave me alone, and he did as I asked, and now I could barely function without him.

"This has become a fine mess," I muttered, as I walked out of school at the end of the day. Before I reached the stairs, Paul Flynn stepped in front of me.

"Hello, Meri," Paul said, in that incredibly cheery and annoying voice of his. "Do you have any plans for tonight?"

I began to say I'd be at the surf shop with Aodhan, and remembered that probably wouldn't be happening. "I don't. Why?"

"I'm having a party. The whole school's invited." He handed me a folded up piece of paper. "My address is on there. Hope to see you later!"

With that, Paul and his sunny disposition bounded away. I watched him disappear into the throng of students, then I descended the main steps. Aodhan was waiting for me at the bottom. When he saw me, he pushed off from the wall he'd been leaning on, and I followed him out to the car park. We were silent as we walked, and as we got into the car. Neither of us said a word until we arrived in front of my house.

"I'm not going to ask if you want to talk," he said without preamble. "I know that you won't talk to me until you're ready, and nothing in heaven or earth can change your mind. Please just know that I'll be waiting for you."

"Thank you. I really do appreciate that," I said, then I got out of his car and walked toward my house without looking back. I was afraid that if I did glance back all my resolve would crumble, and I would be doomed to spending my life cowing to Aodhan's moods.

But would that be so bad?

I squeezed my eyes shut, and imagined a life with Aodhan. Without him. With—gods forbid—someone else. I couldn't figure out what I wanted, and I desperately needed a sign to point me in the right direction. As I wallowed in my inner turmoil, I thrust my hand into my pocket, and felt the paper with Paul's address on it.

If I went to that party, I could experience first-hand what life without Aodhan could be like. Granted, it would only be one evening, but it could help me gain some perspective. After all, I was only seventeen. Just because Aodhan was my first boyfriend, didn't mean he would be my last boyfriend.

I tossed my book bag onto my bed and went straight to my closet. I had a party to dress for.

A few hours later, Kevin dropped me off at a crossroads, and I walked down the hill to Paul's house—or rather, Paul's estate. Whereas I lived in a simple farmhouse that had been occupied by generations of Murphys, Paul lived in an opulent mansion that looked like it had once been a manor home. It was at three stories high, and two wings stretched out from the central building like an enormous limestone hawk. The front gardens were well tended, not like the overgrown hedges that surrounded my house, and the stone pathways appeared to have been freshly swept. Everywhere I looked, the estate was as perfect as a magazine cover, but—and this is hard to explain—the landscape felt hollow. Soulless. As if the people who built this home had died long ago, and a team of hired hands had maintained it ever since. This house hadn't been a home for a long, long time.

My mother's warning about Paul and his father rang in my ears, but I shrugged it off. Paul was just a boy and his father was just a man, and if they or their house had somehow lost their souls, that was their business, not mine. I stepped up to the front door and rang the bell. While I waited, I studied the tall while pillars that framed the entryway, and the intricately carved details on the underside of the portico that stretched across the steps, and offered a bit of shelter from the elements. Even the bottoms of things were decorated around here.

While I traced the delicately carved acanthus leaves with my gaze, Paul himself opened the door.

"Meri! You came!" He grabbed my gloved hands before I realised what he was doing, and drew me inside. "I'm so glad you're here."

"Thank you." I gazed about the grand foyer. It was as over-decorated as the porch, with a marble mosaic floor and a sparkling crystal chandelier dangling overhead. "This is really your house?"

"It is," he replied. "Bit big for just me and Dad, but it's been in the family for umpteen years. Come on, everyone else is through here."

Paul led me through several ostentatious rooms packed with expensive looking artwork and oversized polished wood furniture. It made me wonder if he was bringing me through the grandest parts of his house in an effort to impress me. Little did he know, my mother's family home was a palace made of crushed pearls and roofed with gold.

Eventually, we reached a set of French doors. Through the glass I could see a game room, and some of my classmates were inside, milling about as they played pool and drank beer. All boys, no girls.

"Now, before we enter the party proper, there are rules." Paul indicated a glass bowl filled with keys set on a carved mahogany side table. "No drunk drivers are to leave from this address. Keys, please."

"I don't drink or drive, so no worries there," I replied. When he stared at me expectantly, I added, "I got dropped off, so there are no keys to turn over."

He regarded me for a moment, as if he was contemplating if I was telling the truth. "You'll need to leave your phone out here, too."

"What for?"

"My dad doesn't know about this party. If you call for a lift and you let it get out that the headmaster's son throws wild parties, it would mean big trouble for me."

I looked pointedly at the few people lounging on the couch, and the two boys halfheartedly throwing darts on the far side of the room. "This gathering doesn't exactly appear wild."

"Ah, but the media does like to spin things out of proportion, don't they?"

He held out his hand for my phone. I frowned, but remembered all the rumours and lies that had circulated about my family for years. Perhaps Paul was only being cautious, and not unreasonable. Reluctantly, I handed the device over.

"I'll keep this safe for you." Paul opened the doors and beckoned me inside. "Let's meet everyone, shall we?"

I pulled off my gloves and stuffed them in my coat pocket, and followed him into the party.

...And The Afterparty

I opened my eyes. I didn't know where I was.

Wait. I've been in this room before.

I was lying on a couch. A fluorescent light blazed above me. There were people around me. Classmates. People who went to school with me. People who had never once spoken to me, not on pain of death.

I was still in Paul Flynn's house. He'd done something to me, put me to sleep.

Had I been here all night?

Whatingodsnamehad—

I took a breath and willed myself to calm down. First, I had to get out of here. There would be time to freak out later.

I reached for my phone, but it wasn't in my pocket. Vaguely, I remembered handing it off to Paul when I'd first arrived. No matter, I would just figure out where he'd put it.

I glanced around the room. Thankfully, there was no sign of Paul, and no one else was paying any attention to me. Not knowing or caring where Paul had got to, I grabbed my coat from where it lay beside me on the couch, and went to the French doors. Those doors seemed to be the only way in or out of the game room, and luckily they weren't locked. Not that I was above breaking all that fine glass to make my escape.

Once I was in the outer room, I looked around, intent on finding my phone. The bowl of keys was still there on the side table by the doors, but no phones were alongside it. Interesting. I looked around the room, trying to figure out where Paul would hide someone's belongings. It was one of those old style formal sitting rooms, filled with antique chairs that nobody sat on, and cupboards full of dishes that were too fine for ordinary meals. I went through every drawer and looked behind and underneath every *objet d'art*, and even in between the stacks of plates and saucers in the cabinet. I found nothing, not even a cobweb.

Where would he have hidden the phones so no one could call out?

My gaze moved to the stairs opposite the home's main entrance. They were a glorious affair, worthy of a fairy-tale princess floating down them to meet her prince for a night at the enchanted ball. Pity the only prince here was Paul Flynn.

He must have stashed the phones—along with anything else he wanted to bribe his guests with—somewhere upstairs. Since I didn't want to spend the time or energy needed to search every room in this massive house, I closed my eyes and concentrated on my phone; I thought about what it felt like in my hand, what colour it was, places on the case where I'd touched it. Then I sang a single low note, and asked the music to find anything on the second floor I'd had contact with.

One, two, three heartbeats.

Ping.

I ran up the stairs and turned left at the first landing. I didn't know where I was going, but my song did. It was as if the note had imprinted itself on my phone, and I was on the end of a string being pulled toward it.

My song led me to a set of large wooden doors at the end of the hallway. I pushed them open without thinking, realising only after I'd entered that I was in somebody's bedroom. The centrepiece of the room was an enormous four-poster bed swathed in dark green curtains. Deep blue damask wallpaper covered the walls, and the rest of the furniture was just as large and imposing as everything I'd seen downstairs. Why did every room in this place resemble a museum more than a home?

Hm. Perhaps no one actually lived here.

This couldn't be Paul's room. It was too much for a teenage boy, even a boy as odd as Paul. Perhaps it was his father's room, then? But I'd always thought of school headmasters as academics, whilst this was a room fit for a reclusive billionaire. Then again, the prior headmaster, MacCreehy, had been no academic, and it had taken me an embarrassingly long time to figure that out. Perhaps it was my expectations that needed tweaking.

I spied a large wooden bowl on a table next to the bed. In it were the confiscated phones. I found mine soon enough, and swiped my thumb across the screen. Nothing. I pressed the power button, held it for at least thirty seconds. A dead phone stared back at me.

"Damn it all," I hissed. I rooted through the rest of the phones, hoping a charging cord was in there as well. While I didn't find a charger, I did realise that all of the phones had dead batteries. I was so intent on searching for a stray cord that I nearly jumped out of my skin when someone spoke.

"You can use my charger, if you need it."

I turned around and saw Kelsey McGrath sitting on the floor in the far corner of the room. Her phone was plugged in to a wall outlet.

"Thank you." After a moment's hesitation, I sat next to Kelsey. She took the cord from her phone and offered it to me. As soon as my phone was charging away I assessed Kelsey's appearance.

She was wearing her school uniform, and it was wrinkled as if she'd had it on for several days. Her bright auburn hair, which was usually perfectly styled, was a tangled mess. The shoulder of her shirt was stained, and her makeup had run down her cheeks. What was more jarring than her unkempt appearance was that she was cowering in a corner. The Kelsey I knew wasn't afraid of anything, certainly not a boy like Paul Flynn.

"Why are you hiding up here?" I asked.

"No one's found me yet," she replied. "Even when Paul came in to leave more phones, he didn't find me."

"Have you been here long?"

"Longer than I wanted," she replied. "What day is it?"

"Saturday," I replied, then I remembered that I hadn't seen Kelsey at school the day before. "When did you get here?"

"Thursday," she replied. "I came here right after school."

"Why haven't you gone home?"

"I can't. Paul doesn't want me to leave." She raised her eyes to mine. "He won't want you to leave, either."

A ball of ice formed in the pit of my stomach. "That's too bad, because we're going." I glanced around the room, scanning for alternate exits. I got up and pushed open the first door I saw, which turned out to be a bathroom.

"In here," I said to Kelsey. "Let's get you cleaned up."

And so I spent the next fifteen minutes watching the girl who had tormented me for the past twelve years cry as she washed her face, and her hands tremble as she combed the snarls out of her hair. I didn't ask her how she'd ended up in this house, or why Paul didn't want people to leave. There would be time enough for questions after we got out.

And we were getting out.

As soon as Kelsey was as presentable as she was going to get, I checked my phone. The battery was at forty per cent, so I powered it on and sent a text.

If I send you an address, will you come get me?

I hit send, then I squeezed my eyes shut and waited. He would probably say no. Or he'd demand an explanation and then say no. Or maybe he wouldn't reply at all.

My phone pinged. I looked down and saw one word on the screen.

Yes.

I fired off the address, then I unplugged the charger and grabbed Kelsey's arm.

"We're leaving," I said, then I spied the thin blouse she was wearing. "Have you a coat?"

"I did when I got here," she replied, "but I don't know what Paul did with it."

What had happened to her to make her so helpless and scattered? I grabbed a throw blanket from the foot of the bed and tossed it around her shoulders.

"That'll do, for now." I opened the bedroom door a crack, and sang into the hallway.

"Why did you do that?" Kelsey asked.

"It's to keep anyone from coming near us." I grabbed her hand, and we crept out of the room. "Hurry, it won't hold for long."

We made it across the hall and down the stairs without incident. When I put my hand on the doorknob, I felt magic push against me, keeping the doors closed and us in the house. I sang, and pushed the magic back. The door's spell was strong, but so was I. More than that, something awful had happened to Kelsey and I needed to get her away from this place and sorted out as soon as possible. The spell had just begun to give way when a hand clamped down on my shoulder.

"Leaving, girls?" Paul demanded. "I'd rather you stayed."

I shrugged out from under him. "No."

He reached for my hand and Kelsey screamed. "Don't let him touch you," she shrieked, then she took the blanket from her shoulders, threw it over Paul's head, and kneed him in the crotch. As he staggered back, the spell on the door finally shattered. Kelsey and I pushed it open and fled down the front steps.

When we reached the gravel driveway, I turned around and sang the door seams together, thus making the entrance as solid as a wall. That done, Kelsey and I ran across the front garden and onto the main road. We followed it down to the crossroads and collapsed into a heap in the underbrush, breath ragged and hearts pounding. We were still hiding in the bushes when Aodhan's car screeched to a halt beside us.

Weird Headspace

"**M**eri?" Aodhan got out of the car and came round to us. He stopped short when he saw Kelsey and me sitting in the hedgerow. "Meri, what happened?"

I stood, and swallowed hard before I spoke. "We, ah, were at a party, and we needed to leave. Thank you, for coming."

"We?" Aodhan's gaze refocused on Kelsey, his eyes widening when he realised who I was with. He took a few steps to the side to get a better view of the house in the distance. "The party was there?"

"Yes."

"Meri. Whose house were you in?"

I swallowed again, and desperately wished I could dig a hole and hide in it. "Paul Flynn's."

A muscle twitched in Aodhan's jaw. "What happened to Kelsey?"

"I don't know. I don't think she does, either. When Paul touches you, it—"

"Paul touched you."

"There's something about it, something magical," I continued, ignoring the murder in his eyes. "It only affected me while we were in contact, but Kelsey got the full brunt of it."

Aodhan stared at me for another moment, then he moved toward Kelsey. "Up you go," he said as he helped her stand. "We need to get both of you out of here."

Kelsey and I got into the back of Aodhan's car. I sat behind Aodhan, but Kelsey ended up lying prone with her head in my lap.

"You saved me," Kelsey mumbled, as Aodhan pulled out onto the road so fast we slid across the seat. "Why?"

I hushed her, and said to Aodhan, "As I was saying, Paul has some kind of magic. It's in his skin. Whenever he makes skin to skin contact, it's like you lose your free will."

"Why didn't that happen to me when he shook my hand?"

"I don't know. Maybe he can control it. Maybe it only works on females."

Aodhan looked back at Kelsey, who was nearly senseless. "Meri, how many girls were at this party?"

"Only me and Kelsey. Why?"

"That means that whatever Flynn's doing, he wanted you two specifically."

I stared at my and Kelsey's reflections in the side window. "Yeah. I thought of that, too."

Aodhan pulled into Kelsey's driveway and parked. I don't know how he'd known her address. Maybe he knew the address of every student from The Saints.

He came around and opened the door, then he and I got Kelsey out of the car and onto her feet. "Should we go in with you, and talk to your parents?" I asked. "I don't want you getting in trouble or anything."

"It's fine. They'll just think I was at a party all night." She laughed softly. "Which I was. Look at me, telling my parents the truth." I glanced up at Aodhan, his pinched brow telling me that he felt as awkward as I. Then Kelsey threw her arms around my neck and hugged me.

"Thank you," she whispered. "You saved me. You, of all people. By rights, you should have left me there to rot, but you saved me."

"Past is past," I said. "If you need me, call me."

Kelsey drew back, nodding as she wiped her cheeks. Aodhan and I watched her until she entered her house.

"I can walk home from here," I said.

"Absolutely not," Aodhan said. "Get in."

"Aodhan, I—"

Aodhan rounded on me and grabbed my shoulders. "There's Flynn out there doing who knows what to girls with a single touch." I saw his Adam's apple bob up and down, that muscle flexing again in his jaw. "I am not letting you walk anywhere alone, not while he's still out there."

"Okay," I said. "I won't walk."

"Good. Get in." He released me so suddenly I stumbled. We got into the car, and Aodhan resumed driving.

"You saved me just as much as I saved Kelsey," I said. "You could have left me there, or ignored my text entirely. I was rather shocked when you agreed to come for me."

"What, you thought that just because we had a fight, I'd abandon you? You're still my girlfriend." He reached over to squeeze my knee, but stopped halfway. "I mean, if you still want to be."

Girlfriend. He'd never once referred to me as his anything, and I now knew he'd been considering me his girlfriend for some time. I should have been mad, or at the very least offended. The Meri Murphy of a few days ago would have given him a speech about how she was no one's property and never would be. But now I wanted to be his. Any doubts I'd had about Aodhan were gone like so much morning dew.

I took Aodhan's hand in both of mine. "I'm sorry I got so mad at you, and for how I acted afterward. I should have talked to you right away, like you wanted."

"It's all right, Mer." He leaned toward me and kissed my knuckles, all the while speeding down the narrow roads. That was only slightly terrifying. "I'm sorry, too. I could have handled everything much better." He glanced at me, and asked, "So we're still together?"

"I suppose I have to be your girlfriend," I said. "If anything changed, it might alter our gang."

He laughed. "Is Kelsey the newest member of Murphy's Maniacs?"

"She can be on probationary status, for now."

"Want to go to the shop? It should be quiet there."

"All right."

When we got to the surf shop, Aodhan spent a few minutes talking to Lorcan at the counter. Once they were done, he beckoned me to follow him, and we went into the business office. I sat on one of the guest chairs, while Aodhan claimed the seat behind his desk. He immediately powered on the computer and started typing.

"What are you doing?" I asked.

"I'm searching for Paul Flynn."

"Aodhan, there must be hundreds of Paul Flynns in Ireland," I said. "Maybe thousands."

He frowned at the screen. "There are forty-five million results worldwide. I'll search his dad."

"I bet there are just as many Marcus Flynns." Aodhan didn't say anything, but his frown deepened. "What are you hoping to accomplish with all of these searches?"

Aodhan hit the desk with his palms, then he leaned forward and covered his face with his hands. "I want to find out what kind of monster he is! He's after you, Meri. I've got to stop him."

I went around to his side of the desk and sat next to the keyboard, then I took Aodhan's hands from his face. "You're right, we do need to learn what he is. I just don't think that poking around the internet will give us answers."

"How can you be so calm about all of this?"

"I'm not calm. I'm freaking out. I was terrified earlier, so incredibly scared I'd be stuck in that house forever and never find my way home... Then you said you'd come get me. I haven't been afraid of anything since I read your text."

"You said whatever he did, it's done by touch?" he asked, and I nodded. "Where did he touch you?"

"Aodhan, it wasn't like... like I wanted him to!"

"I know." He stroked his thumb across my knuckles. "I just need to know."

"When I first got there, he kept grabbing my hands," I began. "I was wearing gloves, so nothing really came of that. After I took them off, he kept grabbing at me, but I always stepped out of his reach."

Aodhan squeezed my fingers. "Then what?"

"I was sitting on a couch in the game room, and he tucked some hair behind my ear. I remember his fingers against my ear, my neck... And then I came back to myself and I didn't know what happened or how long it had been." I sobbed at the end. "I didn't know what had happened to me."

"Hush, hush now." Aodhan stood and pulled me against him. "I've got you. Hush." I clung to him as if he were my lifeline, choking on sobs and shame in equal measures. "I'm going to kill him."

"We can't kill him until we know more."

Aodhan drew back and regarded me. "You're all right with me killing a classmate?"

"Of course I am. I probably want him dead more than you do." Aodhan smiled, then he touched my cheek.

"He touched you here?"

"Other side."

He moved to caress my other cheek, then he kissed it as his fingertips followed the curve of my ear down to my neck. His mouth followed his hand until he pressed his lips against the skin just above my collar.

"I'm sorry," he whispered.

I blinked. "For kissing me?"

"For being such a jerk about everything," he said. "I've been in this weird head space, and then Flynn showed up being all smooth and even though I know you don't like him, he so obviously liked you, and I freaked out. I freaked out, and I did that whole display at school to prove to Flynn that I was already with you and you were off limits to him, and all I did was make you mad."

"You did make me mad, but what put you in this weird frame of mind?"

"I." He took a breath, ran a hand over his hair. "I wanted to be with you for so long, and now we're together, but I'm terrified I'll screw everything up."

I draped my arms over his shoulders. "I'm afraid of that, too." Surprise crossed his face. I continued, "If it's any consolation, I've recently had an epiphany and realised I can't possibly go on without you."

"Really," he said, his face split by a massive grin. He moved closer and had barely touched his mouth to mine, when we heard footsteps outside the office door. Aodhan sighed and rested his forehead against my hair.

"Aodhan?" Mr Sullivan called.

"In here, Dad." He flashed me a wry smile. "He always finds us at the best times, doesn't he?"

"Must be parental radar." We laughed, and were still laughing when Aodhan's father entered the office.

"Am I interrupting?" he asked. "Wait, do you two need a minute? Should I even ask that?" He shook his head. "I'm trying to be a cool dad, but I'm still having a tough time remembering that you don't think girls are gross anymore."

"Dad, you've always been the coolest person I know," Aodhan said as he sat in the chair. "Meri and I were just talking."

"Hi, Mr Sullivan." I bit my lip. "Should we tell him what happened?"

Aodhan's brows lowered. "Is that really a good idea?"

"He probably knows more about this stuff that we do, on account of his time with MacCreehy."

"What the hell is going on?" Mr Sullivan demanded. "Are you two in some kind of trouble?"

"Yes, but it's not regular trouble," Aodhan replied, then we told Mr Sullivan everything we knew about Paul, and everything I remembered from Paul's house. By the time we'd finished, I was sitting on Aodhan's lap in the office chair, and his father was sitting cross-legged in the centre of the desk, leaning on the window frame.

"So he can't enthral remotely. He needs physical contact," Mr Sullivan mused.

"I hadn't thought of it as enthrallment," I said.

"The question is, why did he want to enthral you in the first place," Mr Sullivan continued. "You don't have any recollection of what happened while you were out?"

"Everything went black," I replied. "When I woke up, at least my clothes were still on."

I'd meant it as a joke, but my voice caught at the end. I covered my face with my hands and took a deep breath, willing myself to calm down. Aodhan rubbed my back, and murmured that I was safe now.

Mr Sullivan squeezed my shoulder. "I understand, Meri."

I wiped my cheeks with the back of my hand. "I'm sorry. I'll be fine in a moment."

"You don't need to be fine," he said. "Be as upset as you need to be. But don't be sorry about how you feel. You earned those emotions."

"Thank you," I said, but he wasn't done yet.

"And don't be scared anymore, either. Aodhan loves you, which means that I love you, too. I don't let people I love get hurt, not if I can help it. Mark my words, I'll take care of this Flynn dude." Mr Sullivan released my shoulder, then he hopped down from the desk and stretched. "Unless your mother catches him first. Man, I would be terrified if I saw her coming at me with her sword out."

I glanced at Aodhan. His face was as red as a tomato. "Well, your mother is pretty scary," Aodhan said. "Speaking of which, we should probably tell her and your dad about this, too."

I sighed; I really didn't want to tell this story again, but he was right. "There's also the matter of classes on Monday."

"Let's worry about that on Monday," Mr Sullivan said. "Come on kids, I'll drive. Aodhan, did I tell you your mother sold my Mustang?"

"About a dozen times."

INVITATIONS

Mama slammed her palms onto the table and stood. I'd just relayed to my family what had happened at the Flynn house, and while none of them were pleased, she was outright furious. "I'm going to kill him," she seethed.

"Can everyone please stop threatening to kill Paul," I said.

"Give me one good reason why I shouldn't," Mama demanded.

"Yeah," Aodhan said. "He needs to be dealt with."

"Murder is still illegal, for one," I said. "Also, shouldn't we figure out what his game is first? There must be more to him than throwing parties and tricking girls into staying over."

Da and Kevin scowled, but Mama was unfazed. "The real player here is his father. I knew it the moment I saw him. That new headmaster's turning out to be almost as much a problem as your stepfather," she added, with a nod toward Aodhan.

"Donn's a problem?" Aodhan asked.

"What about Headmaster Flynn," I said over him.

"The Saints should be renamed Saint Supernatural," Kevin muttered.

"Guys, give me a second to talk," Mr Sullivan said. "Aoife, you said Donn is a problem. Is Bridgette in danger?"

"I don't know," she replied. "Bridgette has borne him children, so that offers her a degree of protection. It also means she's tied to him, most likely until one of them passes."

Mr Sullivan frowned so hard the cords stood out on either side of his neck. "She has a degree of protection from what?"

"From him," Mama replied. "Bridgette's husband is a sidhe prince."

Mr Sullivan went pale and ashen as a ghost. "What, now?"

"Aye, Donn's a wily one," Mama said. "Been poking around the sand dunes near Lahinch for ages, that one has. Rumour is he's searching for a treasure he buried some time ago, but lost track of."

"My stepdad is a fairy prince." Aodhan glanced at his father, and asked, "Mrs Murphy, forgive me for asking, but why didn't you mention that earlier?"

"It's not for me to judge who Bridgette takes up with," Mama said. "After all, Brian here married a merrow."

Da nodded. "And I'll do it again."

Mama looked at me and sighed. "We can discuss Donn at another time. Right now, the Flynns are my most pressing concern. That, and our invitations."

I couldn't believe Mama was so hung up on her vow renewal she thought her invitations were more important that a classmate of mine who could incapacitate girls with a mere touch. "I'm sure plenty of people will show up to your ceremony," I said, but she shook her head.

"Not invitations to the party," she said. "The king and his council have summoned us back to Kilstiffen."

"Us?" I asked.

"You, me, and Kevin," she replied, then she pursed her lips. "No one else."

No one else meant Da wasn't invited, and didn't that just prove every fear I'd had about being trapped down there below the sea? I'd just been almost trapped by Paul Flynn, and there was no way I was getting myself stuck in Kilstiffen, regardless of what my grandfather the king wanted.

"Excuse me," I muttered, then I pushed back from the table and fled to the kitchen. Once there, I leaned on the counter and stared out the window over the sink, and took a few deep breaths.

Not getting trapped. Not with Paul, and not down there.

"Everything all right in here?" Da asked. I wasn't mad or even surprised that he'd followed me into the kitchen. Ever since he'd started teaching me to cook when I was a wee thing, it had always been our special place.

"Yeah. I just needed a moment." I turned around and faced my father. "Da, I don't know if I want to go back to Kilstiffen. Not yet, anyway."

He stood next to me and leaned against the counter. "I understand. In fact, I may be the only one who understands how you feel, save perhaps Kevin. Those from Kilstiffen don't trust those who live above or below their city, not so far as they can throw them."

"Is that why most of the people treated us the way they did when we went to visit the king?"

"Yes and no. After all this time, they still consider me an outsider, and that's fine with me. However, for the king to invite you and Kevin back means that he sees you two as part of his family."

"Are you sure?" I pressed. "Actually, when we were down there, I felt like he wanted us to stay."

"Perhaps he wanted you three to stay, but not me. I'm the filthy surface dweller." Da leaned close, and added, "If you ask me, I think the old goat wants to make amends with Aoife, and he's using you little ones to do it."

I laughed, picturing Grandfather with goat horns peeking out from underneath his crown. "I can't imagine Mama letting him get away with that."

"No, I can't either." Da went serious. "Meri girl, about what happened at the Flynn house. You're sure he didn't hurt you?"

"I don't really know what he did while I was unconscious." Da winced at the last. "But I don't feel hurt, not physically."

"And you'd tell me if you were?" Da pressed. "If anyone hurt you, even Aodhan?"

"I would. And Aodhan would never," I added.

"In a father's eyes, all boys are suspect," Da said. "And you can be sure I'll say the same to Aodhan."

Da embraced me, and I rubbed my cheek against his old, scratchy jumper. I used to do that when I was small and upset, and the only thing that would ease my hurts was one of his hugs. "I'm sure you've already given Aodhan your big, scary speech."

"I have, a few times. Are you ready to go back to the rest?"

"I am. Thank you for checking on me."

"Any time, Meri girl." Da gave me a final squeeze. "Any time."

Da and I reentered the dining room. Before anyone else could say anything, I announced, "If we're going to Kilstiffen, I think we should bring a fourth person. Someone from above."

"Why is that?" Mama asked.

"Because if we have a surface dweller with us, they won't try to keep us down there," I said. "They'll want us to return the outsider."

Mama nodded, her lips pressed into a thin line. "You'll be wanting Aodhan to accompany us, then?"

"Actually, I thought Mr Sullivan would be best."

"Why not me?" Aodhan asked.

"After everything, I think he'll deal better with the weirdness of the city." I glanced at Mama. "Sorry."

"No, no, Kilstiffen is a strange place," she said. "I've known that my whole life, even before I came above for the first time."

"Is this something you'd do?" I asked Mr Sullivan. "I would understand if you didn't want to."

"Meri, because of you, I'm a free man. I would go anywhere for you," he replied. "Besides, maybe if those underwater city dwellers meet someone from above whose life was thoroughly messed up by Seamus, it will earn your mom some brownie points. But," he added, "what about Bridgette and Donn?"

"I'll stop by the house and snoop around a bit," Aodhan said. "If Donn doesn't know we're on to him, this might be a good time to figure out what he's up to."

Mama nodded. "It's settled, then. Meri, Kevin, Lucas, and I will go to Kilstiffen. Aodhan shall check in on his mother and gather what information he may. And, Brian." Mama paused, and looked at Da. "What will you be doing, Brian?"

Da stretched his arms and clasped his hands behind his head. "I am going to relax, and contemplate the menu for our wedding."

While Mama and Da discussed what sort of soup and other appetisers should be served at their second wedding, with Kevin putting his two cents in, Aodhan and I stepped out to the garden to steal a moment's peace.

"Are you mad I picked your dad to go below, instead of you?" I asked.

"I'm kind of relieved, actually," Aodhan said. "Now that I know Ma's been living with a fairy, I feel I'm needed there more. Not that I wouldn't go if you needed me to," he added.

"I know you would. And you can come next time." I blew out a breath. "Now that I've met the king I'm sure I'll get summoned below whenever he feels like it."

"Hey." Aodhan took my hand, and we sat on the edge of the raised vegetable bed. "Didn't you like meeting your grandfather?"

"I did, and the city itself is so beautiful," I replied. "Even so, I can't shake the feeling that my grandfather wants something from me."

Aodhan stroked my cheek. "Maybe he wants a chance to know his grandchildren."

I moved so I was facing him, and smiled. "You see the good in everyone, don't you?"

"Not everyone," he replied, then he pulled me toward him and kissed me. This time he kissed me hard, as if he'd been waiting too long and the urge had overtaken him. I felt the same, and wound my arms around his neck to keep him as close as possible. I liked being in his arms, and I wanted to stay.

We parted, panting, his brown eyes staring into mine. "Is that what you'd wanted to happen back at the shop?" I asked.

"Yeah. That, followed by endless apologies from me, and maybe dinner."

"Are you ever not hungry?"

"I'll let you know if it happens."

"Meri." Mama came outside, and found Aodhan and I perched on the edge of the vegetable bed. As I slid out of his embrace, she said, "Time to go."

"We're leaving now?" I asked as I stood.

"Best to not keep the king waiting. Aodhan, good luck at your mother's. Remember, even though Donn has no reason to suspect you know what he really is, be careful. Despite what all the stories say there's no such thing as a good fairy."

Aodhan nodded. "I will, Mrs Murphy. Thank you." When Aodhan didn't let go of my hand, Mama smiled.

"Don't worry, Aodhan," she said. "I'll bring Meri and your father back. Kilstiffen's taken enough from us. I won't let them take anything more."

Betrothals And Dalliances

It was much easier for us to access Kilstiffen this time. Perhaps the guards had been told to expect us, and were waiting by the door for our arrival. Although, they should have been expecting us last time, seeing as how we'd been invited by the king for that visit, as well. Regardless of how or why it happened, the gates were speedily opened, and along with the guards, we made the short walk to the palace. The guards didn't even question Mr Sullivan's presence among us, which was odd.

Odder still was that the residents of Kilstiffen were out in plain view as they went about their day; I saw people working in their gardens, hanging out the washing, and doing other mundane tasks about their homes. Some of them even waved and smiled at us, or pointed at Mama and saluted. It made me wonder why the locals had been so unwelcoming during our last visit, and who had put them up to that show of hostility.

When we reached the palace, our escort brought us straight to the throne room. As before, the king was waiting for us.

"My children," Grandfather boomed from his throne. This time, the throne room was packed with onlookers. A group of men wearing the same robes I'd seen on those in the courtroom-like chamber from before were clustered near the king; it seemed that the council of lords had a hand in summoning us below. Every one of them looked down their noses at us. The council was no fan of my family, and frankly, I wasn't a fan of them. "We appreciate your speedy response to our summons."

"Thank you for summoning us, Father," Mama said. "I hope you are not offended, but we did bring a guest."

Grandfather focused on Mr Sullivan. "Aoife, those from above are not welcome here."

"Does that include Da," Kevin muttered.

"He's no ordinary man from above," I said in a rush. "He's Aodhan's father, and he's one of the villagers that were enthralled by Seamus MacCreehy."

The council mumbled and shuffled their feet. Oh, so they knew Seamus's name, and how he'd wreaked havoc across Ireland above. As for Grandfather, his big, bushy eyebrows went so low I couldn't see his eyes. "Aodhan? I do not know that name."

"Aodhan helped me look for Mama," I replied. "We never suspected we'd also find Aodhan's father, but we did. We freed him, along with the merrows and everyone else MacCreehy had kidnapped."

A curt nod, then Grandfather fixed Mr Sullivan in his glare. "Your name?"

"Lucas Sullivan."

"You're not Irish," Grandfather said.

"Not by birth, no," Mr Sullivan replied. "I'm from the US. California, specifically. I came to Ireland around twenty-five years ago."

The king made a second curt nod. "I see what is happening here. We shall adjourn to the day room."

With that, Grandfather descended from his throne in a flurry of velvet robes. Mama shrugged, and the four of us followed him into the room painted like noontime, which was the same room we'd had lunch in during our last visit. The robed councilmen also attempted to enter the room, but Grandfather held up his hand.

"This is a family matter," he said to the men. "I shall meet with you afterward." The men frowned, but didn't attempt to follow us inside the room.

"Why do they want to get in here?" I whispered to Mama.

"That's the council for you," she replied, loud enough for those men to hear her. "Nosy as the day is long. All they've ever done is make things worse."

"Aoife," Grandfather warned. "Have a care."

"I'll have a care when they do," Mama grumbled.

Servants swarmed past the council members and into the room, guiding the five of us to our assigned chairs and placing goblets of ice cold water in front of us. Once our refreshments had been delivered, the servants disappeared, and shut the doors behind them. Grandfather took his place at the head of the table, and regarded each of us in turn.

"Father," Mama began, but the king held up his hand; apparently that was a code for everyone to stop talking. Mama fell silent, but she didn't look pleased about it.

"So you've come to negotiate a marriage," Grandfather said to Mr Sullivan.

"Ah, no, your majesty, I haven't," Mr Sullivan replied. "I'm already married." Both Mama and I gave him a look. "Well, I'm not getting remarried," he added.

Grandfather's gaze darted between us. "Then you wish to claim my granddaughter for your son as compensation for your time with MacCreehy?"

"What? No," I shrieked, loudly enough for servants to come pouring back in. "I will choose whom I marry! There will be no negotiations or compensations involved!"

Grandfather waved away the servants, then he steepled his hands atop his girth. "Is that so? As a daughter of Kilstiffen you were betrothed before you were born. In fact, these betrothals are why you were summoned here today. The council is interested in expediting the process."

"That is... that is." I struggled to form words, my fury making my hands shake and my voice unsteady. "That is not how we do things!"

"Meri, relax," Kevin said.

"She's got a right to be mad," Mama said.

"It is how things are done here," the king said, as he narrowed his eyes at Mama.

"And why are you betrothing me, when you never betrothed my mother?" I demanded, then I noticed Mama staring at the table and being unusually quiet. "Mama? Were you ever betrothed?"

"I was," she began. "But then Seamus began conscripting merrows, and I went above and met your father—"

"We would have overlooked a dalliance with a surface dweller," Grandfather interjected.

"And that boy you found for me was awful," Mama continued. "He was an absolute stranger to me, and you expected me to accept him as a husband?"

"There was a man before Da?" Kevin asked.

"We were betrothed in name only," Mama said. "I never laid a finger on him, nor would I on pain of death."

"Aoife," Grandfather boomed. "You will not insult our allies, no matter that they are not here to witness your behaviour."

"Who are these allies?" I asked. "We could use them for what's going on right now." When Grandfather gave me a sharp look, I added, "I understand you invited us here to discuss these betrothals, but we have more pressing matters at the moment. There are things happening up on the surface and we may need to call upon these so-called friends."

Grandfather regarded me for a moment, then his gaze slid toward Mama. "Explain."

She breathed out the harried king's daughter, and breathed in the calm façade of a warrior. "I believe that a collector has come to our village, and appears to have set his sights on Meri, and at least one other girl."

"And there's a fairy prince after my wife," Mr Sullivan said in a rush.

Grandfather's gaze flicked toward Mr Sullivan, then it returned to Mama. "A single collector cannot be much of a threat. Meri's soul is strongly tethered to her physical form."

"My soul?" I asked. "And what is a collector?"

"Collectors—ankou, we once called them—collect the souls of the dead," Mama explained. "I believe that Marcus Flynn is a collector, which explains his animosity toward Donn; as Master of the Dead, Donn wants all souls for himself. However," she added, as she addressed Grandfather, "this fellow appears to be fixated on the living. He's also got a lackey posing as his son."

"You don't think Paul's really his son?" I asked.

"I don't," Mama said to me, then she faced Grandfather. "This creature in the guise of a human boy is as dangerous as the collector, perhaps more so. He enthralls girls with a touch."

"You think he's a gancanagh?" Grandfather asked.

Mama nodded. "I do. A creature such as that one could lay waste to the land above, even without the assistance of a collector who's decided the living are fair game."

"Is the gancanagh the collector's ally, or servant?" Grandfather pressed.

Mama spread her hands. "That, I do not know."

"And the creature has targeted Meri?"

"Yes," I said. "He tried to trap me in his house."

Grandfather nodded. "Thank you, for alerting me. If these creatures are focused on Meri in any way, they must be stopped. I shall summon our allies at once."

"Who are they? Our allies," I added.

"We have many, but the closest are the sea kingdoms of Ker Ys, Llys Helig, and Lyonesse," Grandfather replied, then he rose and exited the room. My curiosity overruled my manners yet again, and I followed him.

"Meri," Kevin began.

"I'll be fine," I said, then I rushed down the corridor. Behind me, I heard Mama assuring Kevin that I would be safe with the king.

"I've heard of Lyonesse," I said, once I caught up with him, "but where are the other two located?"

Grandfather looked down at me. For a moment, I thought he wouldn't answer, then he beckoned me into a side chamber. On the wall was a massive painting that depicted a map of the northern Atlantic Ocean.

"Ker Ys is here," he said, pointing to a spot off the coast of Brittany. "And Llys Helig is here." He indicated the sea near the Welsh coast.

"There really are sunken cities all across the world." I stepped closer to the map, scrutinising the details. "Where is my aunt stationed?"

"You've an interest in The Shadow?"

It took me a moment to figure out that this Shadow was my aunt. "Of course I do," I replied. "I only recently learned I have an aunt, on your side."

Grandfather grunted. "She is here, in Evonium." He pointed to a spot halfway up Scotland's western coast.

"Is her name really Shadow?"

"No. She moves like a shadow, and the enemy never sees her approach."

"So when I meet her I should call her..."

Grandfather sighed. "You are much like your mother. Scáthach. My eldest daughter is called Scáthach."

"Thank you, for sharing these details with me."

"They are not details," Grandfather said. "By rights this information is yours as much as mine. You are the heiress to Kilstiffen."

"W-What about Kevin?"

"He is the heir." Grandfather turned from the map to a lavish tapestry that hung on the opposite wall. It depicted how Kilstiffen must have looked when it rose above the waves, proud and tall and covered in so much sparkling gold you could hardly look upon it.

"It has ever been the way among the guardians," he continued. "Every monarch has two children, and those children carry on the sacred duty of guarding those who reside below from those above."

His words surprised me; I'd thought it was the other way 'round, and we were guarding the surface from those who lived below. "So you had Mama and Scáthach."

Grandfather's gaze darkened. "I have a son, as well." Before I could fully process that bit of information, Grandfather continued, "Come, Meri. You may assist me in the summoning."

He left the side chamber and continued on down the corridor. I followed a moment later, my head spinning with everything he'd told me. Apparently, I had an uncle, and he didn't seem to be on such good terms with the rest of the family. Based on that revelation, and that the king seemed to be the only royal in this palace, I was starting to think that Grandfather held onto his grudges quite tightly.

I followed the king into a chamber at the end of the corridor. The walls and ceiling of this room were deep blue, like the sea. At the far end of the room was a clam shell so big I could have fit inside it, and sat inside it on a velvet cushion was a pearl as big as my head.

"Pearls are important here, aren't they?" I asked.

"You really are much like your mother," Grandfather said again, although this time he was smiling. "Come, place your hand on the pearl with me."

I did as he asked. The pearl's surface was warm, and soft. Being in contact with it was comforting. "Is this how we summon people?"

"Yes. Now close your eyes, and sing with me."

I followed Grandfather's instruction, and sang to match his notes. My mind's eye was suddenly filled with images of lands I'd never been to or even dreamed of. All of them were surrounded by swirling green and blue seas, and were populated with amazing creatures and people. As the images presented themselves, I noticed one location that remained constant, which was that of a bleached stone palace set on a sandy island in the middle of a calm sea. A curved stone walkway led to the palace gates. The gates opened, and a man and a woman stood on the path. They were beautiful, with long mahogany hair that shone as if polished, and emerald green eyes.

The man looked directly at me, and smiled.

I yelped, and snatched my hand away from the pearl as if it had burned me. When I opened my eyes, Grandfather was watching me intently.

"That man," I began, holding my hand against my breast. "He saw me?"

"He did, and how fortuitous it was," Grandfather replied. "That was Nahel, the prince of Ker Ys."

I swallowed. Hard. "He's the one you intended for... for me?"

"Yes, and his twin sister, Dahut, will be betrothed to Kevin," he replied.

"Why them?" I asked, rather desperately. "If we have all these allies scattered around the globe, why are we getting betrothed to those two?"

"The council chose Ker Ys, not me," he replied. "Let us return to the others."

I followed Grandfather out of the summoning room and back down the corridor. Not only had I never once considered a betrothal, or marriage in general, I had definitely never seen a man like Nahel. He was beautiful, and a prince, and I assumed he was a merrow, or something similar. I wondered if he could sing, and if he liked art, or baking.

We re-entered the noon room, and my gaze immediately landed on Mr Sullivan sitting across from my brother. How would Mr Sullivan feel if he knew I'd just been fantasising about a prince I'd never met instead of Aodhan? For that matter, how would Aodhan feel? Awful, that's how. Guilt washed over me, and I shoved all thoughts of Nahel as far from my mind as they could go. After I did that, I noticed Mama frowning, as if she suspected something had happened in the summoning room.

"I've sent a message to our allies," Grandfather announced. "Meri assisted me."

"Thank you," Mama said. "We shall return home, and await word from you."

Grandfather opened his mouth as if he'd ask us to remain below, perhaps to discuss more of our marriage prospects, then his gaze alighted on Mr Sullivan, and he seemed to change his mind. That glance told me I was right to bring someone from above. We said our goodbyes, and began the walk out of the palace and back to the surface.

"Why does everyone feel like they're trapped down here?" Kevin asked, once we were outside the palace. "We walk in and out as we please. Can't they do the same?"

"They don't want to," Mama replied. "Most who live in Kilstiffen have no idea how to navigate the world above. If I hadn't met your father, I don't think I would have ever attempted to have a life in the village."

"MacCreehy managed it," I began, but Mr Sullivan shook his head.

"MacCreehy had us," he said. "We weren't just his army. We taught him how to pass himself off as an ordinary man. We did his shopping, told him what clothes to wear, everything."

Mama smiled sadly at Mr Sullivan. "I'm so sorry, Lucas."

"Truly, Aoife, none of what he did to us was your fault."

As my mother and Mr Sullivan spoke about the aftereffects of their time around MacCreehy, I tugged at Kevin's arm so he would hang back with me. Once we were about ten paces behind them, I said, "I saw the one Grandfather picked for you. For the betrothal."

"Really," Kevin said, trying and failing to feign disinterest. "What's she look like?"

"She's absolutely beautiful," I replied. "Long dark hair, big green eyes, dressed like the clothes cost her a million euros. Or pearls, or clams, or whatever they use for currency down here."

"Did you catch her name?"

"Dahut. She's the princess of Ker Ys."

"Dahut," Kevin said, rolling her name around in his mouth. "She have a family name?"

"You can't be seriously considering this!"

"And why shouldn't I?" Kevin countered. "It's not like I have anyone, not like you do."

What Kevin said was true; we'd always been loners. "I'm sure you could meet someone if you tried," I began.

"I have tried," Kevin said. "But even though we look like everyone else, we're different. People pick up on that, and it raises their hackles. It's like a primal instinct kicks in, warning others to steer clear of us."

"Are you saying we smell like monsters?" I asked, and he laughed through his nose. "Monsters or no, I can't believe you'd give up everything for a woman you've never met."

"I didn't say I'd give anything up, but what if we got on well? What if we're a good fit for each other?" Kevin blew out a breath, and faced me. "I'm not saying I'm going to grab her hand and marry her. I'm only saying that if I happen to meet her, I won't be rude. Besides, don't you think I'd make a great prince?"

"Technically you're already a prince," I grouched. "Just don't go and leave me all alone up there."

I'd expected Kevin to make a joke or call me a pest. Instead he looped his arm around my neck and squashed me against him in an awkward big brother hug. "Promise you won't leave me alone, either."

"I promise."

Rage Baking

It was late afternoon when we got back to our house. Da was in the kitchen working on dinner preparations, and Aodhan was nowhere to be found.

"How were things below?" Da asked.

"Awful," I replied. "Kilstiffen itself was lovely, but Grandfather thinks he's going to marry Kevin and me off to some allies of his."

Da snorted. "Don't you worry, Meri girl. Steinar's a reasonable man. He always does the right thing, eventually."

"Eventually?" I repeated. "How long will that take?"

"Tough to say." Da took a pot off the stove and drained the contents into a colander. "Grab the reblochon cheese from the fridge for me, please?"

I opened the fridge, and found the cheese sitting on the top shelf in its round package. Da had recently found a bunch of interesting recipes on a French food blog, which in turn led to him ordering fancy cheeses off the internet. "What are you making?"

"I found a new to me recipe for potato casserole, and thought I would try it out. You know how your mother adores potatoes." Da set the cheese on the counter, and started peeling onions. "As for how long it will take Steinar to come to his senses, if you and Kevin aren't for these marriages, I doubt he'll force your hand."

"But what if he does?" I asked, a bit desperately.

"Does it matter?" Da countered. "He may be a king, but he can't force you to marry anyone. A no is a no, and Steinar will just have to deal with it."

Somehow I didn't think the king was used to hearing no. "Where's Aodhan?"

"Out back," Da replied. "No one was home at Bridgette's, but he had a good look around. Now, he's taking out his frustrations on the brambles near the greenhouse. Why don't you go see how he's getting on?"

I darted out the back door without another word. Aodhan was exactly where Da said he would be, waist deep in the ancient raspberry patch. He looked up when he heard me running toward him, and smiled.

"Hey, Mer," he began, then I flung my arms around him and held on as if he was my lifeline. "Careful. I'm all sweaty and gross."

"I don't care." I pressed my face against his chest. "My grandfather and his stupid council want to marry me off."

Aodhan went still. "What? Are you going to do it?"

"No!" I stepped back and stared at him. "How can you even ask me that?"

"I meant, do you have a choice in the matter?" He took my hands. "You can say no, right?"

"I don't know. Maybe. Da thinks I can." I used my sleeve to wipe my face. "My mother refused her betrothal, so I guess I can refuse mine. He's got another one cooking for Kevin, too."

Aodhan swallowed. "Did he introduce you to the, um, the man?"

"No, but I saw him. He's a prince from another underwater city. That one's called Ker Ys." I laughed through my nose. "Apparently it's tradition for the rulers of these cities to marry off their children to one of the other cities."

"He's a prince?" Aodhan asked. I looked up, saw uncertainty splayed across his face.

"I don't care if he's a prince," I said. "My answer is no. And if Grandfather dredges up another prince or a king or a stupid emperor I won't want them, either."

"Then we'll keep them away from you," Aodhan said. "No one is going to tell you who to be with, not even your grandfather. They'll have to go through me to get to you."

"You'd stand between all of Kilstiffen and me?"

He smoothed my hair back from my forehead. "Meri, I'll stand between the world and you."

His words reverberated in my bones and settled around my heart. I had Aodhan, and he had me, and together we were unstoppable. I stood on my toes and kissed him so hard he stumbled backward.

"Sorry," I mumbled.

"It's all right," he said, as he steadied himself. "Kiss me all you want. I can handle it."

"I bet you can."

After we spent a bit more time among the brambles, Aodhan and I joined everyone else in the kitchen. Mama and Mr Sullivan were sitting at the table, while Da was lining up bowls on the counter. Kevin, as usual, was nowhere to be found. He only tended to make an appearance in the kitchen after the food was ready.

"What's all this?" I asked, as I eyed what Da was up to. In addition to the bowls, he'd set out flour, eggs, and sugar.

"Thought you might need to bake something," Da said. "The oven's already warm."

"Despite what you all think, I do not rage bake," I said. "But, a cake would be nice."

While I cracked eggs and measured out the rest of the ingredients, Da greased the cake pan, and Aodhan went back out to the garden and picked a basket of early strawberries. Mr Sullivan wasn't expected to help out, since he was a guest. As for Mama, according to Da food tasted better when she wasn't involved in preparing it. Mama agreed, and sipped her tea while she watched the rest of us work.

Soon enough, the cake was in the oven, and Aodhan's bounty of strawberries was rinsed off and waiting in the colander. I put a copper bowl in the freezer, which Mr Sullivan thought was quite interesting.

"Why'd you put an empty bowl in the freezer?" he asked.

"For the whipped cream," I replied. "It beats up fluffier in a cold bowl."

"You make your own whipped cream?" He shook his head. "I've never considered doing that."

I shrugged. "With the proper ingredients you can make anything."

"Maybe that's what's happening with this collector," Aodhan said. "Does he need to gather certain types of people to make or accomplish something?"

"I'm not sure," Mama said. "Collectors typically only go after the souls of the dead. Why he wants living souls is a mystery."

"What do they do with these souls?" I asked. "Usher them on to the next world?"

"No," Mama replied. "The collectors consume the souls, thus ending that individual's existence both mortally and spiritually."

I shuddered, and reached for Aodhan's hand under the table. "Oh."

"What makes you think he's a collector?" Aodhan asked.

"His appearance, mostly," Mama said. "He resembles a corpse, and a corpse is really all he is."

"Can't we ever get a normal headmaster," I muttered. Mama looked at me sympathetically.

"Perhaps the next will be just a man," she said.

"Do you think this collector might be related to Donn Dumhach hanging around?" Mr Sullivan asked.

"Anything is possible with Donn," Mama replied. "He's been above for a very long time. And you knew him before you met Bridgette, is that right?"

"I did, but I had no idea he was anything other than a regular guy," Mr Sullivan replied. "We met shortly after I opened the surf shop. Actually, he got me a job at his finance company to help me cover the shop's expenses for the first few years." He shook his head, then he turned to Aodhan. "Did you learn anything at home?"

"No one was there, which was nice," Aodhan began. "I also broke a promise I made to myself long ago, and went into Ma and Donn's bedroom." Both Aodhan and his father shuddered.

"Surely it was just a room," Da said, hopefully.

"It was, but they have this huge walk-in closet. It used to be the upstairs office," Aodhan explained, and I remembered that Mr Sullivan had built that house. Just when I thought my heart could not break further for him, I realised that another man was not only living with his wife, it was all happening in what should have been his home. "Anyway, I poked my head in the closet to see what's what, but there aren't any clothes in there. Instead, all the walls are covered in maps."

"Really," Mama said. "Maps of what?"

"Of this area," Aodhan replied. "There's old maps, newer maps, and some that look like military charts with satellite coordinates. Whatever Donn's up to, he's looking for something."

"Didn't you say he's been searching for a lost treasure?" I asked my mother.

"That's the rumour," Mama replied. "Supposedly he left it beneath the dunes in Lahinch, but then he angered some of the gods and they moved it on him. He's been searching for it for, oh, as long as I can remember."

"Wait," I said. "Is Aodhan's stepfather a god? As in, someone who belongs below Kilstiffen?"

"Aye," Mama said. "To both of your questions."

The five of us sat in silence, then the oven timer beeped. Da got the cake out of the oven and turned out onto a rack to cool. I grabbed the copper bowl from the freezer and poured in the cream and sugar, then I reclaimed my seat.

"Who exactly is below Kilstiffen?" I asked, as I began beating the cream with a wire whisk. "Anyone else we should know about?"

Da and Mama shared a look. "That look means the answer is a yes, doesn't it?" I demanded.

"Meri, leave it be," Mama warned.

"Tell me who, and I'll leave it and serve the cake," I countered.

"Yes, let's have cake," Aodhan added.

"Fine," Mama snapped. "My mother's there, along with her father."

I sat back in my chair. I'd wondered why Grandfather ruled alone. "Your mother's a god?"

"She's the daughter of Manannán mac Lir," Da said. "Her name is Niamh."

"And that's why my necklace is called Manannán's Pearl," I concluded. "Have you met her?" I asked Da.

"Meri," Mama said. "The cake."

Right, I'd promised to serve the cake. I got up and retrieved a stack of plates, but I couldn't move on quite yet. "What about your brother?" I asked. "Grandfather said he had a son."

Mama's face darkened. "I do not know where Oscar is right now."

That was definitive. I cut five slices of cake and topped them with the whipped cream and sliced strawberries, then we ate our treats in silence. When we were done, Da asked, "What should we do next?"

"I want to learn more about this collector, and his pet gancanagh," Mama said. "Brian, care to watch the Flynn house with me?"

"Surely," Da said. He was always willing to do whatever Mama needed of him.

"I'll hang around Bridgette's house," Mr Sullivan said. "I might notice something that leads to a clue."

"What should we do?" Aodhan asked.

"Wasn't another girl trapped along with you?" Mama asked.

"Kelsey," I replied. "She got the brunt of whatever Paul's up to."

"Perhaps if you and Aodhan talk to her about what happened, we can determine why the collector wanted her in the first place," Mama said. "Once we know what he's after, we can use that knowledge to figure out how to stop him."

I glanced at Aodhan. "Looks like we're spending Saturday night with Kelsey."

Unexpected Allies

Before Aodhan and I went to Kelsey's, we went to the surf shop's apartment so he could shower and change. While Da and I worked out our issues via cooking and baking, and Mama by stabbing things, Aodhan used physical exertion as his therapist. After learning that his mother was married to a sidhe prince, and hearing my mother describe what collectors do with souls, he finished his cake and went back out to the garden and beat some more weeds into submission. He felt much better afterwards, even though he was a bit dusty. I didn't begrudge him the yardwork, or a shower.

While Aodhan got cleaned up, I sat at the kitchenette's table and sent Kelsey a text.

Meri: How are you?

Kelsey: I'm all right. Better than this morning.

Meri: Want company? Aodhan and I can stop by.

Kelsey: Why are you being so nice to me?

Kelsey: You should hate me.

Meri: I don't. And what happened to you was magical, therefore not your fault, and I'm hoping you can tell us something that will lead to us stopping Paul.

Kelsey: And the headmaster. He's the one in charge.

Meri: Then we can come by?

Kelsey: Come to the back door.

I set down my phone and wondered what the hell I was doing. While it was true that Kelsey hadn't deserved to be singled out by Paul, she had tormented me for as long as I could remember. Why I felt the need to talk to her again, in person, was a mystery; we could have gotten all the information we needed from her through a few text messages. Then again, she'd always tormented me in concert with Sarah, and those two seemed to have parted ways. Perhaps, bereft of her evil companion, Kelsey will turn out to be a good person.

Or perhaps monkeys will fly out of my ear. I know which event I thought was more likely to occur.

I heard the bathroom door open, and instinctively looked up. There was a mirror on the wall directly across from me, and from where I was seated it was angled to reflect the area on the far side of the apartment, which included the bathroom door. When my gaze landed on the mirror's surface, I gasped.

Aodhan was exiting the bathroom, and he was totally, completely naked.

I opened my mouth to, what? Ask him to cover up, or let him know he had an audience? No noise issued forth from my lips, not even a peep. And as for the rest of my face, I couldn't stop staring at him. Aodhan had a beautiful body, lean and well-toned on account of the many sports he played. My gaze dipped lower, and I broke out in a cold sweat.

I'd never seen a naked man before, not in person. As men went, Aodhan was a spectacular example.

Why isn't he getting dressed? Aodhan was wandering around his sleeping area, leisurely picking out clothes and heaping them on top of his dresser. I glanced over my shoulder, and realised what was happening. From where he was standing, he couldn't see me, and I could only see him in the mirror.

Wonderful. I've been spying on him.

"Mer," he called out, and I yelped. "Are you all right?"

"Fine," I replied, my voice cracking on the word. I cleared my throat, and continued, "I'm fine. What are you doing back there?"

"Nothing. Be out in a minute."

I glanced at the mirror. He was still bare as an egg, with his towel draped around his neck and covering up absolutely nothing. Then he turned around, and I learned that the view from behind was as inviting as the front.

Good God, I needed to stop staring at him.

I opened a game on my phone and focused all of my attention on the brightly coloured pixels. In fact, I was so focused on the neon coloured boxes and explosions that when Aodhan put his hand on the back of my neck, I yelped again.

"Sorry, Mer," he said, as he rubbed my neck. "Why so jumpy?"

"No reason," I said in a rush. "I see you decided to get dressed finally," I said, then I bit the inside of my cheek. "I mean, you look nice."

"Thanks," he said, then he gave my shoulder a final squeeze and went to the fridge. "We should have brought the rest of the cake here."

"If we stocked flour and sugar here, I could bake one for you any time," I said. "They only take a few minutes to put together."

"That's a great idea. If we cooked more often, it would make the apartment feel homier."

I opened my mouth, closed it. All I could think about was seeing Aodhan naked, and the last thing I wanted to do was tell him about it. But, I couldn't just sit there mute, not without Aodhan questioning me about my uncharacteristic silence. My gaze alighted on my phone, and suddenly I had a safe topic.

"Kelsey said we can stop by," I said, as I stood up and held my phone aloft as evidence. "We need to go to the back door."

"Back door it is," he said, then he cupped my face with his hands and kissed me like we were in the movies.

"Why are you so nervous?" he asked, when we parted. "Is it because we're here alone? I would never... I mean, I wouldn't try anything."

He was so cute when he got all flustered. "I know you wouldn't. And it's not you," I added. "I've had a weird day, what with getting out of the Flynn house, then going to Kilstiffen and Grandfather talking about marriages, and now we're going to see Kelsey, on purpose." I draped my arms across his shoulders. "This weird day has made me a bit of a weirdo."

"You're my favourite weirdo," he said, then he got serious. "Were you thinking about that Nahel?"

"I was not thinking about him at all," I replied, and that was the truth. In fact, whilst I was watching Aodhan in the mirror, I'd forgotten about Nahel's entire existence. "And I'm going to keep not thinking about him, and that's his problem. Not ours."

"Our problem's Kelsey." He rested his forehead against mine, and added, "And my stepfather, and the Flynns. We've got a lot of problems."

"We've also got each other," I said. "What is it you always say? Together, we can do anything."

"Yeah, Mer," he said, with a smile. "We're unstoppable."

The next thing unstoppable us did was head to Kelsey's. We went around to the back of the house as instructed, and found Kelsey sitting at a table on a rather nice patio, having a drink and smoking a cigarette.

"Took you long enough," she said, when she saw us.

"Next time we'll break the sound barrier to reach you," I shot back. "How are you?"

"Fine." She gestured to the deck chairs. "Have a seat. Want anything to drink?"

"Maybe later." I eyed her glass, and saw that it was wine. "Are your parents home?"

"Yeah, but it doesn't matter. They don't care what I do." She gulped her wine. "They've never cared what I do."

For a moment my heart went out to Kelsey, then I remembered the many, many times she'd gone out of her way to make me miserable. "How did you end up at Paul's house?" I asked.

"Same way you did," she replied. "He asked me to come over. Actually, he was mad when he asked me, made it seem like I was his second choice. I'm guessing you were number one as always, Meri."

"What is that supposed to mean?" I asked.

"You're the prettiest girl in school, the best singer, have the best bad home life story," Kelsey ticked off. "But now your mother's back, so you've got the best reunion story, too. Maybe leave a bit for the rest of us, will you?"

Of all the things I never expected to learn that day, hearing that Kelsey was jealous of me was not it. I looked at Aodhan, beseeching him for help with my eyes.

"When did Paul invite you over?" Aodhan asked. "Was it also for Friday night?"

"No," she replied, shaking her head. "It was Thursday, right after school. I walked onto the main stairs, and he turned around and saw me. Right then, he asked me to go to a party at his house, and we left for his place. I guess it was pretty stupid of me to go there."

I glanced at Aodhan, and his pursed lips and pinched brows told me he'd come to the same conclusion I had: after Aodhan kissed me on the school steps to prove to Paul that I was off limits, Paul had taken Kelsey to his house.

"What happened is not anyone's fault, but Paul's," Aodhan said, to me as much as Kelsey. "He's the villain here, him and his dad." Aodhan nudged my foot underneath the table. Since I appreciated his unwavering support, I nudged him back.

"What happened after you got to the party?" I asked. When Kelsey didn't answer, I leaned across the table and set my hand on her forearm. "I'm not here to judge you. Promise."

Kelsey's eyes darted toward Aodhan. "What about him? He's as much a goody two shoes as you are."

Aodhan held up his hands, palms out. "My only opinion is that Paul can sod off."

"Yeah. We can agree on that." Kelsey stubbed out her cigarette. "I don't really know what happened at Paul's house; at least, not all of it. When I first got there, the headmaster was home. Paul paraded me in front of him, and the headmaster said she'll do, for now," Kelsey said, pitching her voice lower for that last bit. "Again, I wasn't what they wanted, but they would work with me."

I must have gone pale, because Aodhan squeezed my knee underneath the table. "Was the headmaster there for a long time?"

"No. He got a look at me, then he left. I haven't seen him since." Kelsey downed the rest of her wine. "I had a coat with me, but Paul took it and put it somewhere. Then he took my phone, my hat, and my keys. I told him I wanted to leave, then he took my hand and told me to stay." She glanced at me, then away. "That was magic, wasn't it? Like your voice?"

"It was," I replied. "Paul doesn't sing, though. He takes away free will."

She nodded. "He definitely took mine. No way would I have stayed there on my own."

"I believe it," I said. "What else happened?"

"After he told me to stay, he stuck me up in that bedroom, and I lost a great deal of time."

"How much time?" I asked.

"I'm not sure," she admitted. "When I woke up, it was Friday. I found my phone in that big basket yours was in, too, and I had my charger cord in my pocket. I plugged in my phone intending to call for a ride and leave, but Paul came in and found me before the phone was charged up. But, he didn't find my phone plugged into the wall."

And so Kelsey told us of her harrowing day, where she had her phone plugged into an inconspicuous corner to charge while Paul barged in and out of the bedroom, demanding she do things for him. As for the things she did, they were odd, to say the least.

"I made him breakfast. Burned his eggs," she added, with a grin.

"He deserves burned eggs," I said. "Was it all domestic stuff?"

"That's all I remember," she said. "But there was more, wasn't there?"

"I'm really not sure," I admitted. "We think Paul's not a regular person, but instead he's a magical being that works by making contact with his victims. We're trying to figure out how to get rid of him."

Kelsey nodded. "All right. How can I help?"

I blinked. "You believe all of that?"

"Why wouldn't I?" she countered. "I lived it. I lived with him touching me and taking away my right to make a decision, my right to choose. Besides, you said your mother was a mermaid and she would come back one day, and she did. When it comes to magic, you're the expert, not me."

"We have a gang," Aodhan said. "It's called Murphy's Maniacs. There aren't many members right now, so if you join you can be an officer. Are you in?"

Kelsey nodded. "Oh, I'm in. I want to take Paul's magic and shove it so far up his arse it comes out his throat. I want him to regret ever inviting me to his house."

"All right," I said. "You're in."

Confessions

Since I didn't want Kelsey in my home—not yet, anyway—I texted Kevin whilst Aodhan texted his father, and we all agreed to meet up at a pub in the centre of town. When the three of us arrived, Kevin was already there, having secured us a table as far away from the stage as possible. As soon as Kevin saw us, he waved us over.

"Nice table," Aodhan said.

"This is Kelsey," I added, as we sat. Kevin blinked, and did a double take.

"*Kelsey* Kelsey?" he demanded. "The evil one?"

"I'm sitting right here," Kelsey grouched. "And most of the bad stuff was Sarah's idea."

"No, it wasn't," Aodhan and I said in concert. Alone, I added, "But we're moving past that."

"How nice," Kevin said. "Gives me a warm fuzzy feeling."

"Speaking of warm and fuzzy, have you heard from Da?" I asked. We always texted him because Mama hated typing on her phone.

"He said they're fine, nothing to report yet." Kevin signalled the bartender. "We'll start with some pints, yeah?"

"Yeah," Kelsey said, a bit too eagerly.

"I'm only here for the fish and chips," Aodhan said, as he picked up the menu. "No alcohol for me. What with track starting up next week, I need to stay in top form."

An image of Aodhan's top form flitted behind my eyes. I cleared my throat, and said, "Should we really go back to school, what with the headmaster being evil?"

"The last one was evil, too," Aodhan pointed out.

"What was MacCreehy's deal, anyway?" Kelsey asked.

"He coerced people into joining his army, and made it look like they'd died," I replied. "Cliff jumpers, boating accidents, stuff like that."

"So when you tried to jump off the Cliffs of Moher, was that MacCreehy messing with your head?" she pressed.

"Um, yeah. In a nutshell."

Kelsey shook her head. "Good thing you had your boyfriend here to grab you before you went over. When you started running, Aodhan took off after you, screaming his head off for you to stop. It was pretty traumatic for everyone."

I glanced at Aodhan, and saw him blushing. "You were screaming?"

"I was, and I caught you, didn't I?" He took my hand and kissed my knuckles. "Proved I'm faster than magic, too."

"You're not faster than me," Aodhan's father said as he came up behind us. "You're not bad, though. You've got potential."

"Potential," Aodhan scoffed. "I'll show you potential."

"You always have." Mr Sullivan took a seat, and extended his hand across the table to Kelsey. "Hi. I'm Lucas, Aodhan's dad."

Kelsey's eyes widened as she stared between Aodhan and his father. "But, your boat went down. I remember it."

Mr Sullivan ducked his head. "What can I say. Shipwrecks don't stop the Sullivans."

"It's not fair," Kelsey muttered. "You got your father back, and Meri got her mother, but I... but I..." Her eyes welled up and her lower lip trembled, then Kelsey shoved back from the table and stalked across the pub. I rose to follow her, but Kevin was on his feet in an instant.

"I'll go," he said, and he disappeared into the crowd after Kelsey.

"What was that all about?" Mr Sullivan asked.

"She lost her mother, and when we freed everyone from MacCreehy, she thought she might get her back," I explained. "But it didn't work out that way."

"Poor kid," Mr Sullivan said. "She's the one who was at the Flynn house with you?"

"She was," I replied. "Apparently Paul brought her to the headmaster, and he approved her and everything."

"That is creepy," Mr Sullivan said. "When you two were at the school, did you see the headmaster—this ankou, I guess we're calling him—talk to Donn?"

"We did," I said. "Those two did not appear to like each other. You could feel the chill in the air when they were staring each other down."

"So if Donn is against the Flynns, does that mean we're on Donn's side?" Aodhan shook his head. "I don't know how I feel about that."

"Come on, now, Donn's not a bad guy," Mr Sullivan said. "He's not right for Bridgette, but that's another story. Besides, we might need him to help deal with the Flynns."

My phone chimed. I checked the screen, and saw a text from Da. "Speaking of the Flynns, my parents are back from staking them out," I said. "Da also invited you for dinner and an overnight, Mr Sullivan. He thinks it's best if we all stay together."

"Can't argue with that," Mr Sullivan said. "Let's go."

"I'll get Kevin," I said, and I darted toward the bar. I found my brother and Kelsey sitting on a pair of stools, chatting it up.

"Da and Mama are back with news," I said. "We're going back home to discuss our next moves."

"We'll be on it a bit," Kevin said. "Got to finish our pints first." My gaze moved from my brother, to the pints, to Kelsey's uncharacteristically shy smile.

These two were on a date. When had that happened?

"I'll see you at home," I said, since I did not have the spoons to deal with whatever those two had going on between them. I made my way to the sidewalk, and found Aodhan and his father waiting just outside the door.

"Where's Kevin and Kelsey?" Aodhan asked.

"Flirting," I replied. "Let's go."

When we got back to my place, we found a casserole bubbling away in the oven and my parents out back in the larger garden shed. Da was checking the rivets and straps on Mama's shield while she sat at the workbench, sharpening her sword.

"I take it the stakeout went well," I said.

"We learned absolutely nothing," Mama said. "Not a soul was in that house, which means those monsters are out and about somewhere."

"Wonderful," I said. "Only every female in Ireland is at risk of being abducted by Paul."

"You're certain whatever he does only works on girls?" Mr Sullivan asked.

"It didn't work on me," Aodhan said.

"No, it wouldn't," Mama said. "If Paul is truly a gancanagh, he is only able to conscript females."

"Would he affect you?" I asked.

"Yes," Mama said. "Which is why if I see him, I'll cut off his hands before he can touch me."

I watched her slow, methodical movements as she dragged her sword's blade across the whetstone. "You're serious."

"I am," Mama replied. "You know first-hand how dangerous these creatures are. We cannot let one run amok, not if we can stop it."

"We should question him if we catch him, and see if we can figure out what the headmaster's collecting," Aodhan said. "Other than girls, of course."

"Odd that he's collecting anything living at all," Mama said. "If he's collecting in the here and now, he's after something specific. It is imperative that we figure out exactly what he wants."

Later on, after dinner had been consumed and the washing up was done, the grown-ups sat at the kitchen table while Aodhan and I went out to the back porch. The night had gone chilly, so we brought a blanket and sat on the bench with the covering wrapped around us. There was an awning above us, which made the spot cosy, but we still got to see the stars.

"Kevin still isn't back," Aodhan said. "Him and Kelsey sure hit it off."

"I don't even want to think about that." I burrowed further into his arms. Even though the night was cold, with Aodhan I felt warm and safe. "This day felt like it was a million years long. I can't wait for it to be over."

"Want to head back inside?"

"No." I rested my head against his shoulder. "I'd like to stay out here a bit longer. If that's all right with you?"

"Of course it is." He kissed my hair, and my eyes fluttered shut. "We'll stay as long as you want."

The next thing I knew, it was morning. I was still warm and comfortable, but the porch was drenched in sunlight. My first thought was of the people of Kilstiffen, who hadn't seen the sun in over twenty years, and probably wouldn't see it for seven more. According to Mama they could come above whenever they wished, but they chose to remain below. That fact made me lose quite a bit of sympathy for them, since I knew that they weren't trapped under the sea so much as staying below out of spite.

I also wondered about the other drowned cities Grandfather had told me about. Did they also rise and fall according to a set rhythm? If something went awry at Ker Ys, would that Nahel steal the key to the city and put his own life at risk to save everyone? I doubted he had the bollocks to do so. As I contemplated Nahel's lack of courage, I realised I was lying on top of Aodhan.

We must have stayed out here all night. Aodhan was lying flat on his back on the bench, and I was on top of him and underneath the blanket. I stretched my stiff limbs, then I laid my head on Aodhan's chest and listened to his heartbeat. We'd fallen asleep together a few times before, and I always marvelled at how peaceful it was to lie in his arms. My hand snaked upward, and I wound a curl of his hair around my finger. Aodhan's hair was soft and dark and thick, and I'd been wanting to play with those curls for as long as I could remember. While I tugged at his hair, he woke up.

"Hi." I pushed myself up so I could see him. "I see we slept out last night."

"So we did." Aodhan smoothed my hair back behind my ear, then he tucked my head underneath his chin.

"Why didn't you wake me up so we could go back in?"

"It was a nice night," he began, "and now we've got this gorgeous sunrise. Can't have a bad day when you start it like this, eh?"

"No, I suppose not."

"Besides, if we'd gone in, I would have been alone in my room, and you all the way in yours," he continued. "Out here, we got to be together, and waking up with you in my arms is the best feeling in the world."

My face went hot, but since Aodhan couldn't see me I didn't mind. "Does that mean we'll be sleeping on the porch until winter?"

He shrugged, which was an odd sensation coming from underneath me. "If it gets too cold maybe we can sleep in the cottage at the bottom of the garden."

"We can't do that," I said. "There's no electricity, or running water. And it's filthy!"

"We could clean it up really nice." He stroked his hand down my spine; if I was a cat I'd be purring. "Run a line out for electric. I don't know anything about plumbing, though. We'll need help with that."

"Is that what you want to do?" I asked, hiding my face against his neck. I shouldn't have asked that; instead I should have pointed out that we'd only been together a very short time, and we were very, very young, and living together in an old cottage in a back garden was an awful idea. But I didn't mention any of those things. "Have a place for us?"

"I want to wake up with you, and go to sleep with you, and spend every moment I can with you. Is that something you might want, too?"

I propped myself up so I could look him in the eye. "I have to tell you something."

"Something bad?" he asked, his brown eyes wide.

"Maybe. I'm not sure." I took a deep breath, and said, "I saw you naked."

Aodhan blinked, then he laughed. "When was this?"

"Yesterday, when you came out of the bathroom. I was facing that mirror you put up near the door, and, well, that's how I saw you. You should probably move it," I added.

"How much of me did you see in this mirror?"

"Um, not everything. Only about your knees to your head."

He laughed again. "That sounds like everything!"

I hid my face against his chest. "I'm so sorry. I didn't mean to. I just looked up and there you were. Well, your reflection, really." I peeked up at him. "Are you mad at me?"

"Not at all. But I definitely need to sign up for a plumbing course."

"Why?"

He pulled me up the length of his body so my face hovered over his, and said, "We are definitely installing a shower in the cottage, so I can 'accidentally' catch you getting out."

"It was an accident," I said. "You're the one who put up that mirror!"

"A likely story."

BREAKFAST TRUCE

After we made a few more mad plans for the future, Aodhan and I went inside the house. We found my mother already dressed and in the kitchen, making a pot of coffee.

"Where were you two?" she asked.

"Watching the sunrise," I replied. "Does Da know you're touching the coffee pot?"

"I am allowed to make coffee in my own kitchen," she replied. "It's the food he wants me to avoid."

Based on the few things Mama had cooked since she returned to us, I wholeheartedly agreed. I turned around to grab a pan and start making breakfast, when the most awful off-key singing wafted into the kitchen.

"Good lord, is someone murdering a cat?" I wondered.

"I heard the same noise late last night," Aodhan said. "Thought maybe we were being haunted."

"It's not a ghost," Mama said, her words clipped. "It's Kevin."

"Can't he be quiet this early?" I asked. "It's not like he ever sings, anyway. Why assault our ears before breakfast?"

"It's because he's a merrow." Mama glanced at Aodhan and me, then she focused on the coffeemaker. "We sing when we're... happy."

"He doesn't sound happy," I said. "And he was caterwauling last night, as well?"

Aodhan slapped the counter. "Happy! You mean merrows sing when you, um." Mama silenced Aodhan with a glare. "I would like to point out that I have never once caused Meri to sing in such a manner."

"What do you mean, happy? I sing all the time," I began, then I remembered how close Kevin and Kelsey had been at the pub.

"Wait," I said, facing my mother. "You sing during *that*? You mean all the lovely songs I've heard these past few weeks coming from your and Da's room were *that*?"

"Meri," Mama began, but I shook my head.

"And Kevin is with Kelsey, isn't he? I'm putting a stop to this." I stalked toward the stairs, but Aodhan grabbed my arm.

"Mer, you probably don't want to see them, ah, in the middle of it," he said. "I think you've got to let it go, at least for now."

"But it's *Kelsey*," I said. The girl who'd bullied and tormented me for more than a decade was in bed with my brother. I didn't know if I was mad or upset, but I did know that I wanted it to stop, and I definitely didn't want to hear it. "This can't be happening. It's wrong! It's... it's just wrong."

Aodhan wrapped his arms around me, and kissed my forehead. "I know, Mer. I know."

Instead of making breakfast, I went for a walk to clear my head. Kevin was an adult, and therefore could associate with whomever he chooses. However, I did not want to hear, see, or know anything about it. Besides, my true hope was that while I was out walking, Kevin would bring Kelsey home and no one would mention their unfortunate association ever again.

When I returned, I went around to the back of the house, assuming I'd find Aodhan waiting for me on the porch. Instead, I found my traitorous brother sitting on the bench.

"Oh," I said, not bothering to hide my surprise. "I'll go see about breakfast."

"Da's baking something." Kevin slid over on the bench. "Sit with me?"

I did, though most of me wanted to stomp inside like a petulant child. After we sat together in silence for a few minutes, I asked, "How could you? With her, of all people."

"Meri, it wasn't like that," he said. "We hit it off. I didn't mean to like her—"

"You know how she's treated me," I interrupted. "You, of all people, you know."

"You're right. I do know. But you yourself said that things are different now between the two of you."

I remembered the sad girl at school, and how frightened she'd been at the Flynn house, hiding in the bedroom corner. "Just because things are different now doesn't erase what's happened."

"No, it doesn't," Kevin admitted. "But you also know how lonely we've always been, what with us being different, and Kelsey got that about me. She understood things I didn't even know I needed someone to understand about me, and... and we came back here."

I glanced at Kevin, and thought about all the times he'd mentioned me having Aodhan to lean on. Maybe Kevin needed someone, too. "I get that you needed someone, but really. Her?"

"Did you choose Aodhan, or did it just happen?" Kevin countered. "Because you two have the sort of connection I only dream about having with another."

I winced, because I was well aware of how lucky I was to have Aodhan in my life. Everyone should have someone as steady and true as Aodhan Sullivan on their side. "So what, you and Kelsey are in love now?"

He shook his head. "I don't know if I'd call it that. But I like her, and I want to spend time with her. I don't expect you to like her, or to forgive her for how she's acted in the past. But I was hoping, for me, you might consider judging her on how she acts now, and on how she behaves moving forward."

I wanted to say no. I wanted to scream and cry and have a tantrum, but Kevin had a point. He and I were lonely, and if Kelsey made him feel a bit better who was I to argue? At least I didn't have to get in bed with her.

Just because I was agreeing to be the bigger person, didn't mean I couldn't pick on him a bit.

"We all heard you singing," I said, as his eyes widened. "Aodhan, me, Mama. I bet Da and Mr Sullivan heard you, too. You sound like a walrus with a sinus infection."

Kevin laughed through his nose. "Yeah, my voice has never been strong, not like yours has always been."

"I could help you," I said. "With vocal exercises and such. If you wanted."

He smiled, but it didn't reach his eyes. "Thanks, but I've tried those. I don't think I'm meant to sing."

I had no idea Kevin had ever worked on his voice in any way. Now I knew that he'd tried, and felt like he failed. Since I didn't know what to do about that, I concentrated on something I knew made him happy. "Good thing you have Kelsey, then. I mean, if you went for that princess from Ker Ys and couldn't even sing properly, what then?" I wrinkled my nose. "I don't know if that lot are even merrows like us."

"Does this mean we'll turn Dahut and Nahel away together?"

I turned toward the bottom of the garden, and saw the old cottage. No way would I live in that old shack with Aodhan, but I wanted a life with him. Not with some prince from a far-off kingdom, and not with anyone else Grandfather found from his stash of allies. I wanted Aodhan, because he was my choice, and I was his.

Just as Kelsey was Kevin's choice.

"Looks like," I replied. "You really think Kelsey will want to put up with all of this? The magic, the monsters, everything?"

"I don't rightly know," Kevin admitted. "But I owe it to myself, and her, to try."

"All right. I can promise to be civil. But if she acts like an arse I'll give it right back to her!"

Kevin chuckled. "I'd expect nothing less."

We smiled at each other, then Da called us inside for breakfast. The rest—including Kelsey and Mr Sullivan—were already seated around the dining room table; being that there were seven of us for breakfast, we couldn't all fit in the kitchen. Mama was at the head of the table serving up an egg and vegetable frittata and roasted potatoes while Da refilled everyone's coffee mugs. I took a seat next to Aodhan, who was showing his father something on his phone.

"I don't know," Mr Sullivan said. "I think that club requires a membership. Hey Meri, Kevin."

"Good morning," I said. Kevin and Kelsey shared a shy glance at each other, then they focused on their food. "What's this about a club?"

"While you were walking, I did some research on Donn." Aodhan affected a sheepish grin, and continued, "By research, I mean I asked your ma about him."

"And I was happy to help," Mama said with a smile.

"Seems that Donn left a treasure in the dunes near the Inagh River, below an old castle ruin," Aodhan continued. "Since the headmaster appears to be associated with Donn in some way, I figured we could check out the ruin, and maybe get a clue as to what they're after."

"That's a good plan," I said, then I ate another mouthful of my breakfast. Da had added red peppers and feta cheese to the eggs, and it was divine. "But?"

"But the castle is on a golf course, and we don't have a membership," Mr Sullivan said. "We'll either have to sneak onto the course, or shell out for a membership."

"You don't need to do either," Mama said. "Meri can sing her way past the guards."

"She can?" Kelsey said. It was the first time she'd spoken since I sat at the table.

"She commanded an entire army with her voice," Mama said. "I'm sure a few golf course workers will be easy enough to handle."

"Of course Meri can handle it," Aodhan said. "I figure we can go to the golf course, investigate this old castle, and while we're there, Dad can poke around the surf shop."

"Why the shop?" I asked.

"Donn's always been interested in the shop," Mr Sullivan replied. "Odd, for someone who wouldn't be caught dead on a surfboard, but I used to think it was because of our friendship. Now, I'm not so sure."

"Should you really go alone?" I asked. "Maybe one of us should go with you."

All of our gazes turned to Mama. Being that she was the strongest and most feared warrior from Kilstiffen, she was a likely choice to go up against Donn. She set down her fork, and said, "Normally I would be happy to accompany you to the shop, Lucas, but I have business below."

I opened my mouth to ask what sort of business, but Mama shook her head slightly. Apparently, this information was on a need to know basis.

"That's all right," Mr Sullivan said. "If I'm there on my own it will attract less attention, anyway."

"Does that mean me and Kevin are going to the golf course with Meri and Aodhan?" Kelsey asked.

No one spoke, and everyone did their best not to look at me, but it was clear that my vote would be the deciding factor. I wanted to say no. I wanted to say that there was no way I would let myself be seen in public with Kelsey McGrath, no matter what her current circumstances were.

But I remembered everything Kevin had told me out back, and I that loved my brother so much more than I'd ever disliked Kelsey. I didn't want to hold grudges, especially if they might stand in the way of Kevin's happiness.

"It does," I said, and everyone breathed a collective sigh of relief. "Da, would you also like to come with us?"

Da's face darkened. "I'll be going below with Aoife."

"Why won't Mama tell us why she's going below?" I asked Da. I'd followed him into the kitchen on the pretext of assisting with the washing up. Actually, I wanted to interrogate him about this latest invitation below.

"She hasn't told me, either," Da replied. "A messenger arrived with one of those scrolls from the king shortly before dawn."

"And you didn't read it?"

"They're not written in English or Irish or any other language from above," he replied. "Aoife read it over, and immediately went to the kitchen to make coffee. She only drinks coffee when she's thinking."

"If you don't know what it's about, why are you going with her? Is it the same reason we brought Mr Sullivan the last time, to prevent them from trying to keep her below?"

Da scoffed. "I'd like to see them try to contain Aoife. I am going because I was separated from her for fourteen years, and I will do everything in my power to ensure we're never parted again."

"Is that what love is?" I asked. Aodhan's words about wanting to wake up with me every morning were still rattling around in my head. "Always wanting to be near one another?"

"That's a big part of it, yes." Da filled the casserole dish with hot water, and set it aside to soak. "I have noticed that you're always with Aodhan."

"I am. And now it looks like Kevin's always going to be hanging around with Kelsey."

"It certainly does," Da replied. "Are you feeling all right about that?"

"I wouldn't say I'm all right, but I've made peace with it," I replied. "Kelsey and I are different people now. Maybe we'll get on, and maybe we won't, but no matter what, I'm not going to stand in the way of Kevin's happiness."

"You're more mature than I was at your age. You might be more mature than I am now." Da rinsed off another plate and set it in the rack, where it waited for me to dry it. "Speaking of which, you've got that birthday coming up. Perhaps we should plan a party, like your ma suggested. You haven't had one in years."

"I don't need a party," I said. "I would, however, like to request one of your chocolate cakes. With raspberry filling, if it's not too much trouble."

Da smiled. "Never too much trouble for you, Meri girl."

When Da and I returned to the others, my mother was wearing her armour. Her usual sword was hanging at her side, and two others were laid across the dining room table.

"Why are you wearing armour?" I asked. "You didn't the last two times you went below. And what's with the extra swords?"

"I'm dressed as a warrior to remind my father and the rest of the council that I am not to be trifled with," she replied. "I am the guardian of the portal, and I have pledged to protect Kilstiffen from what's above and below. They need to treat me with respect, and not as if I'm a criminal."

"What's below Kilstiffen?" Kelsey asked.

"Gods, mostly," Kevin replied.

"Mostly things you don't want to know about," Mama added, then she touched one of the swords. "This sword is Brian's. I brought out the other in case Lucas felt he needed a weapon."

"You can sword fight?" I asked Da.

"Aoife taught me a thing or two," he replied. "I take it we think your father is upset?"

"I have reason to believe he will be upset after he hears what I have to say," Mama replied. To Mr Sullivan, she said, "Lucas, I trust you learned how to properly wield a sword while in MacCreehy's ranks?"

"I did." Mr Sullivan picked up the sword and gave it a flourish. "Never thought I'd have a reason to use one again, but it's best to be prepared."

"Aye," my mother said. "We don't know what the next few days will bring. I want all of you on alert for anything out of the ordinary. As for you four," she said to me, Kevin, Aodhan, and Kelsey, "don't go anyplace alone, and if you see one of the Flynns reach out to me or Brian or Lucas immediately."

"What if we can't get in touch with anyone?" I asked.

"Then you should run."

Mad Hedges And Secret Tunnels

After my mother's pep talk, the seven of us dispersed. My parents went below, Mr Sullivan returned to the surf shop, and the rest of us went looking for Donn's treasure. Kevin ended up driving to the golf course, which meant Kelsey got to ride in the front seat. It also meant I got to share the back with Aodhan, which was definitely the better option. As soon as we were in the car, Aodhan wrapped his arm around my shoulders and pulled me against him.

"Seat belts, you two," Kevin said, as he watched us in the rearview mirror.

"Eyes on the road, please," I said, as we slid to the other side of the back seat and out of Kevin's direct view. "How far is this golf course?"

"Not too far," Kevin said. "We'll be there soon. Maybe half an hour, if that."

I blew out a breath, and leaned heavily against Aodhan. "Why is everything always so spread out," I grumbled. "Driving around is so boring."

"Why can't you sing us there?" Kelsey asked. "Since you two have these magical voices, and all."

"It doesn't work like that," Kevin said.

"That, and I don't know how to use my voice to transport four people across such a vast distance. Or any distance," I added. "Our mother could do it, though"

"One time, she sang us clear across the country," Aodhan said.

"We started out in County Cavan and ended up on Inis Mór," I said, remembering how Aodhan and I had ended up in the seawater filled Wormhole. "Mama's got a much stronger voice than either Kevin or I do."

"Maybe Rose could help you strengthen your voice," Kelsey said, turning around so she faced me over the headrest. I supposed she was exempt from Kevin's seat belt rule. "She's a professional vocal coach, and she's always wanted you to do more in chorus. It's not just Rose, though. Everyone wants you to sing more."

"Really?"

"You have the best voice in the school, by far," Kelsey continued. "You always have. It's what first ticked Sarah off about you."

"My voice somehow made Sarah angry?"

"When we were, oh, seven? Eight? You got the lead in the children's Christmas pageant," Kelsey replied. "Sarah really wanted that part, and she was furious when you beat her out."

"Wait. You mean to tell me that ten years of making my life a living hell was all over a song in a pageant I don't even remember singing?"

"It was Silent Night," Aodhan said. "You were amazing."

"You remember that?" I asked.

"I remember it, too," Kevin said. "All the teachers were going on about how grown up you sounded, and how clear your voice was.

I'll wager Da also remembers it, because that's when everyone started comparing your singing to Ma's."

"Huh." I only vaguely remembered being in a Christmas pageant, and now I knew that my performance had made an impact on literally everyone else in my life. "Maybe I'll find a few more pageants to sing in."

Aodhan pulled me closer. "Your voice is a gift. Only good things can come of you sharing it."

I kissed his jaw. "You say the best things."

After we got to the golf club where the ruined castle was situated, Aodhan and Kevin went to read the signs near the entrance while I wandered to the far side of the car park. The course stretched out toward the sea, and I could smell the salt air. I closed my eyes, and imagined I was one with the waves.

Fingers glided against my palm, but Aodhan was across the car park with my brother. Wondering who was touching me, I looked to the side. Kelsey was holding my hand.

"I'm sorry," she said. "I'm so, so sorry. We were awful to you, and you should hate us. You should hate me."

"I don't hate you," I said. "But I am curious as to why it went on for so long."

"I don't know," she replied. "When we were kids, we thought it was funny. I think maybe we never grew up." Kelsey scuffed the pavement with her toe. "It stopped being funny a long time ago."

I squeezed her hand. "We can agree on that."

"Not only that, everything you said was true," she continued. "Your mother really is a mermaid. She did go back to the sea to help people, and then she returned home. You always said she would come back, and she did." Tears slipped down Kelsey's cheeks. "Unlike my mother, yours came back."

"What happened to your mother?"

"I'm not really sure. I know she never wanted a family or anything, and when I was around four, she left. My dad remarried a few years ago, and ever since it's been him and my stepmother living their lives, and me living mine without them." She released my hand and wrapped her arms around herself. "I guess no one wants to be in a family with me."

"Kevin does," I said. "And Da cooked you breakfast, and my mother made sure you had coffee with the right amount of sugar in it. Maybe you can hang around with us for a while."

She wiped her cheek against her shoulder. "Why are you so understanding and nice about everything? It's maddening."

"It is, isn't it?" I said, and we grinned at each other. "But be warned, the niceness only goes so far. If you hurt Kevin, either myself or our mother will come after you."

Kelsey looked across the car park toward Kevin, and smiled. "Then I'd better be careful with him. Why isn't his singing as good as yours?"

I shuddered. "I do not want to hear about when or why he was singing to you."

"Don't you sing to Aodhan when you're together?" she asked, her meaning clear.

"Um, no. We've only really been a couple for a short time."

"Well, Kevin and I met yesterday," she said, with a laugh. "If you're of a mind to take advice from a horrible bully like me, don't wait too long with Aodhan. Life is short, and everything changes in a second. You've got to take your happiness whenever you can."

"This morning he was talking about us getting a place," I said, surprising myself. Sharing secrets with Kelsey was a new and not altogether bad feeling.

"Well? Are you?"

"We never got to finish the conversation, thanks to Kevin's awful singing distracting us."

Her cheeks pinked, but she didn't stop smiling. "Sorry. Not really, though. Your brother is—"

"Good God, please don't ever finish that sentence."

Aodhan and Kevin joined us in that moment, the latter's gaze darting between Kelsey and me with a look of mild horror on his face. "What were you talking about?" Kevin demanded.

"You," I replied.

"And you," Kelsey added, nodding her chin toward Aodhan.

"Christ," Aodhan muttered, then he showed me his phone. "There's a map of the course next to the door, and I took a picture of it. Here's the ruin." He indicated the symbol on the map. "Shouldn't be too hard to find. We just need to get in."

"Is there a daily rate?" Kelsey asked, as she opened her purse. "I have some money."

"Members only, and they don't take new applicants on weekends," Kevin said. "Meri, I think it's down to you."

I nodded, though in truth I had no idea how to conjure up a set of membership cards. But walking through the front door couldn't be the only way onto the course. After all, it was out here in the open. We just needed to figure out a way around the club. I ran my hand across the hedge that separated the car park from the fairway, then I peeked between the branches.

"There's no fencing around the green," I murmured. "Only the hedge."

"Really." Aodhan stood behind me, examining the hedge as I had. "Think we can cut our way through?"

"Destroying club property is not a good idea," Kevin said. "I don't want to get picked up for vandalism."

"We don't need to cut a hole in the hedge. We can just ask the branches to move." I sang a single quiet note, and the branches closest to me parted. When I stopped, they moved back together, which I hadn't expected to happen. Then I remembered how MacCreehy had used a dozen merrows to keep all of his stolen warriors in constant thrall, since the spell only worked while the singing went on. Mama explained it as our songs not being able to permanently override a living creature's free will without its consent, and this hedge was certainly alive.

"Oh, so it's like the opposite of when you sang Paul's door closed," Kelsey said. "Turned the door right into a wall, she did."

"I should have stabbed him instead," I muttered. "At least you got him in the balls." I poked at the hedge. "Kevin, I'll need your help."

"My help?" he demanded. "With singing?"

"I need you to follow my lead, and help me hold the notes," I replied. "Otherwise, if my voice gives out when we're only part way through, we might get stuck in the middle, and I don't really know what will happen then." Visions of stiff, sharp branches poking into my ears and mouth danced behind my eyes.

"But, Meri," Kevin began.

"You can do it," I said. "It's who we are. Are you with me?"

Kevin nodded, and stood beside me. "I am. Let's go."

"It's a thick hedge," Aodhan said, giving it a final prod. "We'll need to move quickly once we have a path."

"Then we'll go quickly." I began singing, and a moment later, Kevin joined me. He wasn't that far off key, but he wasn't breathing properly. We'd have to work on that.

Despite Kevin's gasping for breath, the branches complied with our request and curled away from one another, leaving a lovely arched walkway behind. I gestured for Aodhan to go through first, since if we walked into any curious employees or club members he could easily charm them. I sent Kevin next, so his voice could keep the arch open on the other side. Then Kelsey went through, and finally I entered the shrubby tunnel. All was going perfectly to plan, until I tripped over a root.

"Dammit," I said.

"Are you all right?" Kevin asked, which meant neither one of us were singing.

Shit.

I took a deep breath to resume my song, but it was too late. A leafy branch pushed itself into my face, and I coughed and spluttered as I batted it away. I'd just got it away when branches coiled around my arms and legs, pushing my body up and off the ground.

Ahead of me Kelsey screamed, and I heard Kevin's off key notes along with Aodhan's shouting. I tried to sing, but the branches were pressing against my skin and wrapping themselves around my throat like strangle weed. They pulled so tight around my neck I couldn't get a breath, and the sharp wood dug so deeply into my skin it burned. The edges of my vision went black and spotty, and I felt myself slipping from consciousness.

Damn it all, I did not want to die in a hedge.

I heard wood splintering and Aodhan cursing. Through the thin branches I saw him using brute force to rip up sections of the hedge straight from the ground. Kevin followed him, and used his song to work Kelsey free of the branches. Another shriek, and she was free.

Not me, though. The branches wouldn't let up, and I knew I only had a few moments of air left in my lungs. After those moments passed, that would be it.

My vision blurred out, and my thoughts dissipated to nothing—then I felt Aodhan's hands on me as he pulled the branches away from my body, and dragged me out of the hedge and into the light. We tumbled to the ground in a heap of limbs, but I didn't care. I could breathe again, and it was glorious.

"I've got you," Aodhan said, holding me against him as I gasped for breath. "Don't cry, Mer. I've got you."

I tried to tell him that I wasn't crying. Rather, my eyes were watering as a side effect of being throttled, but my voice still didn't work. Instead, I slid my arms around Aodhan's neck, and leaned my cheek against his chest.

"It was crushing us," Kelsey rasped. "On purpose, I think. That bush was mad at us."

"The perimeter might be warded to keep certain people, as in those looking for Donn, away," Kevin said. He had his arm around Kelsey, and kept his body between her and the hedge. "That must mean we're on the right track."

"Must be," Aodhan said, then I felt him move as he looked around the golf course. "How is no one out here? We made a hell of a racket just now. The club is open, but the fairway is deserted."

"Look at the sky," Kevin said. I peeked upward, and saw dark clouds rolling in. "Storm's coming in quick. Everyone's probably inside the club to wait it out."

"Best get moving, then," Aodhan said, and he helped me to my feet. "Are you all right to walk?"

I nodded, then I looked past him and saw the mangled shrubbery. Many branches were broken and cast aside, and the ground was pitted where Aodhan had ripped chunks of the hedge right out of the ground, roots and all. "You murdered a hedge for me," I croaked.

"And I'll murder any others that try to hurt you." Aodhan tipped up my chin. "No one gets to hold you that tightly, except me."

I nodded, not wanting to strain my throat further, and winced at a new pain. Aodhan held up my hair, and frowned when he got a look at my neck.

"You're all scratched up," he said, then he grabbed my hands and pushed up my sleeves. "Your wrists, too. We need to wash these out, and get an antibiotic ointment on you."

"Castle first," I said. "Afterward, you can take care of me."

"That's right I will," Aodhan said, then we set off after Kevin and Kelsey.

Being that the golf course was a mostly flat affair, it wasn't long before we saw the ruined castle in the distance. And what a distance it was. The course was so vast I thought my legs would fall off before we reached the ruin, and to top it all off, it started raining when we were about halfway across.

I glanced up at Aodhan. He had his head down and was pushing ahead, and I envied his ability to focus on the task at hand. I could hardly get past the pain from the many cuts on my neck and wrists, and how they all screamed for attention. Add to that my sore legs and aching feet, and I was a wreck.

"Mer." Aodhan put his hand on my shoulder. "Are you all right? Want me to carry you?"

"You can't carry me." He raised an eyebrow. "I know you're capable of carrying me, but you'll just end up exhausted. I'm okay." I put my hand on top of his. "Promise."

"You know what was strange," he continued. "It was rather easy to get Kelsey out of the hedge. She's also not got a scratch on her. Not you, though. Those branches fought back, like they didn't want to let you go."

I slid my palm against Aodhan's and squeezed. "I felt it, too."

We finally reached the ruin. It was barely a tower, with the rest of the castle having long since fallen away, and it was fully open to the elements.

"Not much left, is there," Kevin said. "We've got two walls and some window openings. Not even a roof to get out of the rain."

"Weird," I croaked. My throat felt a bit better, but I still sounded awful. "How could Donn have hidden a treasure in a tower that doesn't even have a door?"

"He's sneaky," Aodhan said. "He never tells my mother anything. They've been married for six years and I feel like we barely know him. He's hardly ever home, and when he is, we all walk on eggshells around him."

"He sounds like an asshole," Kelsey said. "Why did your mom even marry him?"

"Honestly, I'm not sure," Aodhan replied. "They'd already known each other for years, through my dad. It's not like we needed Donn's money, since my dad had seen to all of that years ago. And now that I think about it they don't act like they love each other. Instead of a marriage it's more like they completed a business transaction."

"But, Donn and your mother have two children," I said, referencing Aodhan's younger sisters.

"Yeah. They do." Aodhan saw something in the inside corner of the tower, and went to investigate.

"It seems like Donn wanted to stay close to your family after your father disappeared," I began; I almost said died, but even though Mr Sullivan had been lost at sea, and presumed dead, we now knew what had really happened. More importantly, we'd freed Aodhan's father from MacCreehy and brought him home. "Maybe he thinks your family has whatever he's looking for."

Aodhan scoffed. "Believe me, there is no treasure in our house," he began, then he crouched down and examined the ground. "Hello, what do we have here?"

The rest of us crowded around Aodhan as he pulled aside some dried grass, and revealed a set of steps that led underneath the tower. "Think what Donn is looking for is down there?" I asked.

"If it is, wouldn't he have found it by now?" Kevin countered. "We've been here a bare five minutes and found it. These steps aren't exactly hidden."

"Unless whatever wanted to keep Meri off the course also keeps Donn out," Kelsey said. We looked at her, dumbfounded. "What?" she demanded, when we all stared at her. "You all think I'm wrong?"

"I think you're absolutely spot on," Kevin said, then we pitched in and helped Aodhan clear the rest of the grass and debris away from the entrance.

"Anyone got a torch?" I croaked. The staircase descended into blackness, and I didn't fancy a tumble in the dark.

"I do," Kelsey said, as she pulled one out of her bag. "I keep a lot of supplies in here."

"Lead the way," I said, and she and Kevin crept down the steps.

"It's a good sized tunnel," Kevin called out, once they'd reached the bottom. "We can stand up straight. Goes on a ways, too."

"All right," Aodhan called back. "We'll be right down." Aodhan tilted up my chin and kissed me hard. "After you, Mer."

Carefully, I made my way down the steps. The last thing I needed was to fall, and add to my already long list of injuries. Aodhan stayed close behind me, with his hand hovering near my back. I don't know if that was for my comfort, or his.

When we reached the tunnel floor, we found Kevin and Kelsey standing in a pool of light that shone from the entrance above us. He had his arm around her shoulders, and her cheek was tucked against his neck. They were standing together much the same way Aodhan and I always stood together, and it struck me then: Kevin and Kelsey were in love with each other, just like Aodhan and me.

Wait, what?

"What was that?" Aodhan asked. Right, I had a habit of muttering to myself, and Aodhan was always close enough to hear me.

"N-Nothing," I replied, unwilling to share with Aodhan that I just divined that I loved him. How I would tell him, I had no notion. Maybe I'd let him puzzle it out for himself. "How far do we think this tunnel goes on for?"

Kelsey swung the torch's beam ahead. The light was swallowed up in the distance. "It's longer than a torch beam," she said.

"Right, then," Aodhan said. "Onward we go."

Since she had the torch, Kelsey remained in the lead. It was a remarkably well-built tunnel, not that I had many to compare it to. However, the smooth walls and level floor did remind me of the tunnels that led from some nearby caves to the edge of Kilstiffen.

"These tunnels remind you of any place?" I asked Aodhan.

"Definitely looks like whomever made those tunnels around Kilstiffen also made these," he replied. "Does that mean they were created by magic? Donn's magic, maybe?"

"I wish we knew if he was on our side," I said, then I saw a glimmer of light up ahead. "Kelsey, put out the torch!"

She did, and the four of us flattened ourselves against the tunnel wall. The light got steadily stronger as whomever held it continued their approach. I'd just grabbed Aodhan's arm and was about to suggest making a run for it, when the light bearer called out.

"Aodhan? How'd you get down here?"

"Lorcan?" Aodhan approached the light, and yes, it was Lorcan, the surf shop's general manager. "What are you doing in a tunnel under a golf course?"

"It leads straight to the shop," Lorcan replied. "I came down as soon as the hedge was breached."

"Wait," I said. "If you know about this tunnel and the hedge, then you also know about what Donn really is."

"I've been keeping him and his away from the shop for a very long time," Lorcan said. "Come on. Lucas has already come by the shop. It's time we all talked."

Tech Duinn

We followed Lorcan through the dark tunnel, with his and Kelsey's torches lighting the way. Eventually, we reached a set of stone steps that were identical to the ones we'd found next to the castle ruin that led below the golf course. These steps led up to a metal door, which in turn led us into the surf shop's basement.

"I never knew this door was here," Aodhan said, after we had all gone through.

"No, I imagine you wouldn't have," Lorcan said. He pushed the door closed, and it blended seamlessly into the wall. I looked around the room, and saw an assortment of shipping crates, and a few battered surf boards that had seen better days. Lorcan had hidden this door in a rarely used corner of the basement. "Lucas doesn't know about it, either," he added.

"But Donn does," I said.

"Aye," Lorcan said. "That he does." He moved toward the opposite side of the basement. "If it's all right with you, Aodhan, I'm going to send the rest of the staff home and close up for the day. Lucas went out to take care of a few things, but he will be back soon. I reckon it will be best if we wait to talk until we're all together."

"Good plan. We'll go up to the apartment, for now," Aodhan said. Lorcan nodded, and went to the retail side of the building, while the rest of us went upstairs.

"Kev, Kelsey, have a seat," Aodhan said, jerking his chin toward the couch. "There's food and drinks in the fridge. Help yourselves. Meri, let's get those scrapes cleaned up."

I dutifully followed Aodhan into the bathroom, where he picked me up by my waist and set me on the counter. I leaned over and looked in the mirror, and frowned when I saw my reflection. I hadn't realised how dirty and dishevelled I was. While Aodhan got out the first aid kit, I picked leaves out of my hair.

"You could have told me about all these sticks and such tangled up in my hair," I said, as I swept the pile of debris into the bin. "I've got an entire forest in here."

"It wasn't so bad." Aodhan lined up his supplies, then he looked at me and frowned. "What's wrong?"

"Nothing!"

"Mer. You're shaking."

I stuffed my hands underneath my legs. "The rain. I-I got a chill from the rain."

Aodhan nodded, then he set his hand on my knee. "It's okay if you're upset, especially after what happened."

"Which part?" I asked. "Being almost eaten by shrubbery, trudging across an endless golf course in the rain, or finding Lorcan's shady tunnel?"

"Points taken. But you're okay?"

"I am." I set my hand on his. "Promise."

He smiled and squeezed my knee, then he tilted his head toward my jumper. "What are you wearing underneath that?" When I blinked, he added, "We should start by washing out your cuts, and I don't want your clothes to get any wetter than they already are."

The fact that he wasn't cracking jokes about seeing me topless told me how rattled he was by the morning's events. I pulled my jumper up and over my head, revealing the thin camisole I was wearing beneath it. "Now what?"

"Now, we'll start with your wrists," he said, and he had me lean over so he could wash out my wrists in the sink. Once that was done, he dried them off, and spread ointment onto the cuts and scrapes. After he'd bandaged them, he scrutinised my neck.

"Can you hold up your hair for me?" he asked. I did, and he dampened a washcloth. He started on my left side, and gently swabbed my neck.

"You take very good care of me."

Aodhan met my gaze, and smiled. "Can't let you be felled by an infection."

"It's not just this." I grasped his forearm. "You're always looking out for me, you've rescued me twice in two days, you never hesitate to charge after monsters for me—"

"Hey. Hey." Aodhan dropped the washcloth and cupped my face with his hands. "I will always be here for you, for whatever you need. Today, tomorrow, forever." He swept his thumbs across my cheekbones, then he kissed my forehead. "Besides, you've rescued me, too."

I placed my palm on his cheek. "Have I?"

"You know you have. If it wasn't for you, I wouldn't have my dad back. For all I know, without you I would be stuck as one of MacCreehy's brainless goons."

"Don't say that." I put my hands on either side of his head, sinking my fingers into his soft, thick hair. "I would never, ever let that happen. And you'll never be without me."

His eyes widened. "Never?"

"Never," I confirmed, though Aodhan's mouth was on mine before I finished speaking. Then his hands were gliding down my back and pulling me off the counter toward him. I wrapped my legs around his waist, and let him take me.

When we parted, he set me down on the counter, then he rested his forehead against my temple. "Christ, I love kissing you."

"Kiss me more often, then," I suggested, and he grinned.

"Let's finish up your neck, first." He washed off the other side of my neck and spread the ointment onto the cuts and scrapes, with his gentle touch driving me crazy in the process. Once he declared the wounds properly tended to, I reached for my jumper, and frowned. My lovely cream coloured jumper was now soaked in a smelly green liquid.

"We must have knocked over Dad's mouthwash," Aodhan said. "I'll throw this in the washer."

"Do you have anything I can wear for now?" Suddenly modest, I crossed my arms over my chest.

"I'm sure I do. Hang on."

He darted out of the bathroom, and returned a moment later with one of his many hooded sweatshirts. It was a soft grey, and had the surf shop's logo—a set of blue waves—printed on the front. The sweatshirt was so long it hung down past my hips, and I had to roll up the sleeves several times, but it was warm and comfortable and, most importantly, it smelled like Aodhan.

"You're swimming in that," Kevin said when we exited the bathroom, jerking his chin toward my too-big sweatshirt. "Want mine instead?"

"I'm fine." As if I would trade Aodhan's sweatshirt for my brother's. "Is Mr Sullivan back yet?"

As if on cue, Lorcan yelled up the stairs that the shop was closed down, Mr Sullivan had returned, and they were ready when we were. Three of us moved toward the stairs, but Aodhan darted into the kitchen for snacks.

"We just had breakfast," Kevin said. "He can't possibly be hungry again."

"I don't think he's ever not hungry," I said. Kevin shook his head, and descended to the shop floor with Kelsey. Aodhan, his arms laden with food, and I followed a moment later.

"Got you a chocolate muffin," Aodhan said, as he held the treat toward me.

"Give," I said, as I grabbed it before he changed his mind. Just to see how he would react, I said, "Sharing food is a love language, you know."

"And I only share food with you," he said, as he kissed the top of my head. "But if you love me too, you'll let me have a bite."

I held out the muffin, and he took a lion-sized bite out of it... then he tried to kiss me with his chocolaty lips. I squealed and ran out of his reach, and almost bumped into a stern-faced Lorcan. "Um, hello," I mumbled.

"Dad," Aodhan said, and he and his father greeted each other with one of those silly one armed man hugs. Mr Sullivan reached for me, but hesitated.

"Are hugs a good thing, or no?" he asked.

"They're good," I replied, and he squeezed me with his other arm.

"Where were you?" Aodhan asked.

"I went back to the Murphy house and left a letter on the kitchen table asking Brian and Aoife to meet us here," Mr Sullivan replied. "It seems that Lorcan has been holding out on us."

"More like I've been trying to keep you away from all of this." Lorcan sighed. "What do you know of Tech Duinn?"

"The legendary Tech Duinn, as in the house of the dead?" Aodhan countered; someday, he was going to have to share his vast folklore resources with me.

"Aye, the house of the dead," Lorcan affirmed. "And it's owned by the sidhe prince, Donn Dumhach."

"Who happens to be Aodhan's stepfather," Kelsey muttered.

"Is that why the tunnel runs from the castle ruin out on the golf course here to the shop?" I asked.

"Aye, lass," Lorcan said. "Tech Duinn is beneath the shop."

For a moment, you could have heard a pin drop. Lorcan had stunned us far past silence and into incredulity. I glanced down at the floor, and wondered how far underneath the shop Tech Duinn was. Could Donn hear us walking around overhead, as if we were upstairs tenants in a flat?

"How long have you known this?" Mr Sullivan asked, thus breaking us out of our amazed silence.

"Always," Lorcan replied. "My kind have kept Donn away from this plot of land for centuries. I'm the last of a long line of guardians."

"Why are you trying to keep him out?" I asked. "If it's his home, doesn't he have the right to be in it?"

"Regardless of ownership, we're all better off keeping Donn as far away from his house as possible," Lorcan replied. "Donn has insatiable appetites for two things: gold and blood. If he were to return to his house, he would become almost unstoppable. The streets would run red with the blood of his victims, much as they did long ago."

"And yet, you let him make my acquaintance." Mr Sullivan took a step toward Lorcan. Kevin put himself between the two men, just in case. "You let him near my family. That bastard married my wife!"

"Firstly, as long as he remains unable to enter his house, he has but a speck of his true might," Lorcan said. "Second, after you disappeared in the storm, we all assumed he'd finally killed you. The safest place for Bridgette and your children was with him, rather than against him."

Mr Sullivan was visibly shocked. "Donn tried to kill me?"

"Several times, in fact," Lorcan replied. "When your boat went down in the bay, we figured he finally did you in. The local selkies confirmed the boat had been tampered with. Just ask their leader, Rose."

Mr Sullivan wiped his hand across his face. "I need a minute," he said, and he walked to the far side of the room.

"Dad's best friend tried to kill him," Aodhan muttered.

"But he failed, and he'll keep on failing," I said. "What did your dad say at the pub? Shipwrecks don't stop the Sullivans?"

"That's right they don't," Aodhan said, then he asked Lorcan, "You said the selkies have a leader? And, there are selkies nearby?"

"Aye," Lorcan replied. "I assumed you kids knew all about Rose. She teaches at The Saints."

"Wait, do you mean Rose Fennimore?" I asked. "My music teacher is a selkie?"

As Lorcan affirmed that yes, Rose had a sealskin stashed in a closet somewhere, Kelsey asked, "Is anyone else a magical creature around here?"

"Near as I can tell, it's about fifty-fifty," Aodhan replied.

"Has Donn ever tried to harm Aodhan, or my girls, Mary and Anne?" Mr Sullivan asked as he rejoined us.

"Not physically," Lorcan replied. "You see, by leaving the shop to Aodhan you thwarted his plans. Donn had wanted to purchase the property after your supposed death, but he knows Aodhan will never sell it. It seems he's been biding his time, waiting for Aodhan to either tire of the shop and sell it, or perhaps go off to university and lose interest in the business."

"He hasn't tried to off me, then?" Aodhan asked.

"It's a trickier thing with you," Lorcan replied. "Because the shop was passed to you, father to son, you've a greater hold on it than if you merely exchanged some coin for a bit of land. You need to give it up of your own accord, and if you die having not relinquished your rights, then Donn might never get his house back."

"You know what's funny," Mr Sullivan began, "when I was writing up the last version of my will, I was going to leave everything to Bridgette. The businesses, the house, everything. It was Donn than convinced me to leave Aodhan the shop."

"Really?" Aodhan said. "I always thought you left me the shop because Mary and Anne aren't into surfing that much."

"That's the exact argument Donn used," Mr Sullivan said. "So you got the shop, Bridgette the house, and your sisters inherited the finance business. At the time, I'd thought it was a fair deal, but now I wonder."

"Aodhan's done a great job with the shop," Lorcan said. "And Mary and Anne seemed quite happy, last I saw them. You did well by them, Lucas."

"Yeah, Dad," Aodhan said. "So what if Donn offered you some advice? You took care of all of us."

Mr Sullivan smiled. "Always, kid."

"So, the treasure Donn's been searching for is really Tech Duinn," I said, and Lorcan nodded. "Are you the one that warded the hedge?"

"I've kept them up, but the wards were originally laid by those that came before me," Lorcan replied.

"That hedge almost killed Meri," Aodhan snapped. "Why did it go after her like that?"

Lorcan shrugged and spread his palms. "Meri's magic must be similar enough to Donn's that it confused the wards."

"I don't have any magic," I said, and the rest scoffed.

"Yes, you do," Kelsey said. "Both you and Kevin are rolling in magic. After meeting your mother, I know where it comes from, too."

Lorcan cocked his head to the side. "Your mother?"

"Aoife," Mr Sullivan said.

"Yes, her name is Aoife Murphy," I said, but Mr Sullivan grabbed my arm and pointed at the door.

"I mean, Aoife is here!"

I looked toward the door and saw my mother, sword out, stalking down the road toward the shop. Keeping pace beside her was my father, and two additional people walked close behind them. When I recognised the newcomers, I swore.

"Who are those two?" Aodhan asked.

I glanced at Kevin. "They are Dahut and Nahel, the heirs of Ker Ys and the ones our grandfather thinks Kevin and me should marry."

THE SEA BULL

"You're engaged?" Kelsey demanded, as she rounded on Kevin.

"I've never even met her," Kevin protested. When Kelsey took a step back from him, he pleaded, "Do you really think I would have chatted you up at the pub if I had a fiancée?"

"I don't know, would you?" Kelsey countered.

"Kevin has never met Dahut," I said. "He's never even spoken to or seen her. Our grandfather mentioned us being betrothed to them only yesterday, and we all refused to let things move forward."

"If things aren't moving forward, then why is she here?" Kelsey asked.

Before I could reply, my mother entered the shop. Mama surveyed the room, then her gaze landed on Mr Sullivan.

"Donn is coming," she said, without preamble. "He's angry."

"Have you seen him?" Mr Sullivan asked.

Mama shook her head. "I was below when a set of wards near the Inagh River were breached. The crack sent ripples all the way to Kilstiffen, and the mages determined that Donn had laid a rather distinct ward on top of the shoddy one near the palace ruin, and was probably alerted the instant it was broken. Since Brian and I knew the children were headed to that area, we returned at once. When we stopped by the house, we found your letter asking us to meet here."

"Those wards must have been on the hedge at the golf course," Kevin said. "That's probably how Meri and Kelsey got trapped in it."

"Any idea who set the ward in the first place?" Mama asked.

Lorcan bowed his head. "My people and I are responsible for the original ward. Your daughter proved too powerful for our meager abilities."

Mama curled her lip at him, then she faced me. "You're all right?"

"A bush tried to eat me and Kelsey." I tugged down my collar and showed her the scrapes on my neck. "But Aodhan and Kevin rescued us. Did you know Tech Duinn is beneath us?"

She looked at the floor. "Beneath our very feet? I assumed it was in the area, but..." Her head snapped up, and she once again fixed Lorcan and Mr Sullivan in her gaze. "How long has Donn been attempting to gain entry to his house?"

"Apparently, longer than he's known me," Mr Sullivan said. "According to Lorcan, Donn befriended me and helped me buy this place all so he could murder me and reclaim the land."

"It's true," Lorcan said. "Donn's done many awful things in his attempts to return here. But then Lucas willed the shop to Aodhan, and since the transference of ownership took place, Donn has been biding his time."

"Biding his time for what, I wonder," Mama muttered, then she asked Lorcan, "You're the only guardian here?"

"I am," he replied. "My people have guarded Tech Duinn for generations, but I'm all that's left."

"Why is Donn using a collector?" she pressed.

Lorcan took a step back. "Is he?"

Before Mama could reply, Da strode into the shop. "I convinced the twins to wait outside," he said, then he sighed as Nahel and Dahut walked through the door behind him. "Not that they paid any attention to me."

Nahel looked from me to Kelsey, and asked, "Which girl is mine?"

"Neither," my mother said, using her sword to bar him from coming further into the shop. "Lorcan, we believe Donn has employed a collector, along with a gancanagh. Why would he do that?"

"What Donn wants is blood," Lorcan said. "A creature like the collector can help him acquire it. You're certain about the gancanagh?"

As my mother confirmed the gancanagh's involvement, I leaned closer to Kelsey and said, "Paul is the gancanagh. That's what creatures like him are called."

She sucked in a breath. "Bloody bastard. If he tries to get us again, what should we do? Set him on fire?"

"A filthy gancanagh touched my betrothed?" Nahel demanded.

"No, because you're not betrothed to anyone here," I snapped. "Really, we have more important things to worry about!"

"Ah," he said, nodding. "You must be Lady Aoife's daughter. I am—"

"A damn fool," Dahut finished. "Forgive my brother. He was dropped often as a baby, sometimes right onto his head. As you can see, it left lasting damage. Where are Donn and the collector now?"

I pointed toward the front windows, and the sea beyond. "Can Donn control the waves?"

Rising out of Liscannor Bay was a giant bull made of seawater, complete with horns that came to a watery point and a gold ring in his nose. That ring looked quite similar to the curved golden tie clasp Aodhan's stepfather had worn to the meet and greet at The Saints.

"That is Donn?" Dahut asked.

"Yes," Lorcan said. "That is Donn Dumhach, Prince of the Sidhe, Master of the Dead. We need to keep him away from this piece of land and everything below it."

Dahut snapped her fingers toward her brother. "We will push him back to the depths. Come, Nahel."

The siblings strode out of the shop and toward the seawall. Before I could speculate as to what they could possibly do against a massive water bull, Dahut and Nahel raised their hands and beckoned spirals of seawater to them. The twins stepped on to the water as if it was solid ground, and proceeded to harry the bull as they spun around him and flung watery missiles against his hide.

"It's like magic carpets, but with water," Aodhan said. "Cool."

I refused to admit anything Nahel did was the least bit interesting. "Why did you bring them here?" I asked my mother.

"We did not bring them so much as they followed us above," she replied. "When they learned of Donn's involvement in the ward's breach, they insisted they could help. They appear to have been correct about that," she added.

I watched as the twins fought the water bull. "Should we go out there?"

"Swords are rather useless against water. Just ask Xerxes." Mama turned around, and faced Kelsey. "I do understand how this looks, but Kevin has no connection with Dahut. He has never laid eyes on her before today, and they've never once spoken to each other."

"Then how are they betrothed?" Kelsey asked.

Mama sighed. "Kilstiffen has some rather archaic traditions, but just because others follow them doesn't mean we have to do the same."

"I won't be following any of them," Kevin replied. "My grandfather mentioned a betrothal to me only one time. No one asked me my opinion on the matter, but here it is. I say no."

"I also say no," I added. "Fancy water powers aren't enough to sway me." Next to me, I saw Da smiling. He liked it when we defied Kilstiffen.

"And those powers are fancy," Aodhan said. I looked toward the seawall and saw the siblings standing back to back on a plume of water. They made an arching motion with their arms, and the water bull bellowed and crashed onto the beach. Thus destroyed, the remnants of the bull flowed out to sea like the water it was.

"Is he gone?" I asked.

"Not likely," Mr Sullivan said. "Donn is nothing if not tenacious. I need to find Bridgette and the girls, and make sure they're okay." Aodhan nodded, then he looked between me and his father, obviously torn between seeing to his family, and staying with me.

"Stay with Meri," Mr Sullivan said. "I can handle it."

"You're sure?" Aodhan asked.

"One hundred per cent." With that, Mr Sullivan squeezed Aodhan's shoulder and left the shop through the back door. Once he was gone, my mother faced us, and began issuing orders like the warrior she was.

"Our first priority is to keep Donn away from Tech Duinn," Mama began. "Lorcan, what defences are already in place?"

"Concealment, mostly," Lorcan replied. "However, it's Aodhan's ownership of the land that truly keeps Donn away."

Mama nodded. "Then we protect Aodhan. We also need to track down the collector and the gancanagh. Where would they be?"

"I know their address," I said. "We can split up, with some of us staying here and some going to the Flynn house."

"If Aodhan's not here and Donn is, that also helps us protect Aodhan," Kevin said. "Us four should be the ones to check out the Flynn place."

"I don't want to get muddled by Paul again," Kelsey said.

"Then stay here," I said. "My parents can protect you. But Paul's touch only works on girls, and Kevin won't let him at you."

"That's right, I won't," Kevin affirmed.

"Perhaps the sea twins can also stay here at the shop, in case Donn returns," Da suggested. "Their abilities seem to be a match for his, and I have a feeling six won't fit in Kevin's car."

"My car's still at the golf course," Kevin said.

"Take mine," Da said, as he handed over the keys. "And mine won't seat six, either."

"Having you four go to the Flynn house is an excellent plan," Mama said. "Brian and I will remain here as well, in case Donn appears in the flesh."

"All right." I sighed, and tried to ignore how my belly had gone sour. "Let's head over to the wretched Flynn house."

The four of us turned toward the door, then my mother said, "Kevin, Meri. A moment, please?"

I glanced at Kevin. He shrugged, and we approached Mama. "What's up?" I asked.

She lowered her voice, and said, "Your grandfather isn't set on this betrothal. It is certain members of the council of lords that want the two of you paired with Dahut and Nahel," she said. "They believe my father has sat on the throne for too long, and as a result, holds too much power. Since neither I nor my siblings have been deemed fit to rule, their solution is to force him to abdicate in favour of one of you."

I gasped. "Can they do that?"

"No, they cannot," Mama said. "Not while he is of sound mind, which he certainly is. But the king has agreed to consider abdication only if and when one or both of you are happily married, and may rule in his place."

Kevin let out a string of curses. "They do realise how utterly unreasonable that is, don't they?"

"Some do, some honestly don't care," Mama said. "We'll talk more about it later. The real question is why they think the heirs of Ker Ys are the solution to problems Kilstiffen doesn't have."

"And why aren't you fit to rule?" I asked.

"Many reasons," she replied. "That may be the only fact the council and I agree on. Be safe at the Flynns, and try not to engage them. Remember, a smart warrior knows when to retreat."

SOULS AND BLOOD

Once we were all in the car, Kelsey asked, "What was that all about? Last-minute instructions from the elder Murphys?"

"More like politics from below," Kevin grumbled. "Kilstiffen's council of lords is tired of our grandfather being the king—"

"Your grandfather is a king?" Kelsey demanded. While Kevin explained our family tree, Aodhan touched my hand.

"It's to be a political marriage, then?" he asked.

"There will be no marriage, political or otherwise," I replied. "The same council that hates my mother apparently also hates my grandfather, and wants him to step down. Their big solution is to have either Kevin or me take over, but not until after we marry those two from Ker Ys."

Aodhan grunted. "Sounds like this arrangement would benefit Ker Ys more than Kilstiffen."

"I hadn't thought of that," I mumbled, then I leaned forward. "Kevin, do you think Grandfather's in danger?"

Kevin scoffed. "Doubtful. Ma made it seem like he was playing along with the council, nothing more. Besides, if they raised a hand to them, they'd have Ma to deal with, and I doubt they're that stupid. Let's get going to the Flynn house," he added, as he started the car. "The sooner we get there, the sooner we can leave."

I didn't have anything to say to that, since Kevin was right. Grandfather was probably only telling the council what they wanted to hear, and nothing more would come of it. Then I remembered something else Mama said.

"Mama also said the council didn't find her or her siblings fit to rule," I said. "How could any of them be unfit?"

"It's hard to say," Kevin said. "Being that we've never met Ma's sister or brother, we don't know what they're like. As for Ma, I'm sure her marrying Da put them all in an uproar."

"The council doesn't like your father?" Kelsey asked.

"They don't like surface dwellers," he replied. "Any of them."

"She did steal the key to the city, too," I added. "That's why they've been stuck below for so long."

Aodhan scoffed. "They hate your ma, when you and she are the ones that saved them. Makes you wonder what good deeds your aunt and uncle have done."

While Kevin drove the short distance to the Flynn house, and answered Kelsey's many questions about Kilstiffen, Aodhan researched gancanaghs on his phone. According to legend, these creatures exuded a toxin from their skin that made others attracted to them and willing to follow their commands, much like how certain tropical frogs secreted deadly poison.

"He's poisonous, all right," Kelsey muttered. "I can't believe we're going back there."

"He won't touch you," Kevin said, in an unusually hard tone. My brother was more likely to influence everyone to get along than to start a fight, but Paul had hurt Kelsey. "Like Ma said, I'll cut off his hands if I need to."

"We should have brought one of the swords with us," Aodhan muttered. "Is there a kitchen in this house? A butcher knife will probably do the job just fine."

I turned away from Aodhan and toward the side window, and stared at the overcast sky. I wanted to ask Aodhan to calm down, but I didn't want to risk angering him further. What if he thought I was somehow defending Paul, or that I'd enjoyed his attentions? I hadn't, and I was fairly certain Aodhan understood that. However, I also understood that Paul had deeply hurt Aodhan, even though he hadn't laid a finger on him, and when people were hurt, they didn't always think rationally.

Besides, if it came down to it and we had to chop off Paul's hands, well, he'd earned his fate.

Sensing my discomfort, Aodhan looped his arm around my shoulders and pulled me to his side of the back seat. When I leaned against him, he murmured close to my ear, "I'm sorry. I know you don't like all this talk of maiming and death. I don't either, not really."

I set my hands on his forearm and squeezed. "I know." He kissed the side of my head, then I glanced out the front window and sat up. Paul's house was visible up ahead.

"That's it," Aodhan said to Kevin. I noticed how Kelsey shrank down in her seat.

Kevin turned onto the long driveway that led to the house, and let out a whistle. "This is quite the estate," he said. "Where's the door?"

"It was there," I said, pointing to a flat brick wall at the top of the front steps. "I sealed the doors to keep Paul from following us."

"Great job, but we're going to need a way in," Kevin said. "Can you un-seal it?"

"Or we can go through the garden entrance," Kelsey said. "When I first got here, Paul gave me a tour. I'll show you the way."

We got out of the car and followed Kelsey around to the back of the grand house. The manicured gardens and slate paths were so well kept they looked like something out of a real estate magazine or tourist brochure. There was even a set of wrought iron patio furniture artfully placed near the climbing roses. "Who maintains this place?" I muttered.

"Probably the girls Paul collects," Aodhan snapped, then he frowned. "I don't mean to be so bitter. It's just that he hurt you."

"I get it." I slid my arm around his waist and pressed myself against the side of his body. "I'm bitter, too. I just want to get this over with, and then never see either one of them ever again."

Aodhan squeezed me against him. "Same, Mer."

"Here's the back entrance," Kelsey called.

Kevin pulled open the back door and had a look inside. "Interesting, that they don't lock their doors."

"They probably eat any trespassers they come across," I said. Kevin gave me some side eye, then he returned his attention to the house.

"Corridor's empty," he announced, and we filed into the house. "Which way?"

"We could go floor by floor," I said, then we heard noises up ahead.

"It's coming from the game room," Kelsey whispered, then she beckoned us down the corridor. When we got to the end, I saw the glass-paned door Paul had led me through on Friday. To my utter shock, the same six classmates I'd interacted with last Friday were still in there, drinking beers and playing at darts and air hockey.

"They've been here for days," I said, covering my mouth in horror. "I can't believe I left them behind."

"They seem to be all right," Aodhan said. "No one looks like they're injured, and they seem to be happy enough. We can figure out how to rescue them after we search for the Flynns."

"And we now know this befuddlement Paul causes works on men, too," Kevin added.

"Paul had nothing to do with this," said a man's voice. The four of us turned as one, and were confronted by our new headmaster, Marcus Flynn. He was standing in the centre of the hallway, wearing the same dark suit he'd worn at school. Coupled with his pale hair and skin, he looked like a ghoul.

"Their souls have already been collected," Flynn continued. "Those bodies you see in the game room are now nothing but empty vessels."

"What gives you the right to take their souls?" I demanded. "They've done nothing to you!"

"A body doesn't need to be my enemy for me to claim their soul," Flynn replied. "Collecting is what I do. It's what I've always done."

"But why are you here now?" I pressed. "Why are you working at our school?"

"What does Donn have to do with this?" Aodhan added.

"Donn is my master," Flynn replied. "He told me to collect as many souls as I wanted, especially from those who were yet living. It's a rare treat for me to have a living soul to snack on. My master only wants the bodies, you see."

"For what?" I demanded, but Flynn never got the chance to answer. Kelsey had circled behind the headmaster and smacked him on the head with the torch she kept in her bag.

"Asshole," she said, as he crumpled to the floor, then she speared me with her gaze. "Well? How do we rescue that lot?"

"I think we'll need to get their souls back in their bodies," I said.

"Okay," Kelsey said. "How do we do that?"

"That's a great question." I watched the six boys in the game room. This wasn't supposed to be a rescue mission, and we didn't have room in the car to get them out of here, but none of that mattered. I couldn't leave them behind and I certainly couldn't let their souls be eaten by Flynn, not when I might be able to help them.

"If Flynn was collecting their souls, he must have put them some-where," I said. "Where would one put something precious? A safe?"

"He didn't call them precious. Flynn called them snacks," Kevin said. "He said he was going to snack on the living souls."

"The kitchen?" I suggested. Kelsey led the way again; since she'd been the Flynns' unwilling maid, she knew the home's layout. Once we were inside the kitchen we ransacked the pantry and shelves, tossing plates and cups aside as we looked for anything out of the ordinary.

"I might have it," Aodhan yelled. He'd climbed up to the top of the pantry, and found a golden urn hidden on the top shelf. "This contraption looks awful special."

Aodhan handed the urn down to Kevin, then he hopped down to the floor. Kevin set the urn on the counter, and we all stared at it.

"How do we know if any souls are in there?" I asked. "Could be the ashes of someone's deceased relative."

Kevin turned the urn around in a slow circle. "There's no inscrip-tions on it, so probably not. If we sing to the souls, do you think they'll answer us?"

"Look at you, wanting to sing," I said; maybe being with Kelsey was finally bringing out his merrow abilities. "Let's sing a bit, and try to match the urn's resonance."

"Ah, okay." Kevin shook out his hands. "You start."

I did, and after a bit of trial and error, I settled on a few midrange notes. Kevin joined me, and with our song we asked the urn if the missing souls were trapped inside. When the urn's lid rattled, we had our answer.

"They're in there, all right," I said, as the lid settled into place.

Kevin grabbed the urn, and we all ran back to the game room. "How do we put the souls back?" Kevin asked, once we were outside the door. "And make sure they get into the right bodies?"

"Maybe set the souls loose and let them find their own way?" I suggested.

Kevin shrugged. "As good a plan as any," he said, then he opened the game room's door. Kevin took the lid off the urn and tossed it into the room, and slammed the door shut. "Just in case they make a break for it," he muttered.

"The souls or the people?" I asked.

"Either."

We watched as the urn rolled to a halt against the air hockey table, then six clouds of mist rose up from the container's mouth and dispersed into the room. When the boys ceased their games and looked about the room, bleary-eyed as if they'd just woken from a long sleep, we knew the souls had found their respective people.

"It worked," I said.

"Probably best to let them sort themselves out," Kevin said. "Better than us trying to explain how they were un-souled for a few days."

"Good point," I said, then a hand clamped onto my shoulder.

"Hello, Meri," Paul hissed in my ear.

I screamed and bent my knees as I tried to duck out from under Paul's hand. He dug his fingers into my flesh, ripping through Aodhan's sweatshirt and then my skin and the muscle beneath. Unlike the last time he'd touched me, he wasn't taking away my free will. This time, Paul's hand was red hot, his fingers like four iron brands burning through me.

He was draining my life.

I felt myself falling, then Aodhan punched Paul dead in the face and yanked me away from him.

"Never touch Meri again," Aodhan yelled. I tried to stand next to Aodhan, but my legs were loose, like jelly. I grabbed Aodhan's shirt so I wouldn't hit the floor. I held on to him, but barely.

"She's mine," Paul spluttered as he clutched his nose. Blood flowed from between his fingers; Aodhan must have broken it. "Donn said I could pick one girl to keep, and I picked Meri!"

"What does Donn want all these students for?" Aodhan demanded.

"He needs blood to reopen Tech Duinn," Paul replied. "The younger the better. He can't get to his home any other way."

"Is he... Is he trapped up here?" I asked. The pain in my shoulder was spreading through my chest and making it hard for me to breathe. I raised my right hand, and saw blood dripping down my fingers.

"He got kicked out of the party down below," Paul said. "Donn hates it up here, but since Kilstiffen hasn't risen in so long he needs to access his house, so he can go below through that portal."

Kevin shoved Paul farther away from me. "Don't blame Kilstiffen for your messes, and don't talk to my sister," he began, then his gaze darted to me and he frowned. "Aodhan, get Meri out of here. We'll see about getting the lads to safety."

Aodhan scooped me into his arms, and stalked out of the house without another word. I clutched handfuls of his shirt, and let my eyes close. The darkness was warm. Comforting.

Shouts rang out around me. I cracked an eyelid, saw the boys who'd been in the game room running past us. An orange glow lit them from behind.

"What's happening?" I mumbled.

"Shh," Aodhan said, his lips against my forehead. "Conserve your strength."

I nodded, and let the world go dark again. As I slipped from consciousness, I heard my brother and Kelsey calling my name.

Healing

When I woke, I was lying on something soft. Whatever it was, it was comfortable, and warm, and totally unfamiliar. My hands ventured away from my body, and I determined I was lying on sheets. I moved my head, and noticed the lavender scented pillow beneath me. A bed, then. I was stretched out on an unfamiliar bed.

I cracked an eyelid, and saw that this bed was in an equally unfamiliar room. The room was small, with ivory and gold tapestries on two of the walls, with the area across from me being taken up by a large cabinet filled with jars and bowls of various sizes. Next to the bed was a small table, on which an oil lamp burned with the flame turned low. The soft lamplight made it seem like I was still dreaming.

The memory of Paul grabbing me flashed behind my eyes, and I sat straight up. Aodhan, who had been sitting beside the bed but behind my head where I couldn't see him, leapt to his feet.

"Meri," he murmured, as he wrapped his arms around me. "Meri, Meri, Meri. I've never been so scared in all my life, not even when you almost jumped off the Cliffs of Moher."

"What happened?" I asked. When Aodhan only held me tighter, I asked, "Where are we?"

"Kilstiffen." He pulled away, I assumed to explain what we were doing here. Instead, he tilted up my chin and kissed me as if he feared he'd never see me again.

When we parted, he sat next to me on the bed, his head close to mine and my hands in his. "There was so much blood," he began, "and no matter what we did, you wouldn't stop bleeding. Kevin called your parents to tell them we were bringing you to hospital, but your ma said to come here instead."

"Blood?" I looked down at myself. My sweatshirt was gone, and red darkened the top of my camisole. There was even a spot on my pearl pendant. Four new shiny pink marks decorated my right shoulder. I remembered when Paul grabbed me there, and the searing pain that came with his touch. "Paul... He hurt me?"

"He did, but they healed you. The people here, they healed you." Aodhan brushed back my hair. "They even took care of the scrapes you got from that angry hedge. Then once they were done, I just had to sit here, wait for you to wake up."

"How did you get down here?" I asked, since Kilstiffen wasn't a fan of outsiders.

"Kevin led us to the set of gold doors, and we banged on them and screamed until someone opened them. When all that ruckus didn't rouse you..." His hand tightened on mine. I squeezed his fingers. He smiled, but it didn't reach his eyes. "Anyway, once the guards opened the door, Kevin demanded to see the king. They were alright with admitting Kevin and you, but not me or Kelsey, and there was no way I was handing you over to an unknown person unless that person was a medic. The guards were about to turn all of us away when Kelsey got in their faces and demanded they bring us here to the palace, whether they liked it or not."

There was a bloodstain spread across the front of his shirt. I set my hand on it, and said, "You carried me. The whole time, you carried me."

He put his hand on mine. "I only let go when the healers took you."

"Even then, he wouldn't go farther than a pace or two away from you," Grandfather said. I looked up, and saw him standing in the doorway. I wondered how long he'd been there. "How do you feel, child?"

"Disoriented," I replied. "And quite thirsty."

Grandfather said something to someone beyond the doorframe, then he entered the room and stood beside the bed. "I imagine you are. The gancanagh's poison was deep within you, and you lost quite a bit of blood."

"Poison?" I repeated, then I remembered Paul's fingers as they dug into my flesh and down to the bone, and that his skin exuded poison. "He poisoned me with his hand?"

"It's why you bled so much," Aodhan said. "According to the healers, your body was trying to purge itself of the toxins."

"Where are these healers?" I asked Grandfather. "I'd like to thank them."

"They've already been well rewarded for their efforts," he replied. "Saving the life of Kilstiffen's heiress is not an act that goes unnoticed."

I nodded, even more uncomfortable with this heir business after what Mama had told me about the council's sneaky plans. "Where's Kevin?"

"He's just in the next room, along with that girl of his," Grandfather replied. "They also refused to go far from your side. This one, however, refused to leave you entirely," he added, nodding toward Aodhan.

"That's right," Aodhan said. "Where Meri goes, I go."

"What happened to Paul?" I asked. "Grandfather, we might need your help against the gancanagh, and the ankou."

"I think they're done for," Aodhan said. "Kelsey set the house on fire with them in it."

So that's what the orange lights had been. "She did what?"

"She didn't want them going after anyone else, and burning the place down was the first thing she thought of," Aodhan explained.

"Who thinks of arson as a first choice?" I muttered, then I shook my head. "Grandfather, remember when I was here last, and Lucas Sullivan told you his wife was in trouble with a fairy prince?"

"I do," Grandfather said.

"This is Aodhan. He's Mr Sullivan's son, and the woman is Aodhan's mother, and the fairy in question happens to be Donn Dumhach. Aodhan's mother really needs our help."

Grandfather frowned. "We are not in the habit of lending aid to surface dwellers, but if it wasn't for you, Aodhan, I might have lost my granddaughter. We shall aid you against Donn, and do what we can for your mother."

"Thank you, sir, but my sisters need help, too," Aodhan said. "My ma, she's got two little ones."

Grandfather bowed his head. "Aye, we'll help the little ones, as well. Now Aodhan, if you wouldn't mind, I would like to speak to Meri privately."

Aodhan glanced at me. When I nodded, he stood. "Yes, sir. I'll just tell Kevin and Kelsey the good news about Meri's recovery."

Once we were alone, Grandfather scrutinised my shoulder. "May I?" he asked, his hand hovering near me. I nodded, and he placed his big, warm hand against my skin. He closed his eyes, and sang softly for a few moments.

"How do you feel?" he asked. "Truly, now."

"Better," I replied. "A bit sore, though. But I also feel as if I'm missing something."

"Missing what, exactly?"

"Honestly, I feel good, all things considered, but should I feel good after an experience like that?" I asked. "Shouldn't I be traumatised?"

"Aren't you?" he asked. When I didn't answer, he used his other hand to tilt my face toward his. "In my experience, when one's body suffers a grave injury, the mind deliberately forgets what happened, at least for a little while. It's a small comfort, but comfort nonetheless."

"Have you had many grave injuries?"

"I've had my fair share."

"I'm sorry."

"I appreciate that," he said. "Our pain makes us stronger, does it not?"

I made a face. "I suppose. We should lift weights instead."

Grandfather chuckled. "Perhaps weights are the answer. You gave us all quite a fright, Meri," he said, as he withdrew his hand. "But the healing is complete. You shouldn't suffer any ill effects from the poison."

"Thank you," I said. "I don't know what would have happened to me if you hadn't been willing to help."

"Even though we're newly acquainted, never forget that Kilstiffen is as much your home as the land above," he said. "Never hesitate to call on me for anything you need."

"Was it also your idea to send Dahut and Nahel above?"

"They went of their own accord," he replied. "Donn has caused his share of misery in Ker Ys, and they were eager to face him. I trust the twins made themselves useful?"

"Yes. They were quite capable in the fight against Donn." I fingered the edge of the blanket. I wanted to ask him about the council, and how they wanted to shove him off of his throne, but I didn't know if it was my place to question him about such things. Instead, I probed for more information about our family.

"Before everything that happened with the gancanagh, a ward attacked me, and apparently it did so because my magic is similar to Donn's," I said. "How could that be? More importantly, what's Donn doing knocking around County Clare if he's a god?"

"Donn is a sidhe prince," Grandfather began. "He belongs in Tír na nÓg, but he was expelled some time ago."

"So, him not being able to access his home in Tech Duinn isn't because Kilstiffen hasn't risen?" I asked, recalling what Paul had said before Kevin shoved him away from me.

"Not at all. Tech Duinn is itself a portal, and it functions independently of what happens here. Donn was exiled from his home for other reasons."

I had a feeling I didn't want to know what those reasons were. "Are we somehow related to him?"

Grandfather blew out a breath. "You are through your grandmother's side. The lineage is somewhat complicated."

"Do I get to learn about this lineage?" I asked.

"Yes, but at another time," he replied. "We'd best have your mother present when I tell you anything about our family. Aoife greatly enjoys disagreeing with everything I say, and I'd hate to get any details wrong, for fear of how she'll punish me later on."

"She is a stickler for the facts."

Grandfather laughed out loud, which both surprised and delighted me. "Stickler? More of a tyrant," he began, then he regaled me with a few stories of Mama as a child. By the time he'd finished his third such tale, I understood that he was also fond of sticking to the facts, and that he loved his family very much. It felt good to have those few things in common with him.

Dinner With Grandpa

Grandfather thought it would be for the best if we all stayed in Kilstiffen that night, and returned to the surface the next day. I didn't really want to remain below overnight, but my newly repaired shoulder remained sore. It would be smart to stay close to those who'd healed me, in case I experienced any complications. Besides, Grandfather had ordered a feast to be prepared in our honour, which meant Aodhan was thrilled to act as a tourist and sample all the foods Kilstiffen had to offer.

After a messenger had been sent above to inform my parents of my recovery, and our plans to remain below as Grandfather's guests for the night, a set of servants showed us to the rooms Kevin and I had been assigned to. They were two large suites situated right across the hall from each other.

"Isn't this grand," I said, as I walked around the front room of the suite assigned to me. Beyond that area was a sitting room, a bedchamber with an adjacent dressing area, and a bathing room. "Do you have many guests in the palace?" I asked Talia, the servant who had escorted me. I imagined that many princes and queens had occupied these rooms in the past.

"This isn't a guest room, my lady," Talia replied. "This is your room, and the one across the corridor belongs to your brother. As soon as King Steinar knew of your impending births, he had these royal suites prepared for you. We've maintained them to the best of our abilities ever since."

"Yeah, Princess Meri," Kelsey said as she bumped her shoulder against mine; luckily she was on my uninjured side. She'd been sent to my room to get ready for dinner alongside me, just as Aodhan had gone with Kevin into the other room. "Getting the royal treatment, aren't we?"

"Is this lady your handmaiden?" Talia asked. I eyed Kelsey, as a dozen well-earned retorts waited on the tip of my tongue. But Kelsey had proven that she was more than who she'd been, and I owed it to her to do the same.

"This is Kelsey, my brother's girlfriend. Consort? Yes, consort is a better term." Kelsey raised an eyebrow at my wording, only to laugh when Talia got all flustered and curtsied.

"Excuse me, my lady," Talia murmured. "I meant no disrespect."

"No worries," Kelsey said. "I'll introduce you to Kevin later on."

"We've already met," Talia said. "In fact, I recall when Aoife was first carrying him, and when both of you were presented as infants to the court. The royal children have always been my charges, and that charge now extends to you, and Kevin," Talia explained.

"You've looked after all of the royal children, even my mother and The Shadow?" I asked. "And their brother?"

Talia blew out a breath. "If I can survive looking after Scáthach, not to mention Oscar, I can survive anything. There's a sound reason why Aoife has always been the king's favourite child."

"Is she? I thought rulers weren't supposed to play favourites."

"After the antics the older two got up to, my kindly sweet Aoife was a pleasure to raise," Talia said. "If you'd like, I'll share a few stories about her and the other two hellions while you get ready for the feast."

"That would be wonderful," I said.

"Do we get to wear these clothes?" Kelsey asked, as she swept into the dressing area and grabbed a frothy blue gown from the closet.

"You certainly may," Talia said. "While you're enjoying dinner, I can have your surface clothes laundered and pressed. I've already mended that hooded garment you arrived in," she added, with a nod toward me.

"Thank you, Talia," I said, as Kelsey mouthed the words "surface clothes" behind Talia's back. "Do we have time to wash up?"

"Of course," Talia said, and she led us into the most amazing bathroom I'd ever seen. The tiled walls and floor were gleaming mother-of-pearl set with mosaics of tiny iridescent shells, and everything from the stately pillars to the dressing table and mirror was edged in gold. Instead of a regular bathtub, in the centre of the room was a massive sunken pool. It could have easily fit five or maybe even ten people inside, if they all got on well.

Or, based on Talia's face, it was perfectly sized for two people: Kelsey and me.

"As you can see, the bath is ready for both of you," Talia said. "Would you like me to assist you with washing?"

"We'll be fine," I said. "Thank you, Talia."

"Looks like we're taking a swim together," Kelsey said, as Talia arranged stacks of towels and tiny, colourful soaps near the edge of the pool. "Think it'll be salt water?"

I sighed. "Let's just get this over with."

The tub was not salty like the sea. Instead, it was filled with pleasantly warm fresh water. After we'd bathed—separately, mind you—Kelsey and I set about donning our fancy dresses. Talia returned after we'd put them on, and were picking out our shoes. She took one look at our still-damp tresses and declared she would help us style our hair.

"Mine is fine the way it is," I said, only to have Kelsey and Talia share a look. "What?"

"Meri, down here, you're royalty," Kelsey said as she picked up one of the delicate shell combs and began dragging it through my hair. "You've got to look the part. Think of your grandfather. He ordered this whole dinner for you and Kevin, and since he's the king, the least you can do to thank him is look like a princess."

"I do agree, my lady," Talia said. "And you need to look the part as well, Lady Kelsey."

Kelsey blinked. "What? Me?"

"As Prince Kevin's consort, you must present yourself according-ly," Talia said. "After all, if the two of you marry, you will someday be our queen."

While Kelsey's face went white, then red, I asked, "Would the council of lords accept a surface dweller as a queen?"

"The council's opinion isn't as important as they like to think it is," she replied. "They represent all off the sea kingdoms, not just Kilstiffen, but their opinions amount to little more than recommendations. Ultimately, they have no power over us."

"Really." Finally, Talia was giving me the unvarnished truth about how things worked down here. "Then why did they dredge up those twins from Ker Ys for Kevin and me?"

"The council did that to make their own lives easier, but pay them no mind. As you know, your father isn't from here, and neither is your grandmother. The royal family has always been free to marry whomever they wished." Talia patted the bench in front of the mirror. "Now, if you'll both have a seat, we'll have your hair properly coiffed in no time."

After a bit of hair pulling and pinning, Talia declared our hair fit for dinner. Kelsey had ended up with her hair held back from her face with a set of abalone combs in a shade of blue that perfectly matched her eyes. For my hair, Talia had produced a bowl of gold pins set with crystals and pearls, and arranged them around the crown of my head like a creamy halo. It was reminiscent of those tiaras Aodhan was always teasing me about, and I had to admit I did like the effect. I found myself hoping he would, too.

"Well, now, ladies, I'd say we're done," Talia announced, as she set down her combs. "Enjoy the evening."

Kelsey and I thanked Talia, then we stepped into the corridor and found Kevin and Aodhan waiting for us. They'd also got the full brunt of Kilstiffen's wardrobe department, and were wearing the undersea version of men's formal wear. Aodhan looked like an eighteenth-century gentleman, complete with an ivory shirt buttoned up to his neck topped with a cravat, deep blue pants and a matching frock coat, and pointy black shoes. I'd never imagined he could be so handsome, and I've thought he was handsome since we were in play school.

"Don't you look nice?" I said to him, and he grinned.

"Far cry from a wetsuit, isn't it? And you are beautiful, as always," he said as he took my hand and kissed my knuckles. I was wearing a sleeveless white dress that draped from a wide gold collar, with a sheer white shawl wrapped around my shoulders. The dress was cinched with a thin gold belt, and I had matching gold slippers on my feet. I'd arranged the pearl necklace so it sat atop the dress, nestled just above my breast. Talia had cleaned the last spatters of my blood off the pearl, and it was a perfect match to the silken fabric.

Kevin took Kelsey's hand, and I watched as he smiled and she blushed. They were dressed similarly to Aodhan and me, though Kevin's formal wear was charcoal grey, and Kelsey's dress was the extra lacy blue one she'd insisted on. I'd thought it a bit much, but Talia had said it would set off Kelsey's red hair nicely, and it certainly did.

Aodhan offered me his arm. "Shall we?"

I tucked my hand into his elbow, but before we could move, Kevin shouldered his way in front of us. "I'm older, so I go first," he said.

Kelsey looked back at us and stuck out her tongue. I reciprocated. Laughing, the four of us walked down the corridors and, after we asked a few of the palace staff for directions, we entered the dining hall.

"Wow," Aodhan said.

"How much money does this place have?" Kelsey asked.

"A lot," Kevin said, and by the look of things, he was right. The dining hall was even more opulent than the throne room, with polished white marble walls and floors and hammered gold details on the columns and candelabras. Brightly coloured stained glass windows ringed the room, and every table and chair was draped in white silk. Dozens if not hundreds of candles were scattered throughout the room, giving everything a hazy, dreamlike glow.

"I am reminded of your mother's massive dowry," Aodhan whispered in my ear, referencing the multitude of gold bars she'd inherited after marrying Da. "Like as not, it didn't make a dent."

"It doesn't seem that way," I murmured, then I straightened as the king strode toward us.

"My grandchildren have arrived," he announced. "Don't you all look splendid? I am pleased you have accepted my offer to remain with us this evening."

"Thank you, Grandfather," Kevin and I murmured in unison, while Aodhan and Kelsey bowed and curtsied.

"Come, children," Grandfather said. "You're to sit with me. We have another honoured guest that will also be dining with us."

"Who's that?" I asked.

"Gradlon, the monarch of Ker Ys," Grandfather replied. I saw Kevin's shoulders stiffen, but that was his only reaction. "You met his children earlier, did you not, Kevin?"

"Yes," Kevin replied. "They were a great help against Donn. Thank you, for sending them."

"I did no such thing," Grandfather replied. "They were told that help was needed above, and being that they're people of honour, they did what needed to be done. Here we are." We arrived at a round table set with six chairs; one of the chairs was made of opulent gold, another one was slightly less rich in silver, and the remaining four were carved dark wood. I assumed the four wooden chairs were for regular people like me. "Kevin and Meri, I'd like one of you to sit on either side of me."

We dutifully arranged ourselves around the table per Grandfather's instructions. Once we were all seated, Grandfather took a moment to beam at us. "I am overjoyed to have you both with me this evening. And your companions, of course."

"Are we your only grandchildren?" I asked.

"Yes, Meri, you are, which makes you all the more precious to me. Kevin."

"Yes, sir," Kevin said.

"You said earlier you've assisted Meri in a few songs," Grandfather said. "I trust that means your voice is strengthening?"

"I surprised myself when I held the notes as long as I did," Kevin replied. "If only I hadn't stopped singing earlier today, Meri and Kelsey wouldn't have been trapped in that hedge."

"A hedge trapped them?" Grandfather asked.

"It was near where Donn Dumhach supposedly left his treasure," I replied. "The ward was, um, warding the place against Donn, and it got a bit confused. When Kevin and I both stopped singing, it decided we were the enemy."

"I'm so sorry for dropping the tune, Meri," Kevin said.

"You were amazing," Kelsey said. "You can't hold yourself responsible for how an evil bush acts."

"Your lady speaks the truth," Grandfather said, then he stood. "Ah! Here's Gradlon now."

Across the hall, the king of Ker Ys had entered and caused quite a commotion. He looked much like a younger version of Grandfather. Gradlon's hair and beard were mahogany instead of grey, and he wore sunny yellow and gold robes rather than the greens and blues Grandfather favoured. Gradlon stopped to speak to the council of lords' table, and took the time to laugh at their jokes and clap them all on the back as if they were great friends. For all I knew, they were.

"Are his children here?" Kevin asked.

"I don't see them," I replied. "Let's not mention them, and hope he doesn't, either."

After Gradlon had put on a suitable show so we all knew how well-liked he was, he strode to our table and greeted Grandfather.

"Steinar," Gradlon said, and they embraced like old friends. "Yet again, your hospitality amazes me. How are you?"

"Well, though not as well as those in Ker Ys," Grandfather replied; I wondered what that meant. "Allow me to present my dear grandchildren, Kevin and Meri, and their companions, Kelsey and Aodhan. Children, this is Gradlon Mor, the king of Ker Ys."

"A pleasure," Gradlon said as we stood to bow and greet him appropriately. His gaze lingered on Aodhan and Kelsey for a few moments, then he took his seat. "What are we having this evening, Steinar? Let me guess, clams?"

Grandfather chortled like an undersea Father Christmas. "I do love a good clam stew, but tonight I thought we'd dine like our brethren in Armorica. You brought us a bull for roasting, did you not?"

"Aye, and a case of our finest wine." Gradlon signalled a servant, and crystal glasses filled with a fizzy orange liquid were delivered to our table. "Please, everyone partake."

I brought my glass to my nose and sniffed. "It smells fruity."

"Like blueberries," Kelsey said, then she took a sip. "Yes, it's very berry."

"We harvest the berries that grown near the shore, and our vintners make good use of them," Gradlon said. He eyed Aodhan and me over the rim of his glass. "I notice you two aren't drinking. Is my wine not to your liking?"

"It's not that," I said. "We don't really drink alcohol, but we can make an exception tonight. Right, Aodhan?"

"Absolutely," Aodhan said, then he took a small sip. "It's wonderful. Thank you for sharing it with us, sir."

Since everyone else had tried it, I drank some of the orange wine. It was so fruity and thick it tasted like carbonated jam. "Quite lovely," I said.

"It pleases me that you enjoy it," Gradlon said. "Now, Steinar, tell me everything that has happened in Kilstiffen since I was last here. I've heard that you regained the key!"

"We certainly have," Grandfather replied, and he proceeded to tell Gradlon everything that had occurred in this corner of the sea since his last visit. It was quite the list.

Dinner went on that way, with Grandfather and Gradlon trading stories and lobbing gentle barbs at one another across the table, while the rest of us looked on. Even though their conversation seemed friendly, I got the impression that even though Gradlon boasted and postured about how great his city was, Ker Ys was in some way worse off than Kilstiffen. What's more, it seemed that Gradlon thought Grandfather could do something about it. I supposed that like everything else around here, there were reams of backstory between the two lands.

As far as the food went, it was mostly good. The bull Gradlon had bragged about supplying for our dinner had been transformed into rather tender and tasty steaks. The steaks were served alongside roasted sea vegetables; honestly, I could have done without that bit. Dessert was a smooth, mild cheese topped with nuts and honey, which was unusual but delicious.

The evening ended up going rather smoothly, which was a relief. In fact, after Gradlon had bullied us into drinking his wine he paid almost no attention to anyone other than Grandfather, and the lords seated their nearby table. Our reprieve from his notice ended when our after dinner coffees were served.

"It's like espresso," I said, marvelling at the dainty cups. Each coffee was served in a delicate white nautilus shell, and was set in a silvered cage to keep it upright. "How lovely."

"I see you wear Manannán's Pearl," Gradlon said, as he nodded toward my necklace. He startled me so much I almost spilled my coffee. "It is fitting that a daughter of Kilstiffen has earned such a treasure."

"I wouldn't say I earned it," I said, my hand fluttering atop the pearl. "It was in my mother's things, and I came across it."

"Your mother the warrior," Gradlon said. "Still calling herself the guardian of the portal, is she?"

"Aoife remains our greatest warrior," Grandfather said.

"As Dahut remains ours," Gradlon said. "Kevin, what did you think of my daughter? You met her today, did you not?"

"I did see her earlier, but that was all," Kevin replied diplomatically. "We did not have the opportunity to be properly introduced."

Gradlon grunted, then he swung his gaze toward me. "And you, Meri."

"Me?" I squeaked.

"What was your impression of my son, Nahel?"

"Um, he has very shiny hair." When Gradlon frowned and Grandfather laughed, I added, "We really didn't have time for introductions. They'd come above along with my parents, and soon after they arrived, Donn Dumhach decided to attack us from the bay."

Gradlon's frown deepened. "How did Donn appear?"

"As a bull made of seawater," I replied. "Your children defeated him."

"Defeated him for now," Grandfather said. "If I know Donn—and I do, quite well even—he merely retreated to regroup and plan his next offensive."

I shuddered. "I don't ever want to see that water bull again."

"That's one of Donn's favored forms," Grandfather said, "but fear not, Meri. Donn has been put in his place before, and we will do so again."

"Meri," Gradlon said, as a servant refilled his crystal glass with more of that sickly orange concoction. I wondered how many of those he'd had. "That's an unusual name for one from Kilstiffen."

"I'm named for my grandmother on my father's side," I replied.

"Granny Mer," Kevin said, with a grin. "She makes a cake so rich, one bite and you'll forget your name."

"Remember that four tiered monstrosity she made for Easter one year?" I asked. "Those cakes were so heavy everything listed to the side!"

"It was like a pastel Leaning Tower of Pisa," Kevin added.

"Think she'll bake a cake for your weddings?" Gradlon asked, and Kevin and I shut our mouths.

"Meri's quite a good baker, herself," Aodhan said, rescuing us all.

"You'd make me bake my own cake?" I scoffed. "I would happily prepare one for Kevin, though."

"You're the best sister ever," Kevin said, raising his coffee cup to toast me. "Definitely the best one I've ever had."

I glanced at Gradlon; his face was red, and he looked to be gearing up to give us a piece of his mind. Luckily, Grandfather also noticed Gradlon's agitated state, and defused the situation.

"It is getting late, and I fear I'm not as young as I once was," Grandfather said as he stood. "I mean to retire. Meri, you should get some rest, as well."

"Yes, Grandfather," I said. "I will certainly take your advice."

"We all will," Kevin added.

The rest of us got to our feet, and followed Grandfather as he left the hall and walked toward the residential side of the palace. I didn't know why Gradlon was accompanying us, but I thought it best not to question his presence. When we reached the corridor that led to our rooms, Grandfather said, "I trust your sleeping accommodations have been worked out?"

"Yes, sir," the four of us responded as one. Gradlon's gaze darted between Kelsey and Aodhan, and I remember what Grandfather had said to my mother, that a dalliance with a surface dweller would be overlooked. Is that what was happening now? Had everyone decided to overlook a few dalliances that in my case weren't even happening?

I shook my head, and decided to leave off such speculation, at least for now. "I appreciate your help so much. Thank you," I said, then I embraced Grandfather. He was startled, more so when Kevin embraced us both.

"I do like having a grandpa," Kevin said; seemed not just Gradlon had too much wine.

"And I find you both quite delightful," Grandfather said, as he patted our backs. "I look forward to having breakfast with you. All of you," he added.

We nodded and smiled, then the four of us continued on down the corridor. When we reached our rooms, Kevin looped his arm with Kelsey's, and they disappeared behind his door without a backward glance. Which left Aodhan and me alone, standing in front of the entrance to my sumptuous suite.

Oh, dear.

Know Your Enemies

"I suppose we'd best get inside," I said in a rush. I shoved the door of my suite open. It banged against the wall as I entered the front room. Aodhan followed, and gently closed the door behind him. "And here we are."

"Mer." Aodhan approached me, and caressed my cheek. "Why are you so nervous? We've been alone before."

"I know, it's just." I paused, and gestured wildly at the rich furnishings. Someone, probably Talia, had thought to light the lamps, and the resulting romantic glow was enough to give me heart palpitations. "We've never been someplace like this. We're always at my house, or school, or at the surf shop. This is like the honeymoon suite at a posh hotel."

"True, but we don't need to stress about it. It's just a room, nothing more." When I wouldn't meet his eyes, he said, "There's a couch in the sitting room. I'll sleep there." Aodhan squeezed my fingers, and walked toward the very comfortable looking velvet couch. It was more than long enough for him to stretch out on, and there was a woollen blanket tossed over one of the arms. There were even a few cushions for him to lay his head upon. Aodhan would have a great night's rest on that couch.

My heart lurched. I couldn't let him sleep all the way out there in the sitting room. I couldn't let myself sleep without him.

The idea of Aodhan leaving me all alone in Kilstiffen was terrifying. He would only be in the next room, and within earshot if I called out during the night, but I needed him in this strange land that kept getting stranger. I hoped he needed me, too.

"Aodhan." He halted, and faced me. "Don't sleep on the couch. Sleep in the bed. With me." When he didn't move, I said, "Please." Aodhan crossed the room in two long strides, and cupped my face with his hands.

"You're sure?" he asked, and I placed my hands on top of his.

"I am."

"All right, I accept your offer. But just for sleeping," he added. "I don't want to—I mean, I do, but not here."

I gulped down my panic; it had sounded like I was propositioning him for more than just a night's rest, but at least he thought that would be a bad idea, too. "I agree. Not here."

Aodhan kissed my forehead. "Let's see if that fancy closet of yours came stocked with any pyjamas."

We parted, and entered the dressing room. The back of the massive wardrobe had an assortment of nightgowns, each one lacier than the last, but there was nothing resembling boys sleepwear. I imagined that when Grandfather had this room set up for me, his only granddaughter, he hadn't thought anyone would be sharing it with me. Certainly not while I was an unmarried teen, and definitely not a boy from the surface world.

I never thought I'd be sharing a room with another person in such a way, either, but waking up with Aodhan on the back porch that morning had woken something deep within me. The more time we spent together increased my reluctance to be apart from him, even when we were sleeping. Maybe Aodhan was right, and we should get a place for the two of us. But where would that lead?

I pushed this latest worry aside, and concentrated on finding something to wear to bed. I was always telling Aodhan we needed to tackle one problem at a time, and I needed to follow my own advice. Otherwise I'd go batty.

"This one looks promising," I said, as I pulled out a blue cotton nightgown that was only edged in lace on the cuffs and neckline. I would have preferred more flannel and less lace on my sleepwear, but my options were limited.

"I guess I'll wear this one," he said, holding a plain ivory night shirt aloft. "I'll, um, change out there."

With that, Aodhan left me alone in the dressing room. I sighed, then I kicked off my golden shoes and removed my silk dress, and slipped the nightgown over my head. My newly healed shoulder protested the movements, and it was a tricky thing to get the dress off and then the nightgown on, but I managed. The nightgown fit rather well, though the sleeves were a bit long, and the lace was soft rather than itchy. I reentered the bedchamber, and found Aodhan clad in his nightshirt and standing in front of the full-length mirror, frowning.

"It is comfortable, I'll say that," he said when he saw me.

I stood behind him and slid my arms around his waist. "You're as handsome as ever," I said, as I peeked around his arm at our reflection.

"In that case," he began, then he spun around and snatched me into his arms. I squealed, but he kissed me hard, then he picked me up and carried me to bed. He set me down as gently as if I was made of glass, and began tugging the pins out of my hair.

"Can't sleep with these in your hair," he said. "These pearls are lovely, but I prefer your hair down."

"Do you?"

"Yeah." Having finished with the pins, he raked his fingers through my hair. "Softest thing I've ever felt, your hair is. So soft I can hardly feel it."

I put my hand on his. "If you can hardly feel it, how do you know it's soft?"

"I know." He took his handful of hairpins and deposited them on the bedside table, then he walked around to the far side of the bed and pulled back the blankets.

"Why are you all the way over there?" I asked. "Are you going to set up a barrier between us, too?"

"Whatever it takes to get you to behave." Despite his words, Aodhan moved toward the centre of the bed. I did the same, and nestled myself against him. "Sweet dreams, Meri."

"You too, Aodhan."

When I woke, I was once again in an unfamiliar bed, but this time I knew the arms around me as well as I knew my own name. I rolled over, and Aodhan smiled at me.

"Hello, sleepyhead."

"Have you been awake for a while?"

"I have. Talia's been in and out a few times, too. She brought back our clothes." He nodded toward the dressing room. I could see our clothes sitting in two tidy piles on top of the bench, freshly washed and neatly folded.

"And you didn't leap out of bed to put trousers on?" I teased, since he was still wearing his borrowed nightshirt.

"Nah. I wanted to stay here with you."

I laid my hand on the bed between us, and Aodhan covered it with his. I'd always loved our early morning talks, when it seemed like he and I were the only two people in the world. "What did Talia say about finding us like this?" I asked.

"Not a thing," he replied. "Kilstiffen seems to have a rather relaxed attitude with regard to premarital relations."

"How progressive of them." Not that anyone here was having relations. "You slept well?"

"I did." His hand hovered over my shoulder. "May I check your shoulder?"

I nodded, then Aodhan pushed the too-big collar of my nightgown aside, and frowned when he saw my shiny new scars. "How does it feel?"

"Hurts." I left off how I could still feel Paul's fingers tearing my flesh apart, and how in my dreams last night I saw his manic grin as he insisted I was the girl he'd picked to keep. That part of my trauma had nothing to do with my physical wounds, and it would take some time to heal. "But it's getting better."

Aodhan glided his fingers over the marks, then he tugged my nightgown back over my shoulder. "Tell me if you need help with anything at all. There's no shame in asking for help, especially while you're healing."

"I know." I traced little circles onto his chest. "Last night, I was thinking about what you said. About getting a place for us."

"Yeah? And what did you think about my mad idea?"

"Maybe it wouldn't be so bad." I looked up at him. "But not the old cottage."

"We can agree on that. Besides, there is the matter of it being my turn to catch you exiting the shower, and that cottage is shower free."

I swatted his arm, but gently. "I'm never telling you anything ever again."

Aodhan raised an eyebrow, which usually meant the teasing was on. He never got to say whatever was on his mind, because Talia reentered the room.

"Lovely to see you awake, Meri," Talia greeted, then she saw how close Aodhan and I were. "I'm not interrupting, am I?"

"Not at all," I replied, as I sat up against the headboard, and not just to prove I was still dressed. "Thank you, for seeing to our clothes."

"You are most welcome," Talia said. "If you're of a mind to rise, breakfast will be served shortly."

"I love breakfast," Aodhan said.

"Will it be in the same great room we dined in last evening?" I asked.

"Oh, no," Talia replied. "The king has requested an intimate meal with only his guests. You'll be seated in the noon room, which he favours. When all of his children were small, and Lady Niamh was still in residence, that room was where he preferred eating."

"Why isn't Lady Niamh in residence now?" I asked.

"She's below for the time being," Talia replied. "She divides her time between both worlds, though I must admit, we all miss her when she's away."

"Even the king?" I asked.

"Especially the king," she replied. "He does get a bit melancholy without her. Perhaps, now that you and your brother are accustomed to visiting us, you will come by more often. Then King Steinar will have a reason to use the noon room again."

I imagined a younger version Grandfather in the noon room surrounded by children. From what Talia had told us, they had all been little terrors running amok in the palace. Since I wondered who else Talia knew, I asked, "Have you ever met my father?"

"I certainly have," Talia replied. "Even when I first met Brian, it was plain how he adored our Aoife. We can talk more later, but I fear breakfast will be served soon and we don't want to delay the king. Would either of you like help with dressing?"

"We'll be fine," I said. "Thank you again, Talia, for everything."

Talia curtsied and left the chamber. Once she was gone, Aodhan asked, "What grown human needs help getting dressed?"

"Yesterday, she tried to give Kelsey and me a bath." I got out of bed, and caught a glimpse of my reflection in the mirror. My nightgown was a great deal sheerer than I'd realised. I grabbed my clothes and took them into the bathroom, and announced that I'd get changed in there. Hopefully, neither Aodhan nor Talia had noticed that literally all of me was on display.

Soon enough we were both properly dressed, and combing our hair with the delicate shell combs Talia had left for us. Aodhan's hair got fluffier the more he did to it, and I was searching through the crystal trays and bowls for something I could use to put my hair up. My elastic band seemed to have disappeared, and I desperately needed a ponytail.

"Why don't you use these pins from last night?" Aodhan asked, as he set some of the pearl and crystal pins on the table in front of me.

"I wouldn't even know how to put my hair up with those," I said.

"Can't be too hard," he said, then he grabbed a handful of my hair, twisted it, and pinned it up. He repeated the action a few more times, and I ended up with a fluffy bun that sat just above the nape of my neck.

"I suppose that works," I said, eyeing the stray tendrils of hair grazing my shoulders. Overall, the effect was rather becoming. "Ready for breakfast?"

Aodhan clutched his chest as if I'd wounded him. "How can you even ask me that? Of course I'm ready for food."

"Come on, you goof." We stepped into the corridor, and found Kevin and Kelsey standing in front of our door. "Waiting for reinforcements before going down to breakfast?" I asked.

"Strength in numbers," Kevin said, then he jerked his chin toward my right shoulder. "Quite a fancy repair."

"Seems solid," I said. Talia had repaired the holes Paul Flynn had ripped into Aodhan's sweatshirt by embroidering them shut with four delicate seashells, and she had used actual gold thread. Add to that the gold and pearl pins in my hair, and I was worth more than a new car.

Speaking of my hair, Kelsey went behind me and scrutinised the bun Aodhan had created. "This is interesting."

"I didn't have a hair elastic." I took Aodhan's hand. "Shall we?"

Kevin offered his arm to Kelsey. "Let's see what they eat for breakfast down here."

"I hope it's not squid," Kelsey said. After a collective moan of disgust, we were on our way to find out.

When we reached the noon room, it was set up much as the last time we'd eaten there with Grandfather, right down to the oversized pearl and silvered coral centrepiece. What was new was our supposed friend King Gradlon seated across the table from Grandfather.

"Good morning," I said, too startled by Gradlon's appearance to be anything other than polite.

"Meri, Kevin." Grandfather stood and held out his arms. We went to him and had a proper group hug. "I trust everyone slept well?"

"We did," Kevin said. "Thank you, for providing breakfast for us."

"Yes, thank you," I added.

"Think nothing of it." Grandfather released us, and Kevin and I seated ourselves on his right and left, respectively. That meant Aodhan and Kelsey had to sit next to Gradlon again, but at least it would be over soon.

Breakfast proved to be omelettes with tiny shrimps and chives folded in; Da would have been impressed. Instead of coffee, we were given steaming cups of tea. It tasted salty, as if it had been brewed with seawater. Well, five of us drank tea. Gradlon sipped a clear liquid that I suspected was the undersea version of vodka.

Speaking of Gradlon, he'd come to breakfast with a surly air about him, and remained mostly silent during our meal. I wondered if he'd indulged in a bit too much of his sickly sweet wine, and was nursing a hangover.

After we'd finished our omelettes and our plates had been whisked away, and our salty yet tasty teas were refilled, Grandfather folded his hands upon the table and addressed us. "Aodhan Sullivan and Kelsey McGrath," he began.

"Yes, sir," Aodhan replied, as Kelsey went white as a sheet.

"I am sure you're both aware that the location of Kilstiffen is not widely known to those above, or below," Grandfather began. "Nor do we welcome outsiders. Kevin, I do understand why you brought them here, and I do not fault you in the slightest. Bringing Meri here for healing was the best course of action."

"Ma insisted we bring her here," Kevin said. "We were on our way to hospital and turned right around."

Grandfather bowed his head. "Aoife was correct to tell you to do so. Aoife has a history of correct judgements, but if you tell her I said so, I may deny it." His eyes twinkled underneath his bushy grey brows. "As for the two of you, Aodhan Sullivan and Kelsey McGrath, know that for your actions toward securing aid for Meri, you have my gratitude. May I have your solemn vows that you will not speak of Kilstiffen, nor reveal its location, to any surface dwellers so long as you draw breath?"

"Absolutely, sir," Aodhan said.

"It's a yes from me, too," Kelsey said. "Most wouldn't believe me, anyway," she added, with a grimace toward me.

"Thank you," Grandfather said, as he bowed his head toward them. "Henceforth, you will be considered friends of Kilstiffen, and may return below at your pleasure."

Aodhan and Kelsey murmured their thanks, both acknowledging that Grandfather had bestowed a rare honor upon them. Not to be outdone, Gradlon stood and set two small leather sacks on the table, one in front of me, and the other in front of Kevin.

"I'd like to present each of the heirs with a gift," Gradlon announced, as he stood beside Grandfather. "Within these parcels are measures of salt from the deepest well in the ocean. It lies underneath Ker Ys, and only we have access to it."

"A true treasure," Grandfather said.

"Thank you," I said, as I leaned closer to the parcel. "If the salt is so rare, must it only be used for certain meals? Holidays, perhaps?"

"Oh, this salt is not for eating," Gradlon said with a chuckle. "The grains are as sharp as razors. The combination of this salt and your voices will make you more than a match for any foe, including a certain sidhe prince who has been harrying you."

I grabbed Aodhan's hand. "We could stop Donn, save your mother and sisters, all of it," I said. Aodhan smiled tightly, and indicated Gradlon with his eyes. I turned back to the king, and saw him staring pointedly at my and Aodhan's joined hands.

"I do want to be clear, Meri, that by accepting my gift, you are also accepting your betrothal to Nahel," he said, slowly as if I was dull witted. "And you, Kevin, will accept your match with Dahut."

"That is... that is..." My hands trembled as I felt hot blood rising in my neck and face. How dare he try to use his fancy salt to corner me and Kevin into marrying his children! "That is unacceptable."

Gradlon, his face a mask of fury, took a step toward me. Aodhan leapt to his feet and put himself between us. "Let's all take a breath and relax," Aodhan began.

"Remove yourself, surface dweller," Gradlon said. "I am speaking to the heiress."

"And the heiress has had just about enough of you," I snapped. "Is that all the king of Ker Ys thinks of my brother and me? That our lives and hearts are worth nothing more than a bit of salt?" I pushed the leather sack onto its side. "Keep your gift. I'll defeat Donn without you." I took Aodhan's hand and moved to leave.

"You won't," Gradlon began, but I rounded on him.

"You doubt me?" I countered. "I stopped Seamus MacCreehy, and ensured the safety of Kilstiffen and all of those below. I commanded an army of stone, and I rescued dozens of captive merrows and enthralled people. Where were you when all this was happening? Where were your magic children and your precious rare salt? You weren't what Kilstiffen needed then, and you're not what I need now." I turned my back on the spluttering old fool, and faced my grandfather.

"I appreciate everything you have done for us, from the bottom of my heart," I said. "But we'll be leaving now."

With that, I grabbed Aodhan's hand and dragged him out of the breakfast room and through the palace. I heard Kevin and Kelsey following behind us, but I didn't look back. No, looking back would be even madder than telling off a powerful king who commanded an entire undersea army. Best to keep moving.

"Meri, you weren't wrong, but you weren't very smart about that, either," Kevin said as we hurried toward the exit.

"She was amazing," Kelsey said. "That guy needed a shot of truth."

"He certainly got it," Aodhan said.

I glanced up at him, and asked, "What, you think I was wrong, too?"

"I think you're brilliant, and strong enough to speak your mind," he said, then we reached the main doors. Guards on either side of the exit crossed their spears over the doors, keeping us inside. As I wracked my brain trying to think of what notes I could sing that would make them let us leave, Grandfather approached us.

"Guards," Grandfather boomed, his voice as layered as a full choir. "Leave us."

The guards withdrew. Slowly, and with my heart in my throat, I turned to face the king of Kilstiffen.

He was smiling.

"Why are you happy?" I blurted out. "Are you going to throw us in a dungeon?"

Grandfather stepped closer, and said, "We don't have a dungeon. Kevin!"

"Here, sir." Kevin stood next to me, his back as straight as an arrow.

"I assume you share your sister's opinions?"

"Yes, sir. Mostly." Kevin glanced at me. "Not all of them."

"Traitor," I hissed.

"I share them as well," Grandfather said, and I felt a weight lift off of my shoulders. "Gradlon has sought a union between his kingdom and Kilstiffen's heirs for some time. Being that all of his schemes have fallen through, it would seem that fortune has other plans for our family, and his."

"Then you're not angry with me?" I asked.

"Not in the slightest," Grandfather replied. "Go, and continue your fight against Donn. I'll deal with Gradlon."

"Will you be all right?" I asked, which was ludicrous. Grandfather wasn't called Steinar the Immoveable because he couldn't handle his houseguests. "Sorry! I didn't mean to be disrespectful."

"You weren't," Grandfather said. "Gradlon forgot one of our oldest laws, which is that a gift must be freely given without guile or deceit, yet he offered you the salt on the condition you marry his children. He is the one in the wrong." He glanced between Kevin and me, and asked, "I'm to assume we'll have no weddings in the summer months?"

"Not this summer, no," Kevin said. "But as for next year, who's to say?"

"There will be Mama's wedding," I said. "She and Da are renewing their vows in a few weeks. You'll come, won't you?"

Grandfather's smile widened. "I look forward to it. Go now, with my blessings, and keep a sharp eye out. I've summoned a few allies to aid you against Donn. Help will be on the way soon enough."

I threw my arms around his neck. "Thank you, for everything."

"You are very welcome, my Meri." Grandfather patted my back, then I withdrew and took Aodhan's hand. The four of us walked through the palace doors, and we left Kilstiffen without so much as a backward glance.

Regroup And Return

"That was a shite show," Kevin said, for the third time. We were walking up the steep, narrow tunnel that led from Kilstiffen to the field where he'd left the car, and he just couldn't resist offering up a few brotherly observations. "Think Grandfather is still fighting with Gradlon?"

"Would they fight?" I wondered. "That doesn't seem like very royal behaviour."

"Yeah, well, Gradlon doesn't behave like someone who was ever taught good manners," Kevin said. "He really thought we would up and take his children as spouses without us even knowing them!"

I shrugged. "I suppose that's the way it's done in these drowned cities. Remember, Grandfather wanted to make this happen as well, until yesterday, and all to placate that sketchy council. I wonder what changed his mind?"

"Aodhan did," Kevin replied. "He tore into the palace carrying you with your chest pressed against his, and his hand clamped over your shoulder, stanching the blood. He refused to put you down or let anyone have a look at you until a proper medic arrived with bandages."

"Did he?" I peeked over my shoulder, saw Aodhan and Kelsey walking a few paces behind us. "Well, brother dear, I was told all about how Kelsey ordered around half the guards and convinced them to let us into the palace."

Kevin grinned. "That she did. Seems we both made better choices of partners than these kings did. Here we are."

We reached the car, and I pulled open the back door. When I saw the rusty stains on the seat, I gasped.

"Hang on," Kevin said, as he popped the boot. "Da's got a blanket back here." Kevin handed the blanket to me, and I spread it across the seat. "Guess we'll have to get the interior detailed."

"Yeah." I smoothed out the blanket to hide the evidence of my near death experience, then I took a seat and shut the door. Aodhan got in from the other side and took my trembling hands in his.

"You're okay, Mer." He kissed my knuckles. "I won't let anything hurt you."

"What, you're my protector now?"

"Always have been." He looped his arm around my shoulders and pulled me against him. "Can't let anything happen to you now. Who will eat all those chocolate muffins Dad bought the other day?"

I smiled against his chest. Those muffins were our love language. "Yeah. Wouldn't want them to go stale."

Kevin drove slowly and carefully back to the village; it seemed that our breakfast with Grandfather and Gradlon, and subsequent fast exit, had affected him more than he let on. After Aodhan sent and received a few texts, we decided to head to the surf shop. My parents were already there, as was Lorcan. Mr Sullivan hadn't yet returned from when he left to find Aodhan's mother and sisters, and he had responded to only one of Aodhan's texts with a curt "talk soon". I had no idea where Dahut and Nahel were, and I couldn't care less what they'd got up to. Hopefully, they had collected their disagreeable father and the three of them had gone back to where they came from.

Aodhan's phone set off a series of pings. "What's that about?" I asked. "Your dad?"

"No, it's the shop's pages," he replied. "I haven't updated the surf conditions for a few days, and people are asking about it. Hang on."

I watched as he pulled up his phone's weather app, and transferred the water temperature and wind readings to the shop's social media accounts. "You're taking this rather seriously."

"I mean to," he said. "What I'm ultimately trying to do is come up with new ways to increase revenue, and I figured making the shop more of a regular destination, rather than just a place to buy a one off board, would be a start. Since surfers always need to know the shore conditions, I thought this was a good starting point."

"Why do you need to increase revenue?" I asked. "Is the shop in trouble financially?"

"No, not at all. We turn a great profit, actually." Aodhan put down his phone, glanced at me, and then looked at his hands. "But I reckon I need to start planning for the future."

"Oh." I worked my fingers into his. "I used to think about the future all the time, but it never involved staying in Clare. I always imagined going to Dublin or maybe Europe, and starting a new life, but I haven't thought about that in some time."

He traced the ridges of my knuckles with a single fingertip. "Does that mean you want to say in Clare?"

"Yes." I tightened my hand against his. "I think that's a good plan."

We finally reached the town proper, and Kevin turned onto the street that led to the surf shop. Kelsey twisted around in her seat, and asked, "What do we think about Lorcan?"

"He's been the shop manager longer than I've been alive," Aodhan said. "Dad's always trusted him. I trust him, too."

"But he lied to you," Kelsey said. "Maybe not outright, but is withholding the truth that much different?"

Aodhan frowned. "I think I need to talk to Dad about just how well he knows Lorcan."

I squeezed Aodhan's hand. "We'll figure it out. Have you had any more updates from your dad?"

Aodhan glanced at his phone. "Not yet."

Kevin parked the car, and we walked toward the surf shop. Only a few weeks ago I only would have approached the shop by taking the village streets, being that I'd promised Da to stay as far away from the sea as possible. Based on the few times I'd heard the sea's call back then, and nearly drowned, Da was right to caution me. Now I walked on the road next to the seawall like every other resident and tourist in the village, and I knew the water was my friend.

But then again, the sea had let Donn attack us. I glanced at the waves, and resolved to remain wary.

As soon as the shop was in sight, I felt better. We'd survived not only the monsters in the Flynn house, but a night in Kilstiffen, too. I was starting to believe Aodhan was right, and that together we could do anything.

The shop door opened, and my mother strode toward us. She was still wearing her armour, her gold mail winking in the sunlight, along with her sword and shield. If anyone out and about in the village thought her gear was odd, they wisely kept their opinions to themselves.

Mama strode directly to me and swept me into her arms. "Meri, I've been so worried," she said as she squeezed the life out of me.

"I'm all right," I said. "You were right to send us there. The healers fixed me right up."

"Kilstiffen's healers are the greatest in the world, above or below," she said. "I wish I had been there with you."

"It was all right. Grandfather took good care of us, and we met Talia."

"Och, Talia. She was like a second mother to me."

"Talia told us a few stories about you, and your siblings," I said. "She said you were everyone's favourite."

"Of course I'm the favourite. Out of that lot, I'm the only one that knows how to behave." Mama drew back, then her gaze caught on the golden repair work on the shoulder of my sweatshirt. "That's where he got you?"

"His fingers went right through me," I said, shuddering at the memory. "As much as I appreciate the medical care, I feel bad about Talia wasting her golden thread on a sweatshirt."

"That's how we do a repair in Kilstiffen," Mama said, as she smoothed back my hair. "We aim to fix things in such a way they end up better off than they were before."

"We might have wrecked a few other things while we were down there," Kevin said, as Mama brought him in for a hug. "That Gradlon's a—wait, where are his kids?"

"Unknown at the moment," Mama replied. "Before we deal with them, tell me how you left things with the collector and his pet?"

"Kelsey set them on fire," I replied.

"An effective tactic," Mama said, nodding. "That won't likely kill them, but it will slow them down for a time. Good work, Kelsey. All of you, come inside the shop. Brian's in there, keeping an eye on Lorcan."

We entered the shop, and found Lorcan in his usual spot behind the counter while Da observed him from the far side of the room. Da saw me, and held out his arm. Taking the cue, I hugged him.

"I am beginning to wish you didn't take after your mother as much as you do," Da said. "You're all right?"

"I am, but I missed you."

"Missed you too, Meri girl." Da gave me a final squeeze. "How were things with the old goat?"

"Grandfather was good to us, but he and Gradlon don't seem to be on the best of terms," I replied.

"It's been that way for some time," Da said. "Ever since your ma ditched Corentin and came up here, Gradlon's not made things easy for Steinar."

"Who's Corentin?" I asked, then I remembered how my mother had refused a betrothal of her own. "Is he the one that was supposed to marry Mama?"

"There was no way that was going to happen," Mama said, as she made a cutting motion with her hand. "MacCreehey's mad plans were just beginning to gain supporters, and while I was in the midst of trying to stop him, Gradlon threw his foolish brother at me." She paused, and added, "Not literally."

"I assumed not," I murmured. "Wait, is Corentin the man Da punched in the face?"

"Da slugged someone?" Kevin asked. "Did you knock him out cold?"

Da stared at Kevin and me for a moment, then he turned to Mama, and demanded, "Aoife, you told our daughter I hit someone?"

Mama shrugged. "It happened. Laid him right out, your father did. Even so, Gradlon insisted I accept the man as my husband, and there was no way that was going to happen."

"How did you get them to leave you alone?" I asked.

"I stole the key to Kilstiffen and fled above," Mama replied. "My actions had the dual benefit of stopping Seamus's plans from advancing, and having me declared a criminal. Gradlon's a greedy old fool, but even he doesn't want a thief in the family."

"He tried to bribe us with tiny bags of salt," Kevin said, and Mama nodded.

"The salt from beneath Ker Ys is powerful, indeed, but we'll manage without it," she said. "Did you learn anything about Donn's plans at the Flynn house?"

"According to the ankou, Donn wants blood," I replied. "It's how he will reopen Tech Duinn."

"Then that's why Donn employed the collector," Lorcan said. "With their souls gone, Donn would be free to drain the captured bodies whenever he wished, and the blood he collected wouldn't have the memory of the lives the people had lived."

"Blood has a memory?" Kevin asked.

"Oh, yes," Lorcan said. "It's why so many rituals depend on blood."

Since I didn't want to talk about blood any longer, I said, "We freed the all of the souls he had. At least, I think we got all of them."

"There was no one else in the house," Kelsey said. "Would Donn have put some of his captives elsewhere?"

Mama glanced at Kelsey, then she asked Aodhan, "Have you heard from Lucas?"

"No," Aodhan replied. "Other than a two word reply, he never checked in after he went looking for my ma and sisters."

"Have faith," Mama said. "Lucas is a canny warrior. If anyone can rescue Bridgette and the girls, it's him."

Aodhan nodded, but he didn't look convinced. "I'm going to make a few calls," he said, then he went up to the office. I wanted to go with him, but I had more questions for my mother.

"We also learned that Donn was booted out of the gods' home below Kilstiffen," I said. "Any idea what he did to deserve that punishment?"

Mama pursed her lips, and looked out the front window toward the sea. "Gods draw their power from their worshippers," she began. "Years ago, Donn attempted to convert some of the lesser gods into his followers, and therefore increase his own power. In time, he attempted to unseat Danu herself."

"And that's why he got the boot," I concluded. "Was Danu scared of him causing a revolt?"

"Danu isn't scared of anything," she replied. "However, conscripting another god's power broke one of her cardinal rules. Donn was a very strong warrior, but he was also greedy. He didn't want to work with the other gods, only take what was theirs."

"Is Donn stronger than you?" Kevin asked.

"No," Mama and Lorcan said in unison. Startled, Mama faced the shop manager. "What do you know of it?"

"I know that Donn was expelled from the land of youth long before you became the guardian of Kilstiffen, and he's almost breached the portal several times," Lorcan replied. "However, since you've been standing between him and those below, he's been trapped up here, and has been desperate to come up with new schemes to return to his home."

"Are you saying I forced his hand?" Mama asked.

"Not at all," Lorcan said. "Only that Donn never expected to encounter a warrior his equal. While he's above his strength is diminished, and your lineage gives you an edge he wasn't prepared for."

"Lineage?" I repeated. "Because you're from Kilstiffen?"

"I am, but my own mother is from Tír na nÓg ," she replied.

"And Tír na nÓg is where the gods live," I finished.

Before my mother could say anything further, the front door banged open and Aodhan's father strode into the shop, with Mrs Dumhach close behind. They each carried a young child in their arms. Aodhan's sisters.

"Where's Aodhan?" Mr Sullivan demanded, then Aodhan himself came thundering down the stairs.

"Dad," Aodhan said, then he stopped short when he saw the rest. "You found them!"

"They were at Donn's place in Cork," Mr Sullivan said.

"He trapped us there," Mrs Dumhach said. "For days we were confined to the apartment! We couldn't leave, not to go to the park or get the messages or anything, not until Lucas came for us."

"You're safe here," Mr Sullivan said, as he handed off the girl he was carrying to Aodhan. "Get Nora and Roan settled in upstairs. I need to talk to Lorcan."

Aodhan and his mother disappeared upstairs with the girls. Mr Sullivan watched them go, then he faced Lorcan. "Donn had his apartment enchanted so they couldn't leave, but I had no problem getting in," he said. "And I was able to get everyone out."

"Donn does like his wards, but it is odd that the place wasn't warded against you," Lorcan said.

"Maybe he forgot to update the ward," I suggested. "For many years, everyone thought Mr Sullivan was dead."

"Not likely," Mama said. "Donn isn't sloppy. If anything he warded the place to alert him when you entered, Lucas."

"Which means he followed me, and is on his way here." Mr Sullivan wiped his hand down his face. "What do we do now? Retreat, or make a stand?"

"We cannot let Donn access Tech Duinn," Lorcan said. "He must not go below."

"Why shouldn't we send him down there to receive his punishment?" I asked. "Surely a bunch of gods could deal with him better than we can."

"That's just it," Mama said. "They can't. Along with gods, the souls of the righteous dead populate Tír na nÓg . With so many souls feeding into his power, Donn could become nearly invincible—so much so that he might attempt to steal the greater gods' powers again."

"That's... that's terrifying," I said, my mind reeling with the concept that a single being could wield that much power. "When he tried all of this before, who stopped him? That's who we need now."

A wave violently crashed against the shop's front window. I turned toward the glass and felt fear grab my heart.

The sea bull was back.

THE SEA GOD AND THE BULL

"How far do the shop's wards extend?" Mama demanded, as a second wave crashed against the shop's windows. Seawater advanced under the front door and retreated just as quickly.

"They reach all the way to the seawall," Lorcan replied. "Donn shouldn't be able to make any sort of contact with the shop!"

"That's why he's come as the water bull again," I said, as yet another wave, this one taller than the last, arched over the seawall and splashed down on the walkway. "He's using the sea's momentum to propel him up and over the wards."

"Why isn't he using the dead to come after us?" Mr Sullivan asked. When we all looked at him as if he'd lost his mind, he added, "I don't want to deal with a bunch of zombies, but if he's the Master of the Dead and all, why isn't he taking advantage of that?"

"He can't," Lorcan replied. "Until Donn reenters his home, his powers over the dead are nullified."

"Which is why we will keep him out of this house," Mama declared. "Lucas, guard your family. Lorcan, see to the shop. The rest of you, with me."

"Even me?" Kelsey squeaked.

"Stay behind me," Kevin said, then the five of us left the shop and approached the watery form of Donn Dumhach, the Master of the Dead. My mother got on top of the sea wall for a better vantage point, and helped me up beside her. A moment later, Aodhan ran out of the shop and hopped up next to me.

"You were going to fight the monster without me?" Aodhan asked.

"I'd rather not fight him at all," I said, then I turned toward the beach. The sea was farther out that I'd ever seen, and the wet sand reflected the light like polished stone. "Is it low tide?"

"This isn't like any low tide I've ever seen." Aodhan shielded his eyes with his hand, and squinted at the beach. "The sea never goes back that far. Is Donn holding back the ocean?"

"Not Donn, but I'd wager that someone who can help us is holding back the sea," Mama said. "Brian, do you think he's on his way here?"

"We can only hope," Da said. Before I could ask who this mystery ally was, a horse made of sand erupted from the beach. "Aoife, there!" Da yelled.

Mama spun to face the horse, and sang a note so high it could shatter glass. The horse shuddered, and collapsed into a sandy heap.

"That was Donn?" Aodhan demanded, and Mama nodded.

"He's coming as sand now?" I asked.

"He will take any form he can manage," Mama said.

"What can we do against a being that can use all of nature against us?" Kevin demanded.

"We use nature against him," I said, and I remembered the little leather sacks Gradlon had offered us that morning.

"What about salt?" I asked. "If we sing the salt up from the sea, perhaps we can use it to neutralize him?"

"Ordinary salt won't work," Mama said. "Not on a being as powerful as Donn."

"What about the salt from below Ker Ys?" I pressed. "Gradlon claimed it could easily defeat Donn."

"That would work, but we would need to petition Gradlon for a measure of his salt," Mama replied. "We don't have the time for that, and he'd likely decline."

"What if we don't petition him, and use it anyway?" I asked. "We can borrow a bit, just enough to send Donn on his way."

She faced me. "If we do that, steal Gradlon's salt, we will have started a war," she said.

"Perhaps, but if we also save Ireland above and below from Donn, won't that be more important?"

Mama pursed her lips, then she looked past me to Da. "War's been brewing between Kilstiffen and Ker Ys for a long time," Da said. "If it's going to come to a head, might as well make it mean something."

"You're right, and I have been wanting to end the bad blood between our lands once and for all," Mama said, then she focused on me. "This is a dangerous plan, Meri, but it should work. As for the consequences, they may be significant."

"We'll worry about them later, after we send Donn packing." I took her right hand, and Kevin took her left. "Let's grab that salt. You take the lead."

My mother glanced at me, clearly amused I was making her the point person for my plan, then she faced forward and began singing. The notes were low, which made sense since we would be sending our voices tunnelling into the sea floor far below Ker Ys. I wondered how far down that was. Kevin and I lent our voices to her song, and cones of salt began pushing their way up from underneath the sand. Soon enough, the beach was littered with them like a tiny white mountain range, but those cones were regular salt.

We needed Gradlon's precious stores.

I took a deep breath, and pictured the little leather sacks Gradlon had so carefully placed in front of Kevin and me on the breakfast table. I imagined the sacks splitting open, and the salt moving toward us like dandelion seeds on the wind. My mind's eye tracked their movements as my voice kept tone and pace with my mother's and Kevin's, and tiny hillocks of Ker Ys's salt formed on the beach. It looked different from the regular sea salt; it was greyer, almost like powdered silver, and where it caught the light, it had an iridescent sheen. Magic vibrated from the salt, and I wondered how powerful it really was.

Gradlon was going to be furious. He was already furious, what with how I'd rejected his stupid idea of my brother and me marrying his children. I didn't regret what I'd said, but nor did I want my actions to make Grandfather's life more difficult. Then again, when we were leaving, Grandfather hadn't seemed the slightest bit upset at me. Perhaps he and Gradlon weren't such great friends after all.

Another cone of iridescent salt grew out of the beach, this one larger than the rest. Despite all the possible ramifications of our salty theft, I smiled. This scheme of mine was going to work.

Suddenly, Nahel was standing in front of me. "Hey!"

"I'm busy," I snapped, then I resumed singing.

"Why are you stealing our salt?" Nahel demanded.

"We need it to stop Donn," I said quickly, then I resumed my song.

"We already stopped him," his twin, Dahut, said. Wonderful, they were both here.

"You just made him mad," Kelsey said, and she pointed toward the sea. Dahut turned, and I watched her eyes widen as the sea bull rose up over the waves.

"Impossible," Dahut said. "We have never been defeated."

"Let us use the salt and he will be defeated," Aodhan said.

Nahel looked as Aodhan as if he was a bug, then he said to me, "I will allow you to use our salt, but then you must become my wife."

"What? No," I said, so disgusted I stopped singing altogether. "That is absolutely not going to happen."

Nahel raised his hand, and a wave crashed onto the beach and scattered every one of the salt cones we'd so carefully assembled with our song. "No marriage, no salt," he said.

"What is your problem?" I demanded. "We're trying to fight off the Master of the Dead here, and all you can think about is getting a girlfriend? You're an idiot."

"You were promised to me," Nahel said, then Aodhan stepped between us.

"Back off," Aodhan said. "Meri said no."

"Is this your surface dweller pet?" Nahel asked me, while ignoring Aodhan. "You can keep him, if you like. I have pets, too."

"Get away from me," I said, then I resumed singing.

Dahut clapped her hands together, and commanded, "Stop."

Mama, Kevin, and I fell silent; a heartbeat later, I realised Dahut had somehow stopped us from singing. Based on Mama's incredulous face, she hadn't been silenced often. "Watch yourself, wave dancer," Mama warned.

"Watch yourself, merrow," Dahut retorted. "I am the guardian of Ker Ys, and I will not allow you to steal from us."

"And I am the guardian of Kilstiffen and what lies beneath," Mama shot back. "I keep all of those below safe, including the gods your father so desperately wants to be part of!"

A wave crashed onto the salt free beach. Riding the wave's crest was the sea bull. "Are you implying that the gods owe you, halfling?" the bull asked with Donn's voice.

Mama jumped down to the beach and drew her sword. "Face me with honour, Donn," she yelled at the sea bull. "Leave off these tricks!"

The bull's face contorted, and it reared up to strike.

I screamed, terrified my mother would never make it off that beach. At the last moment, I transformed my scream into a song.

My voice reached deep below Ker Ys, deep into the salt mines and brine pools below the city. I grabbed every crystal of salt they had and flung it all toward the sea bull. The grains erupted from the beach like a geyser and sliced through the water toward the man within. Inside the sea bull, I could see Donn as he tried to evade the salt.

The sea bull roared, and became a deep red colour, then a shocking blue. The water flowed away from Donn's body in two fast moving streams. Mama turned away from the brunt of the spray as the sidhe prince fell to the beach, pale and immobile.

I gasped, and clapped my hand over my mouth. "Is he dead?" I whispered.

"He's not moving," Aodhan said.

"I didn't mean to... I only wanted to keep him back..." Donn groaned, and I let out a breath. "Oh, thank God."

Dahut arched an eyebrow. "You don't seek to kill your enemy?"

"I've never killed anyone," I admitted. "I would have in order to save my mother, but I'd rather not."

Dahut nodded. "I understand. Ending a life is not something to be taken lightly." She moved to say more, but the tide decided to come in all at once. Mama jumped atop the sea wall moments before the waves lapped against the concrete. As for Donn, his limp form was floating on his back, but I worried he'd roll over and drown at any moment.

"What's happening now?" I asked, my voice going shrill. "Why did the water return in a rush like that?"

Da pointed toward the horizon. "He's coming."

"Who's coming?" I asked, then a small wooden boat came into view. Standing in the centre of the boat was the tallest, broadest man I had ever seen. His hair and beard were as white as sea foam, and his clothes were the greenish blue colour of waves when the sunlight shone through them on a clear day. He wore a heavy gold torque and armbands, and held a golden sceptre topped with a cluster of gilded shells. While he was amazing, I was equally fascinated by the woman that was next to him. She stood with her back straight and her gaze forward, and had the most beautiful golden hair I'd ever seen. What's more, she looked familiar.

The boat bumped into the sea wall. We all stared at each other like fools for a moment, then the tall man spoke.

"I held the sea back as best I could," he said to Mama. "I thought we would arrive long before Donn made his way here. Forgive me my lateness, Aoife."

"I think I shall thank you for your help, instead. It was timely, and much needed," Mama said, then she turned to the woman. "I wasn't expecting you to see you today."

"I wasn't expecting to come, but here I am," she replied, then she stepped off the boat and embraced Mama. "I've missed you so, mo chroí."

"Mo chroí," I repeated, wondering who in the world would use such an endearment toward my mother, when Da put his hand on my shoulder.

"That's Aoife's mother, your gran," he murmured, then he moved on to tell Kevin the same news.

"That's Niamh," I whispered to Aodhan. "Which means that he—"

"Is Manannán mac Lir," Aodhan finished. "Mer, these are actual gods."

Manannán raised an eyebrow, and asked Aodhan, "You've heard of me, then?"

"A bit, sir," Aodhan replied. I did not understand how he was calm enough to speak to a god as if he were an ordinary man. I felt as if my knees would give out at any moment.

"Kevin, Meri," Mama said, thus snapping me out of my awed state. "Come meet your grandmother."

Kevin and I dutifully went to her side, and I saw Niamh up close. She was wearing an orange silk dress bordered with gold embroidery, and a golden torque and earrings set with pearls. I also noticed that her eyes were the same clear blue as my mother's, and my own.

Mama began to introduce us, but Niamh held up her hand. "Steinar has told me so much about you both I feel like I already know you," she began. "Kevin, your grandfather is quite impressed with your courage, and your loyalty. He foresees that you will be a great leader one day."

"Thank you," Kevin murmured, as he grabbed Kelsey's hand for support. "Truly, thank you."

"Is this your lady?" Niamh asked.

"Yes," he replied. "This is Kelsey."

"Kelsey," Niamh said, as she cocked her head to the side. "What a lovely heart you have. You see who Kevin truly is, don't you?"

"I do." Kelsey looked up at Kevin, and smiled. "I really do."

"And you, Meri," Niamh said, as she turned to me.

"It's lovely to meet you," I blurted out, and immediately wanted to go off and bury myself in a hole. Niamh, unaffected by my awkwardness, smiled.

"It's lovely to meet you as well, Meri," Niamh said. "All of Tír na nÓg knows how you've helped protect Kilstiffen, and us."

"Everyone?" I squeaked.

"Everyone." Niamh looked past me toward Aodhan. "You're the one who saved Meri?"

"The healers saved her," Aodhan said. "I just brought her to them."

"Not yesterday," Niamh said, as she shook her head. "I mean at the Cliffs. You caught her before the voices compelled her to jump."

I gasped, wondering how Niamh could possibly know such a thing, while Aodhan replied, "I had to save Meri. I couldn't let her go over."

"Because you couldn't imagine your life without her," Niamh said. "No wonder your hearts beat in time with each other's."

I stepped back, physically shocked by what she said. Aodhan's arm came around my waist. "I'll always look out for Meri," he said.

"Of that, I have no doubt," Niamh said, then her gaze alighted on my necklace. "Da, Meri wears the pearl."

"That she does," Manannán said. "The pearl means you may call on me in times of need. Which means that you, Kevin, will need a talisman of your own." He broke a golden whelk off from his staff, and handed it to Kevin. "If you have need of me, do not hesitate to call."

While Kevin thanked Mannanán for his most excellent gift, Niamh looked beyond Aodhan and me, and smiled. "Brian," she said, as she held out her arms.

"I'm surprised you remember an old fisherman like me," Da said, as they embraced.

"How could I forget the love of my daughter's life?" Niamh countered. "Steinar tells me you will renew your vows to one another soon."

"Father knows?" Mama said, a bit panicked. "Who told him?"

"Um. I did," I said.

"What, Aoife, are we not invited?" Niamh asked.

"Of course you are," Mama said. "I just didn't know if you could come above for it."

"We will both be there," Manannán said, then he raised his sceptre and levitated Donn's unconscious form from where it bobbed on the surf and deposited him in the bottom of the boat. "Now, I'm afraid we must take our leave of you. Donn won't remain inert for much longer, and when he wakes, I want him to be well away from anyone he could harm. I am glad to have seen you, Aoife and Brian, and to have met your children."

Everyone murmured their appreciation, and out of the corner of my eye I saw Nahel standing off to the side wearing that same smug grin from when I first glimpsed him, thanks to the summoning pearl, standing in front of the bleached palace. I touched my pearl necklace, and said, "Manannán—Mr mac Lir—you said I can call on you if I have need to?"

Manannán faced me. "Of course, Meri. Have you need of my assistance?"

"Are you familiar with the king of Ker Ys? He's decided Kevin and I should marry those two," I replied, pointing at Dahut and Nahel. "We don't want to."

Manannán, nodded, then he faced the twins. "How do you feel about this arrangement?"

Dahut shrugged. "If it's not a match between Kevin and me, I can live with that. I am perfectly able to work out my own marriage.

Besides, that one already has a partner," she added, nodding toward Kelsey.

"The partners they have don't matter," Nahel insisted. "Meri was promised to me!"

"And I have declined," I said. "Don't make me sing you back to where you came from!"

"I would like to see you try, little one," Nahel said with a sneer.

"Enough," Manannán said. "Meri and Kevin have refused the betrothals, and I stand as witness. The matter is closed."

"But I was promised," Nahel whined.

"And you are now un-promised," Manannán said. "Abide by my ruling, or suffer the consequences." Nahel tried to speak, but his much wiser sister told him to stay quiet. Manannán gave Nahel one final stern glare, then he faced us again.

"Now, we must depart," he said, as Niamh joined him on his boat. "Farewell, my children." As he spoke, the boat receded into the sea, then a mist enveloped them, and my grandmother and the sea god were gone.

"We met gods," Aodhan murmured. "Meri, we met actual gods and you're related to them."

"Don't remind me," I said, since I already felt like my head might explode. "I'm still processing everything."

Aodhan kissed my hair. "Same, Mer."

"We will take our leave of you as well," Dahut said. Her brother was sulking off to the side. "I understand why you wanted our salt, and I do not fault you for using it against Donn. However, I do not know how my father will feel about this turn of events. I will try to impress upon him that Manannán's will was done, but I make no guarantees."

"Thank you, Dahut," I said. "I'm sorry things didn't go better between us."

"What do you mean?" she asked. "We got to fight a massive water bull, and we met the king of the sea. This was a wonderful trip."

"Father won't like this," Nahel warned.

"Father cannot overrule Manannán mac Lir," Dahut snapped. After her brother turned away, she smiled a bit too widely at me, then she turned to Kevin. "Good luck."

"And to you," Kevin replied.

With that, a stream of water rose up from the tide and carried Dahut and Nahel away, hopefully all the way back to Ker Ys. "Why do I feel like we'll be seeing them again?"

"I'm sure we will, Meri," Mama said. "Gradlon's not one to let to let something like this pass."

"What did Nahel mean about Gradlon not liking Manannán's ruling?" Kevin asked.

"I'm not sure," Mama said. "It seems things aren't well in Ker Ys. Hopefully ,they keep their problems to themselves, but when has that ever happened?"

"Something isn't adding up," I said. Mr Sullivan's question about why Donn was attacking as a bull and not the Master of the Dead was knocking around my brain. "Donn comes to fight us as a bull, Gradlon's children show up and fight him, then we go below, and Gradlon feeds us a bull."

"Gradlon fed you a bull?" Mama asked. "You didn't tell me that."

"He brought one to Kilstiffen, and the cooks turned it into steaks," I said. "He bragged about it quite a bit."

"I imagine he did," Mama said. "Ker Ys's sigil is that of a bull rampaging on the waves. It's an interesting choice for him to bring to a dinner in Kilstiffen."

"Like Donn, as the sea bull," Kevin said. "Rampaging on the waves."

"It's not just that," I said. "Grandfather told me that Donn's well known in Ker Ys, and that was why the twins came up in the first place."

Kevin grunted. "Think Donn and Gradlon are in cahoots?"

I shuddered. "I hope not. Nothing good could come from that pairing."

Problems At The Saints

After the gods from below and the heirs of Ker Ys departed, the six of us climbed down from the seawall. I watched as Da held out his hand to Mama and helped her down, and how she smiled and blushed as she accepted his assistance. Even after all these years, and the extended period of time when they were forced to be apart, they were still very much in love with each other. I wondered how it must feel to adore another person so much they became the centre of your world. Then Aodhan jumped down from the wall, grabbed me by my waist, and set me down in front of him. He smiled at me, and my heart actually fluttered. Maybe I already knew how it felt to love, and be loved in return.

"You're okay after all that?" he asked.

"Physically, yes," I replied. "My mind's a bit blown, though. What if Gradlon really did send Donn after us?"

"We don't know if he did, but we can work on figuring that out next." Aodhan pushed my hair back from my forehead. "Niamh said that our hearts beat in time with each other."

"What does that even mean?" I grumbled. "Organs don't sync up like that."

"It means we're unstoppable together, just as we always thought. It also means I was meant to look out for you," he added, and after a glance at my newly healed shoulder, he faced the rest. "We should probably get back inside the shop."

"Agreed," Mama said. "Who knows what other beasties are lurking about the bay in Donn's shadow."

"Wait, you mean there could be more monsters coming after us?" Kelsey demanded. "Like more water bulls?"

"We never know what'll come next," Kevin said, as he put his arm around Kelsey and kissed her cheek. "I told you it's never boring around here."

"I'd love a little bit of boring," I said, and everyone else voiced their agreement. We went back inside the shop, and were met by Aodhan's parents. His father was leaning against the counter, while his mother paced across the sales floor, muttering and wringing her hands.

"How did it go?" Mr Sullivan asked.

"Is Donn gone?" Mrs Dumhach demanded, as she took a step toward us. "As in, gone for good?"

"Manannán took Donn away," Aodhan said. "I don't know if he'll ever be back. Do people come back from there?" he asked my mother.

"Not often," Mama replied. "For now, I'd say we're all safe."

Before we could enjoy a collective sigh of relief, Lorcan came out of the stockroom with his phone in hand. "I'm on the line with Rose," he said. "We've got problems at The Saints."

"What sort of problems?" I asked.

"The ankou and the gancanagh are there, and they're racking up a body count."

We immediately left the shop and headed to The Saints. Kevin, Kelsey, Aodhan, and I were in one car, while Mr Sullivan followed in his own vehicle with Mama and Da. Lorcan stayed behind at the shop to defend Mrs Dumhach and the girls, along with Tech Duinn beneath.

As we drove toward the school, I moved so I was in the centre of the back seat, and watched the road ahead through the windshield. I'd travelled this road hundreds of times, both by foot and in cars, and I'd dreaded going to school many times. However, I'd never before gone to school to face the creature who'd almost ended my life, and I was a mere breath away from falling apart.

I clenched my fists and gritted my teeth. I was not going to let Paul beat me, physically or mentally.

Aodhan put his hand on the back of my neck, and I turned toward him. He gathered me against him, and laid his cheek against my forehead. "I won't let him hurt you."

"You didn't let him hurt me before," I said, as I fisted my hand in his shirt. "He just did it anyway."

"That was his last chance. If he comes at you again, I'll deal with him."

"Deal with him how?" When Aodhan didn't reply, I drew back and met his gaze. "Don't do anything you'll regret."

He caressed my cheek, and said, "The only thing I will regret is if something happens to you, when I could have stopped it."

"We'll stop him together," I said.

"That's right, Mer." He stroked his thumb across my cheekbone. "Together."

When we arrived at The Saints, Kevin skipped the car park entirely, and screeched to a halt directly in front of the school's steps. Rose was standing at the top of the steps directly in front of the double doors. She was wearing her usual outfit of black jeans, boots, and a fitted black blouse, but today she also had a pale brown sealskin draped across her left shoulder.

"Are both of the Flynns here?" I asked, as we ran up the steps.

"You don't have to refer to them by their fake names," Rose replied. "Lorcan explained to me what they truly are. As for which of them is here, the collector's already got a few of the students. I don't know where the gancanagh is."

"When we went to their house, the collector had put all of the souls he'd taken into an urn," Aodhan said. "We were able to restore those souls to their rightful bodies, and save them. Maybe we can restore these souls, too."

Rose's face darkened. "You can't restore this lot. There's nothing for these souls to go back to."

"Oh," I said, as I covered my mouth with my hand. "That's awful."

"It is, which is why we need a plan of attack," Rose said.

"The plan is we stop him here," Mama said as she joined us. "We fight hard, and don't let up until we see both of their bodies. How strong are you with your skin?" she asked, nodding toward Rose's sealskin.

"Strong enough to deal with a rogue collector." To prove her point, Rose grabbed one of the metal door handles and crushed it like tissue paper. "But if the gancanagh gets his hands on me, he could turn me against the students."

"Then we won't let him near you," I declared. "Paul only affects females. We're eight, so if we split into two groups with two men in each, no females need to engage him."

"Isn't Paul's skin burnt?" Kelsey asked. "He's got to be pretty messed up after that house fire. Maybe he's not as poisonous as he was."

"We can't assume he's been weakened in any way," Mama said.

"Aoife's right," Mr Sullivan said. "These beasts from below are sneaky, and damn resilient. No offense," he added, with a nod toward Rose.

"You humans are rather resilient, too," Rose said. "I saw what Donn did to your boat all those years ago. When I heard you were back, I was shocked."

"Shipwrecks don't stop the Sullivans," he said. "After we split up, what's next?"

"We need to get the students and teachers to safety," I said. "They're our top priority. Once that's done, we can decide what to do with the monsters."

"If I encounter the gancanagh, I'll kill him first and ask questions later," Mama warned.

"So will I," Aodhan said, then he glanced at me. "Or I'll just punch him in the face again."

"Will anything bad come of killing him, or the collector?" Kevin asked. "They won't transform into angry spirits, or something else worse than what they already are?"

"Good question," Mama said. "I'm certain the gancanagh is a mortal creature, so that one we can kill on sight, but I'm not sure about the collector. We should only incapacitate him until we know more." Mama withdrew two of her knives, and handed one each to Kevin and Aodhan. "Do you have a weapon?" she asked Kelsey.

"I have my lighter, and a brolly," Kelsey replied. "I can set them on fire and poke their eyes out."

Mama nodded approvingly. "Meri, your voice is the only weapon you need," she said to me. "Although, should it come down to it I believe a bit of Gradlon's salt is still lying about on the beach. Be safe, my lamb." She set her hand on my cheek for a moment, then she exchanged a few quiet words with Kevin.

"All right, we'll take the ground floor and work our way up," I said, nodding toward Aodhan, Kevin, and Kelsey. To the adults, I said, "You four go to the top and work down. We'll meet in the middle."

Da set his hand on my good shoulder. "If you need us, yell. I'll be there in an instant."

I set my hand on his. "Same goes for you."

With that, we barged into The Saints. The adults split into two groups before they headed up each of the staircases, while us youngsters began searching the ground floor. What we found was not reassuring.

The corridors resembled something out of a disaster movie. Book bags and papers were strewn across the floor, and there was a red stain on the wall near the main entrance. Thankfully, that one bloody splotch was the only gore in sight.

We checked the classrooms one at time, with Aodhan and me taking one side of the corridor, and Kevin and Kelsey the other. All of the rooms were as trashed as the corridors were. They were also empty, which was a relief. Although, it did make me wonder where everyone was.

"The Flynns couldn't have got them all, could they?" I whispered to Aodhan after we cleared the fifth empty room. "If both of their abilities work on touch, that would be an awful lot of students and teachers for them to go through, one by one."

"That's if they only work by touch," Aodhan said, then he stopped in the center of the corridor and jerked his head toward the closed library doors. "If you saw the headmaster and his creep of a son turn into a pair of nasty monsters, you'd hide, right?"

"That, or run for my life," I muttered. "You think everyone's holed up in the library?"

"Conversely, the Flynns could be in there waiting to spring a trap," Kevin said, as he and Kelsey joined us.

"Good point," Aodhan said. "I'll open the door. Kevin, you have your knife ready. Kelsey, be ready to beat them with your brolly."

"And me?" I asked.

"Can you sing in such a way to keep anyone inside the library from moving?" Aodhan asked. "Just long enough for us to know what we're dealing with."

I nodded. "I can, but I won't be able to hold it for long."

"We only need a minute, tops," Aodhan said.

"A minute it is." I took his hand. "Let's go in."

Aodhan squeezed my hand, then he approached the library doors. Kevin and Kelsey took up positions on either side, with their respective weapons raised. I watched as Aodhan pushed the door handle, then he frowned.

"And the doors are locked," he said.

"Hang on," I said, then I sang a few notes I hoped would unlock the doors. I heard the mechanism slide open, and breathed a sigh of relief. At least that had gone well.

From inside the library, a woman shrieked, "Not again, you soggy devils!"

"That voice sounds familiar," I said. Aodhan and I shared a look, then he flung the doors wide open. Standing in front of the circulation desk was Sister Mary Katherine holding a push broom aloft as if it was a sword.

"Oh, children, thank God you're all right," she said, as she lowered the broom.

"Sister, have you been in here long?" I asked.

"The Flynns arrived shortly after the first bell, and began reigning chaos," she replied. "I rounded up everyone I could find, and we've been in here ever since."

"Everyone?" I repeated, then I looked past Sister. Hiding among the stacks and research tables were dozens of students and teachers.

"Sister, I believe you've rescued half of the student body," Aodhan said. "Who's watching the back exit?"

"Father Flaherty pushed a few bookcases in front of those doors," she replied. "Having only one way in or out makes the room easier to defend."

"True," I murmured, impressed by Sister's defensive skills. I wondered if she'd picked up this knowledge while enthralled by MacCreehy, or over the years as a teacher. "We're sweeping the school for the Flynns now. Have you any idea of where they might be?"

"The last time I saw Marcus, he was headed into the auditorium," she replied. "I have no idea what's become of the other one."

"Can we leave now?" one of the students asked.

"Actually, you're much safer in here," I said. "Until we have the Flynns contained, I recommend you stay put."

Sister nodded, and raised her broom. "I'll guard the door."

"Kevin, Kelsey, you stay, too," I said. "Lock the door behind us, and don't open it for anyone but Aodhan or our dads. Paul can't affect boys," I explained to Sister.

Kelsey raised her umbrella. "Paul is not getting past me."

"Or me," Kevin said. "I may not sing as well as Meri can, but I get my point across."

"You don't have to sound good," I said. "Just keep them out."

"I can do that," Kevin said, then he set his hand on my good shoulder. "Be safe, both of you."

Aodhan and I stepped into the corridor, and waited until we heard Sister lock and barricade the doors. "To the auditorium?" he asked.

I nodded. "Let's end this."

The Collector's Gift

When we got to the auditorium, the first thing Aodhan did was prop open the doors as wide as they could go. "Are you expecting people to come from behind us?" I asked.

"Having the doors open gives us a better view of the room, so Flynn can't sneak up on us," he explained. "Although, the seats do present a problem." He gestured toward the rows of wooden seats nailed to the floor. I could imagine the collector slithering between them like a pale serpent.

"How will we ever figure out if he's in here," I began, then I felt four spots of heat searing into my shoulder. "Aodhan, I think Paul's close."

"Why?" Aodhan demanded, as he got in front of me and shielded me with his body. "You see him? Hear him?"

"My shoulder." I reached toward it, wincing. "Where he grabbed me. It burns."

"Let me see it."

I pulled the neck of the sweatshirt to the side, and Aodhan examined my shoulder. "It looks fine," he said, then he placed his hand against the scars. "It doesn't feel warm at all. Regular skin temperature."

"It hurts so much," I whispered. Aodhan held my face close to his.

"I believe you, but I don't think this is a physical hurt," he said. "I think it's magical."

"What difference does that make?" I demanded, rather desperately.

"Maybe you can magic it back to him."

Could I do that? I'd used my voice to stop the magic of others, but never once had I tried to undo anything... Or perhaps I had. I'd unlocked doors, and unfurled tangled string. The other day I sang apart the branches of a magic hedge. If I could undo a few locks and knots and branches, I could probably untangle Paul's magic from me, as well.

I sang a few high notes, and visualised the sound waves removing the heat from my shoulder and tossing it in Paul's face. The pain appeared in my mind's eyes as threads, thin enough to slice into my flesh if pulled taught enough. The magic was tenacious, and was wound deep into my muscles and tightly wrapped around my bones. I cried out even as I pulled the tendrils free of my flesh.

"What's happening?" Aodhan demanded.

"It feels like I'm pulling a piano wire through my body." Tears leaked from my eyes and my hands trembled. I feared I might pass out from the pain. With a hand on Aodhan's chest to steady me, I added, "Make that four wires."

"Can you feel what they're tethered to?" he asked. "Or what direction the wires are coming from?"

I pointed toward the auditorium's stage, then my knees gave way. Aodhan caught me before I hit the floor, then he lifted me in his arms and carried me toward the stage.

"We're getting closer," I said. The pain had spread from my shoulder and was burning a path all the way down my side. "I think the pain gets more intense the closer we get."

"I want to find him, and stop this once and for all." Aodhan stopped moving when I whimpered, and glanced down at me. I must have looked especially awful, because he said, "I'll bring you back to the library, and come back with Kevin."

"No," I protested, albeit weakly. "Let's get this done."

"You are the bravest girl in the world, Meri," Aodhan said, as he brought me onto the stage. "I don't deserve you."

"What you deserve is a life with no monsters," I began, then I screamed as an unseen hand wrenched my shoulder so hard it dragged me out of Aodhan's arms and onto the ground. As I fell onto the cold, hard stage, laughter came from above.

"Some think my sole purpose is to fetch the loose souls who have left their hosts, but my true gift is death," Marcus Flynn said from the balcony. He was standing just behind the railing, wearing his usual dark suit. The contrast of the black fabric against his white skin was blinding. "When Paul touched you, Meri, he killed a portion of your body. That means I have four portals by which to get inside, and control you."

Marcus clenched his fist, and pain squeezed my body. I curled into a ball and screamed, unable to think past the agony. Then I heard Aodhan yell, and there was a crash in front of the stage.

More importantly, the pain in my shoulder had ended just as suddenly as it had begun.

"Meri," Aodhan said as he knelt beside me and gathered me in his arms. "Mer, please be okay. I'm sorry I brought you in here. We've only just begun to really be together and now you're hurt, again you're hurt, and if I hadn't been so hell bent on getting revenge on Paul none of this—"

"Aodhan." I placed my hand on his cheek. "I'm okay."

"Thank God," he said, as he rested his forehead against mine. "I am going to get us a place, and I am going to spend every day and night holding you. I'm going to take care of you until the end of time."

"That all sounds wonderful," I said, confused but happy to be with Aodhan, though I didn't understand how I'd suddenly become pain free. I peeked over his shoulder, and saw Marcus Flynn crumpled in a heap in the main aisle. "What happened?"

"He was doing something to you," Aodhan whispered. "Even though he was all the way on the balcony, he pulled you right out of my arms! Then you were on the floor writhing in pain, and when he said death is his gift and I thought he was going to kill you. I took the knife your ma gave me and I flung it straight at him. He fell over the edge and crashed down to the floor."

"Great aim," I said, as I eyed the distance from the stage to the balcony. "Where did you hit him?"

"I aimed for his face." Aodhan pushed my hair back from my forehead. "You're really all right?"

I never got to answer. Behind Aodhan, Marcus Flynn bonelessly rose from the ground as if he was a marionette controlled by unseen strings. His black suit crumbled away, and soon he was swathed in nothing but filthy grey rags. The knife Aodhan had thrown at him protruded from his left eye, and the bright red blood smeared across his face was the only colour on his form.

"He really is like death," I whispered. "He's the Grim Reaper, come to collect." Aodhan turned toward the seats as the collector pulled the blade free from his face, and moved toward us.

"Meri, run!" Aodhan yelled, as he shoved me behind him.

But I couldn't run and leave Aodhan behind to face the collector alone, not when I could keep him safe.

And my voice could do just that.

As I began to sing I remembered what my mother had said about Gradlon's salt. My song increased in intensity and emotion, and I retrieved all of the leftover grains of Ker Ys's bounty that were still scattered across the beach in front of the surf shop. The silvery crystals formed a tiny whirlwind of salt in front of me, then I sent that salty tornado straight into the wound on Marcus's face.

His shriek was as painful as his magic.

Aodhan and I fell to our knees with our hands clamped over our ears as Marcus screamed so loudly the very walls shook. And it wasn't just the walls. I could feel his voice inside me, twisting my organs and rattling my bones. The pain was unlike anything I'd even felt before, and was far worse that what Paul had done to my shoulder.

For a moment, I doubted I'd survive.

"I... I can't..." I gasped.

"Hang on, Mer." Aodhan crawled toward me, and held me so one of my ears was pressed against his torso while his arm blocked the other. "Please. Hang on."

Blissfully, the collector's screams faded, along with the pain. Aodhan and I crumpled into a heap on the stage, panting and crying and enjoying the blissful silence. Then I heard it, a steady beat that was as comforting as the screams had been terrifying.

Thump thump thump

"Is that a drum," I began, then I put my hand on Aodhan's chest. It was his heartbeat.

Curious, I placed my other hand over my own heart, and smiled. Niamh was right.

"Our hearts do beat in time," I said, as I took Aodhan's hand and set it over my heart. "It's amazing."

"You're the amazing one," he said, then we heard shouting. My parents and Aodhan's father burst into the auditorium from the main corridor, yelling our names. When I turned toward them, I saw Marcus's body lying in the middle aisle and contorting like he was possessed, then the collector vanished into thin air.

"Is he dead?" I asked.

"Not likely," Rose said from behind us; she'd come through the dressing rooms offstage. "A more likely explanation is that he went back to where he came from to lick his wounds."

"As long as he's gone," I murmured. "Did you find Paul?"

"There's no trace of the gancanagh anywhere in the building," Mama said, as she circled the spot on the carpet where Marcus had fallen. "You used Gradlon's salt?"

"I didn't know what else to do," I said. Mama nodded, then she and Da exchanged a look. "Was that wrong? And what about Paul?"

"No one I've spoken to has set eyes on the gancanagh since he first arrived," Rose said. "Perhaps Kelsey was right, and the wounds he got in the house fire finally did him in."

I shuddered, and burrowed deeper into Aodhan's arms. "Perhaps."

"As for the salt, no, you weren't wrong to use it against the collector," Mama said. "And I'm the one who suggested it in the first place, so if there's any blame to be had, I will take it."

"If I wasn't wrong, why do you look worried?" I asked.

"We used the salt twice in one day without permission," she replied. "Gradlon will do his best to make us suffer for it."

Rose scoffed. "If he had a drop of sense he would laud all of you as heroes, instead of complaining about a resource that readily replenishes itself. Ker Ys is not in a position to make enemies, especially not with a powerful kingdom like Kilstiffen."

Mama nodded. "That's true, but when has Gradlon ever been able to see past his pride?"

The Next Part

In the days that followed Donn Dumhach and the Flynns' defeat our routines changed quite a bit, but almost all of the changes were for the better.

Our first order of business was contacting the authorities, and evacuating the survivors from The Saints. After the garda had taken dozens if not scores of statements, the official explanation for the carnage was that Headmaster Flynn had a psychotic break and ran amok through the school, terrorising students and teachers alike. I supposed that was a better story than the one they'd cooked up about the returning jumpers that had been enthralled by the former headmaster, Seamus MacCreehy, being brainwashed by a cult.

One thing neither the garda nor the school administration could explain was where the Flynns came from in the first place. Not only were there no records of Marcus Flynn applying for and subsequently being interviewed for the position of headmaster, no one could turn up a single piece of evidence proving that he or Paul actually existed. My family and I understood that this was because Donn had somehow used magic to install Marcus into The Saints as his lackey, but it did leave the school administrators with egg on their faces.

The next day, we organised ourselves into groups and searched the village and all the surrounding areas, including their burnt shell of a house, and found no trace of Paul or Marcus Flynn. Mama was confident that Paul had perished, perhaps at Marcus's hand, and according to her, it was unusual for collectors to harry the living without the support of a local deity. Since Donn was also out of the picture, that meant we were safe, at least for now.

There was a double funeral held for Marcus and Paul, though none of us went. What we did attend was each and every funeral for the students Marcus had murdered. We'd lost eight students, which was eight too many. Sister Mary Katherine was hailed as The Saints' hero for her quick thinking, and for saving as many students and teachers as she did. Hopefully, that meant she would get her literature classes back.

We'd also gained four more people into our ever-growing family circle, with three of them being Mrs Dumhach and her youngest daughters, Nora and Roan. Aodhan's father had moved back into the family home, and while he and his former wife hadn't completely reconciled—I understood Mr Sullivan was sleeping in the guest room for the time being—they were getting along with each other again. What greatly helped matters was that the girls adored Mr Sullivan, and he treated them as if they were his own children.

Our fourth new member was, of course, Kelsey. She and Kevin spent almost every waking moment together, and since she'd effectively moved into his room, they were together as they slept, too. I often wondered what Kelsey's parents thought of her new living arrangements. I also wondered why Aodhan and I were still confined to separate rooms while Kevin had his girlfriend right there in his bed. Then again, I wasn't so certain I wanted to share a room with Aodhan just yet, and if there was anything I wouldn't do, it was rush things between us. We had our entire lives ahead of us, and I wanted to do things the right way. For me, that meant letting our relationship deepen naturally.

One thing that we did take care of right away was soundproofing all of the bedrooms. When Aodhan told Kevin about his idea to keep *those songs* contained, they obtained the materials and finished the job in a weekend.

Now that we regularly hosted ten for supper, Da was truly in his element. He loved cooking for a full house, and his dream of owning a restaurant seemed closer than ever. The next step in his plan was catering his and Mama's vow renewal ceremony, which made my mother equally proud and apprehensive.

"It's not that I don't want your father to do the cooking," Mama said, while we were sitting at the kitchen table having coffee. We were two weeks out from our victories, and the ceremony was to occur next weekend. "It's just an awful lot of work, and Brian should enjoy the day."

"Da's happiest while he cooks," I reminded her. "Besides, Kevin and I are here to help, and I've seen the menu. It's nothing we can't handle."

"And my parents are coming," Mama continued. "You know how the king can be toward surface dwellers."

"But Niamh doesn't seem to share his opinions." Somehow, I could not refer to her as my grandmother. "At least, not towards Da."

"True. Brian greatly impressed my mother when they first met, and he's remained on her good side ever since." Mama eyed me over the rim of her mug, and said, "I'm sure you want to know exactly what happened between Corentin and me."

"If he was anything like Nahel, I already know what happened," I said. "This Corentin is Gradlon's oldest son?"

"Actually, he's Gradlon's younger brother," Mama replied. "Ever since my parents found one another, and introduced a godly bloodline into our family, Gradlon's thought that Kilstiffen somehow has a leg up against the other sea kingdoms. As if the gods show us favours that are withheld elsewhere."

"I'd say our situation is quite the opposite. When I got stuck in the hedge, it was because the ward Lorcan's people laid around the old palace thought I was Donn, and it was keeping me out." I paused, and asked, "Does that mean we're closely related to Donn?"

"I think what it really means is that Lorcan's wards are shite," Mama said. "Everyone below is related to everyone else in one way or another. The gods have existed for a very long time, and the family tree is a bit gnarled. Donn is a cousin on my mother's side, though I'm not sure how many times removed."

"Have you been there? To Tír na nÓg ?"

"I have. It's a strange place, but I suppose a place filled with that much magic would have to be."

I nodded. "Then, Gradlon also wants an invitation below?"

"He wants to be related to the gods," Mama replied. "Gradlon is a greedy man, and can't stand it when he feels someone has more than him."

I snorted. "Greedy people tend to end up with nothing."

"Very true, Meri girl," Mama said. "Manannán does have a habit of bestowing gifts among his family members, such as your necklace, and the shell he gave Kevin. However, Gradlon wants a very specific item, and thinks that he can only obtain it by marrying into our family."

"If he wants something so badly, why doesn't he just ask for it?" I wondered. "Surely he'd have a greater chance of success by being forthright."

"I don't think he'll succeed either way," Mama said. "The item Gradlon covets would grant him immortality."

"I can see why the gods wouldn't want that one around for eternity," I said, and Mama laughed. "And Gradlon assumed pairing you with his brother would make all of this come to pass?"

"Traditionally, the monarch of each city has two children, and they marry into another one of the royal families when they come of age. As I was the younger sister, Gradlon imagined I'd be a match for Corentin. At our first meeting, it was clear that Gradlon was mistaken."

"I'm sure that soggy prince had nothing on Da," I said, and Mama grinned. "Who did Gradlon marry? A princess from one of the other cities?"

Mama leaned across the table, and said, "Gradlon has never married, but he did have a brief relationship with one of Ran's daughters, and that's how the twins entered the picture."

"Who's this Ran?" I asked. "Another cousin of ours from below?"

"We're not related. Well, not that I know of. Ran is a lovely Nordic lass with influence over the cold northern seas. She had nine daughters, all of them wave dancers, and one of them caught Gradlon's eye. A year later, she left two newborns on his doorstep. It was quite the scandal," she added.

"I bet." I recalled Dahut and Nahel's water-based magic, and realized they were also descended from people with power over the sea. "So Gradlon is related to gods."

"Aye, but Ran and her husband are no friends to Gradlon," she replied. "Rumor is the twins haven't seen their Norse relations in quite some time, and Gradlon himself isn't allowed to travel northward ever again."

"He irritates everyone he meets, it seems," I said. "Is that what Rose meant when she said Ker Ys is in no position to make enemies of Kilstiffen?"

"Most likely," Mama said. "Ever since the northern kingdoms turned their backs on Ker Ys, the city has had a significant loss of revenue. They're not nearly as wealthy as they once were."

I recalled the casual displays of wealth in Kilstiffen. Everything was covered in gold and pearls, not to show off, but because the city had an abundance of them. After he'd overstayed his welcome, greedy Gradlon probably tried pocketing the cutlery on his way out the door. "Do you think that's why Gradlon turned to Donn? Because an exiled god might want to help a king no one liked?"

"Perhaps, but we don't know for certain if Gradlon and Donn are associates," Mama replied. "However, we'd best keep our eye on both of them."

I nodded, though I didn't want to monitor either of those two. Instead, I asked, "After the match with you fell through, no one tried to set up Corentin with your sister?"

Mama scoffed. "Scáthach has stated many times she will never marry, and anyone who doesn't believe her is a fool. Instead, she oversees a training academy in Evonium. Many heroes learned the art of combat from her."

"Did she teach you?"

"Yes. She put a sword in my hand as soon as I could walk."

"Do you miss your siblings?"

"I do. I am hoping Scáthach attends our gathering next weekend. As for my brother, I don't know where Oscar is right now."

"Perhaps, once the gathering's behind us, we can go looking for him."

Mama smiled, and sipped her coffee. "That's a fine idea, Meri. Between the two of us, we'll have him tracked down in no time."

After Mama and I finished our coffee, she went off to handle something for the impending vow renewal ceremony, and I went out back to find Aodhan. Since he was more of a fan of eating than of cooking, his contribution to the ceremony was cleaning up the back garden. He'd rallied his father, Kelsey, and even Lorcan and Rose to the cause, and I had to say the garden looked better than it had in years.

I found Aodhan near the old greenhouse wielding a paintbrush and a bucket of whitewash. "Will this be where we duck in, in case of rain?" I asked.

"Oh, maybe." Aodhan set down his paintbrush, then he took my hand and drew me inside the greenhouse. "Remember when you said you wanted to restore the greenhouse so you could grow more plants, strange vegetables and fancy orchids and such? Now, you can."

He gestured toward the interior, and I gasped. The broken pots and heaps of debris were gone, and in their place orderly tables and benches lined the sides of the house. A large round table sat in the centre of the room, and on top of it was a set of new terracotta pots. There was even a gravel floor underfoot, instead of the packed dirt that had been here before.

"You did all of this for me?" I asked, unable to take my eyes from the work he'd done.

"Mer, I would do anything for you." He draped his arm around my shoulders. "All we need to do now is go shopping for plants."

"We'll have plenty of time, since school's cancelled again." What with the garda reporting that Headmaster Flynn had attacked and killed several students, and the Flynns' missing and presumed dead, and The Saints was having a hard time finding a new headmaster. Not surprising, since they all tended to disappear under mysterious circumstances. "Do you think the Flynns are really gone?"

"Probably not," he replied, "but if they come back, we'll deal with them. We're getting pretty good at sending these supernatural threats on their way."

"We are." I laid my head on his shoulder, and shoved away all the nagging little voices in my head that insisted these good days wouldn't last, and that the Flynns and Gradlon and god awful Nahel would be back. I wanted to enjoy every moment I spent with Aodhan, and not worry about things that may never come to pass.

"What will your next project be?" I asked, and not just to drown out those voices. "Fixing up the old cottage?"

"I thought I might fix up the shop's apartment instead," he replied. "Now that Dad's gone back home it can be just us again. If you'd like that?"

I felt the next part of our relationship unfold in a beautiful, natural way. "I would like that. I'd like it very much."

Keep scrolling for a sneak peek from Book 3, Manannán's Pearl.

Manannán's Pearl: Chapter One

"Meri," my mother yelled as the bedroom door banged open. "Meri! Are you awake?"

I blinked my eyes open. "I am now."

"Get ready," she said. "The merrows will be arriving soon!"

I sat up and looked at the window. It was pitch black outside. "They're arriving before sunrise? But the ceremony won't be until four."

"Yes, well, down below, they do things their own way," Mama said. "Where's Aodhan?"

"Here, Mrs Murphy," Aodhan said, as he raised an arm to reveal his location. He was clear across the room, curled up in the armchair and nestled under a blanket. I'd been shuttled to his room the day prior so Aunt Donna and her wife could use mine while they stayed with us for my parents' vow renewal weekend. Since my room used to be Donna's, it was only fair. Besides, I liked being in Aodhan's room.

"How can I help?" Aodhan asked. "Just point me toward what needs doing."

"Aodhan, you are a treasure," Mama said. "I'm not really sure what we need to do first. Make some coffee for the guests, maybe? Or tea?"

"I can handle both," I said, as I stretched the last bits of sleep from my muscles. "We also finished all the baking yesterday, so we'll be able to put together a nice breakfast for whomever shows up in these predawn hours. Why don't you let us worry about all of that, and find someplace quiet so you can relax for a bit?"

Mama crossed the room and kissed the top of my head. "Meri girl, I don't know what I would do without you. Thank you, my lamb."

With that, Mama swept out of Aodhan's room, and proceeded to barge into Kevin's across the hall. While she harangued my brother and Kelsey, Aodhan left his uncomfortable looking chair and slid under the blankets with me. "Good morning, beautiful."

"Good morning." He gathered me against him and tucked my head underneath his chin, and all was right with my world. "When did you go to the chair?" I asked, since we'd fallen asleep together in the bed last night.

"After you went to sleep," he said. "I didn't want to violate any versions of your dad's 'no air mattress' rule."

I giggled, because I remembered that rule all too well. Aodhan and I had just got in trouble at the Cliffs of Moher Visitor Centre, and Da came to rescue us. After he heard Aodhan's mother go on about how she found us sleeping on an air mattress, Da had banned them from the house as a euphemism for Aodhan and me not getting in bed together. "That was a stressful day."

"It certainly was, and it's all the more reason to make sure things go smoothly today." Aodhan caressed my cheek, then he kissed me. "Let's go have a vow renewal, shall we?"

"Let's."

I snuck into my room to get ready, and managed to change into a tee shirt and shorts without waking either of my aunts. That done, I went to the kitchen and found Da already hard at work.

"You should not be up this early," I admonished. "At this rate, you'll be dead asleep when you're supposed to be exchanging vows."

"Don't you worry about me, Meri girl," Da said, as he whisked a few pastry shells out of the oven. "I'm far too excited to sleep. Get me the pastry crème from the fridge, please?"

I did as asked. "What are you making? I thought all the baking was done."

"These are a few special tarts, for Aoife's ma," he replied, as he rinsed off some berries.

"You make special tarts for a goddess?"

"That I do, and how that came about is a fine story," he replied. "One day, shortly before Kevin came along, I was trying out new dessert recipes. Your ma had gone into the town for something, and, as you know, it's nice to cook in a quiet house."

"It is," I agreed. "Can I help with these tarts?"

"Melt the apple jelly for me, so I can use it as a glaze, if you wouldn't mind," he said, as he filled a piping bag with the crème.

I found the jar of jelly, and scooped some into a pan. "You said you were trying out new desserts?"

"Ah, yes. I was. I had just pulled a batch out of the oven when there was a knock at the door. I opened it, and standing there on the stoop was a woman with long golden hair who claimed to be a friend of Aoife's. I invited her in, made her some tea, and fed her a few berry tarts. And that's how I met Niamh."

"You won her over with a tart," I said, remembering how Niamh had warmly greeted Da when they'd seen each other following Donn Dumhach's defeat in front of the surf shop.

"That I did, and we've got on well ever since," Da said. "Speaking of which, best heat up that clam stew you made for the old goat. He doesn't have a sweet tooth like his bride."

"Do you get along with Grandfather at all?" I asked, as I hauled the stew pot out of the fridge and set it on the stove.

"Yes and no," Da replied. "Steinar loves his children very much, and more than anything, he wants them to be happy. Aoife is happy with me, therefore he is happy with me. However," he paused to take the apple jelly off the hob, and pour it through a fine sieve, "we met under rather awkward circumstances."

"Was it when you hit Corentin?" I asked, eager for undersea gossip.

"That boy got hit because he wouldn't take no for an answer," Da said. "Your ma was wearing this dress that didn't cover one of her shoulders, and he put his hand on her bare skin. She knocked his hand away and told him to stop. He did it again, so I took it upon myself to persuade him to leave Aoife be."

"The way I heard it, you left the prince lying in a puddle of blood," came a voice from the doorway. I turned, and saw a woman who was a taller and more heavily muscled version of my mother leaning against the doorframe. She was wearing a bronze coloured sleeveless shirt and matching pants, brown boots, and gold bracelets that matched the pair my mother always wore. She also had a long blonde plait, and striking blue eyes.

"Corentin claims you disfigured him for life," she continued.

"That will teach him to touch a woman without her permission," Da said. "Meri, meet your Aunt Scáthach."

"You're The Shadow?" I blurted out.

"That old nickname," Scáthach said, with a smile. "Hello, Meri. Brian, what have you made for me?"

"I roasted a joint of mutton in a fire out back. You can go at it with your teeth." Da wiped his hands on a tea towel, then he and Scáthach embraced. "Good to see you."

"And you," she said. "Is that clam stew I smell?"

"Meri made it," Da said. Scáthach sidled over to the stove, and had a sniff.

"May I try it?" she asked.

"Of course." I got a clean spoon and handed it over. "It's still a bit cool, but you'll get the idea."

She sampled a spoonful, and grinned. "Oh, you'll be the old goat's favourite after he has this."

"Why does everyone call Grandfather a goat?" I asked, then I heard the thunder of Aodhan galloping down the stairs. He bounded into the kitchen, and stopped short when he saw Scáthach standing over the stove.

"Um, hello," Aodhan said. "I was just going to go out back, and start setting up chairs."

"I'll help," Scáthach said, then she strode out of the kitchen door and into the garden.

"Two questions," Aodhan began. "Who is that, and is there breakfast?"

"She's my Aunt Scáthach, and I will make you breakfast." I set a skillet on the stove. "How hungry are you? Ravenous as usual?"

"You know me well." Aodhan smiled at me, nodded toward my da, then he followed my aunt into the garden.

"Mama was right about merrows arriving before dawn." I grabbed a bowl, and started cracking eggs into it. "At this rate, we'll run out of food before noon."

"If we've enough food to keep Aodhan fed, we've enough for every-one," Da said. The pastry shells had cooled, and he was piping in a layer of crème. "My true worry is the cake my mother is bringing."

I stopped moving, my whisk motionless in the eggs. "Granny Mer made a cake?"

"Claims she outdid herself," Da said. "Said it'll put her Easter cakes to shame."

"Oh, dear."

Get your copy of Manannán's Pearl here, or wherever books are sold.

Glossary Of People, Places, And Pronunciations

Ankou (AN koo) – a creature who collects the souls of the dead and brings them to hell.

Aodhan (AY den) Sullivan – owner of Sullivan's Surf Shop, son of Lucas and Bridgette, and Meri's partner in all things.

Aoife (EE fah) Murphy – a merrow and warrior from Kilstiffen. Mother of Kevin and Meri, wife of Brian, sister of Oscar and Scáthach, and daughter of Steinar and Niamh.

Brian Murphy – a fisherman with dreams of running a restaurant. Father of Kevin and Meri, husband of Aoife.

Céilí (KAY lee) – a gathering where those in attendance dance and play traditional Irish music. These gatherings may be held in a home or a public location.

Cliffs of Moher – sea cliffs located at the southwestern edge of the Burren region in County Clare, Ireland. They run for about fourteen kilometres. At their southern end, they rise one hundred twenty metres above the Atlantic Ocean at Hag's Head, and, eight kilometres to the north, they reach their maximum height of two hundred fourteen metres just north of O'Brien's Tower, then continue at lower heights. The closest settlements are the villages of Liscannor six kilometres to the south, and Doolin seven kilometres to the north.

<u>Corentin (kor en tin)</u> – prince of Ker Ys and younger brother of Gradlon.

<u>Dahut (DA het)</u> – princess of Ker Ys. Daughter of Gradlon, twin sister of Nahel.

<u>Donn Dhumach (don DOO mahk)</u> – sidhe prince and master of the dead.

<u>Evonium (ee VO nee um)</u> – a lost city off the western coast of Scotland.

<u>Gancanagh</u> – a male fairy known for seducing women.

<u>Gaol</u> – prison.

<u>Garda</u> – The Garda Síochána is the national police and security service of Ireland. It is more commonly referred to as the Gardaí or the Guards.

<u>Gradlon Mor</u> – the king of Ker Ys, father of Dahut and Nahel, older brother of Corentin.

<u>Great Famine</u> – also called the Great Hunger, was a period of mass starvation and disease in Ireland from 1845 to 1849.

<u>Kelsey McGrath</u> – classmate of Meri, partner to Kevin.

<u>Ker Ys (Kerr Iss)</u> – a mythical city on the coast of Brittany that was swallowed up by the ocean.

<u>Kevin Murphy</u> – half merrow and heir of Kilstiffen. He is the son of Aoife and Brian, brother of Meri, partner to Kelsey.

<u>Kilstiffen</u> – a lost city beneath the Cliffs of Moher which sprawls grandly over the Atlantic Ocean on the western coast of Ireland. The city once rose every seventh year, but now it remains submerged until the golden key to the gates is found.

Lucas Sullivan – father of Aodhan, Mary, and Anne. Former surfing champion from California, he was held captive by Seamus MacCreehy for eight years.

Manannán mac Lir (MAH na non mac LEER) – god of the sea, father of Niamh, grandfather of Aoife.

Meredith "Meri" Murphy – half merrow and the heiress of Kilstiffen, she commanded a stone army and defeated Seamus MacCreehy. She's the daughter of Aoife and Brian, sister of Kevin, and partner to Aodhan.

Merrow – a mermaid or merman in Irish folklore.

Milesians – the Milesians (sons of Míl) are Gaels who sailed to Ireland from Iberia. When they landed in Ireland they fought with the Tuatha Dé Danann. The two groups agreed to divide Ireland between them: the Milesians took the world above, while the Tuatha Dé Danann took the world below.

Mo chroí (moh cree) – my heart in Irish.

Nahel (NA hell) – prince of Ker Ys, son of Gradlon, twin brother of Dahut.

Niamh (neev) – daughter of Manannán mac Lir, wife of Steinar, mother of Aoife, Oscar, and Scáthach.

Ogham (og hmm) – an Early Medieval alphabet used primarily to write the early Irish language, and later the Old Irish language.

Oisín (oh sheen) – regarded in legend as the greatest poet of Ireland. He spent three years in the Otherworld with the sea god's daughter, but it was three hundred years in mortal time. When he returned to Ireland the centuries caught up to him, and as soon as his foot touched Irish soil he withered and died.

Oscar – son of Niamh and Steinar, brother of Aoife and Scáthach.

Press – Irish term for a cabinet or cupboard.

<u>Saint Senan and Conainne's Academy (The Saints)</u> – the school Meri and Aodhan attend.

<u>Scáthach (skah hoch)</u> – the head of the combat training academy in Evomium. Daughter of Steinar and Niamh, sister of Aoife and Oscar.

<u>Seamus MacCreehy (Shay muss Mah kree hee)</u> – a merrow and once captain in Kilstiffen's army who attempted to permanently raise the city. He was defeated by Meri.

<u>Selkie (sell key)</u> – creatures that can shapeshift between seal and human forms by removing or putting on their seal skin.

<u>Sidhe (shee)</u> – the fairy folk of Ireland, said to live in underground palaces or forts called sidhe.

<u>Steinar (STAI nar) the Immoveable</u> – king of Kilstiffen, husband of Niamh, father of Scáthach, Oscar, and Aoife.

<u>Tech Duinn (tek doon)</u> – literally the house of the dead, where Donn Dhumach collects the souls of the dead.

<u>Time Team</u> – long-running British archaeology programme.

<u>Tír na nÓg (teer nah nogue)</u> – In Irish mythology, Tír na nÓg or Tír na hÓige ('Land of Youth') is one of the names for the Celtic Otherworld.

<u>Tuatha Dé Danann (too AH de Dan an)</u> – literally, "the folk of the goddess Danu". They comprise the Irish pantheon of gods who dwell in the Otherworld.

ACKNOWLEDGEMENTS

Here we are with another badly written, semi-forgetful acknowledgements section. Away we go!

First of all, we have yet another cover created by the brilliant and talented Lisa Amowitz. Can she get a round or two of applause?

Much like Merrowkin, I had a lot of help with Death's Door. The bulk of it came in two forms: my online critique group, and my new day job. interestingly enough, my critique group never read a single passage from Death's Door, but the advice and suggestions they've given me on other projects (one of which s a novella set in this world) have made me a better writer overall. Thanks, guys! And as for the day job, I went from being treated like a second rate seat warmer to an actual adult. This has led to a marked reduction in stress, and corresponding increase in creativity, and you know what that means: more stories!

Finally, a big thank you to my Patrons: Jessica Worthy, Bobbi Coburn, Aurora Slinkman, Amanda Raymond, and Keri Maniquet. Your support means more to me than you know.

ALSO BY JENNIFER ALLIS PROVOST

The Chronicles of Parthalan, a six volume epic fantasy (and one short story collection)

Heir to the Sun

The Virgin Queen

Rise of the Deva'shi

Pieces of Parthalan: Six All-New Stories From The Land Of Parthalan

Golem

Elfsong

Sunfall

The Copper Legacy, a four book urban fantasy:

Copper Girl

Copper Ravens

Copper Veins

Copper Princess

A duology based in the Copper world:

Redemption

Salvation

Poison Garden, an urban fantasy filled with seers, witches, and one seriously hot detective:

Belladonna

Oleander

Bleeding Hearts

Thornapple

Wolfsbane

Mistletoe

Mandrake

**Gallowglass, an urban fantasy set in
Scotland and New York:**

Gallowglass

Walker

Homecoming

**Winter's Queen, an urban fantasy set in
Scotland and Elphame:**

Touch of Frost

Giant's Daughter

Elphame's Queen

**Merrowkin, an urban fantasy set in Ireland
above and below**

Merrowkin

Death's Door

Manannán's Pearl

Changes, a contemporary romance:

Changing Teams

Changing Scenes

Changing Fate

Changing Dates

About The Author

Jennifer Allis Provost is a native New Englander who lives in a sprawling colonial along with her beautiful and precocious twins, a dog that thinks she's a kangaroo, a parrot, a junkyard cat, and a wonderful husband who never forgets to buy ice cream. As a child, she read anything and everything she could get her hands on, including a set of encyclopedias, but fantasy was always her favorite. She spends her days drinking vast amounts of coffee, arguing with her computer, and avoiding any and all domestic behavior.

Find Jenn on the web here: http://authorjenniferallisprovost.com/

For up to the minute sale notifications, follow her on Bookbub here: https://www.bookbub.com/profile/jennifer-allis-provost

For exclusive content, follow her on Patreon: https://www.patreon.com/jenniferallisprovost/

Friend her on Facebook: http://www.facebook.com/jennallis

Follow her on Instagram: @jenniferaprovost

Happy reading!